# ANDREW POST

# CHOP SHOP

This is a **FLAME TREE PRESS** book

Text copyright © 2019 Andrew Post

**FLAME TREE PRESS**
6 Melbray Mews, London, SW6 3NS, UK
**flametreepress.com**

Distribution and warehouse:
Baker & Taylor Publisher Services (BTPS)
30 Amberwood Parkway, Ashland, OH 44805
btpubservices.com

Thanks to the Flame Tree Press team, including:
Taylor Bentley, Frances Bodiam, Federica Ciaravella, Don D'Auria,
Chris Herbert, Matteo Middlemiss, Josie Mitchell, Mike Spender,
Cat Taylor, Maria Tissot, Nick Wells, Gillian Whitaker.

The cover is created by Flame Tree Studio with
thanks to Nik Keevil and Shutterstock.com.
The font families used are Avenir and Bembo.

Flame Tree Press is an imprint of Flame Tree Publishing Ltd
flametreepublishing.com

A copy of the CIP data for this book is available from the British Library
and the Library of Congress.

HB ISBN: 978-1-78758-285-9
PB ISBN: 978-1-78758-283-5
ebook ISBN: 978-1-78758-286-6
Also available in FLAME TREE AUDIO

Printed in the US at Bookmasters, Ashland, Ohio

# ANDREW POST

# CHOP SHOP

**FLAME TREE PRESS**
*London & New York*

# CHAPTER ONE

Frank Goode was having a nightmare about being back in prison. Even if it was a client ringing his doorbell that woke him up, he was fine with that. He sat up, his throat sore from sleeping with the air conditioner going full blast all night. A hangover blossomed in his skull as he sat up, blood moving back through the booze-burned parts of him.

The doorbell rang again. Three quick pulses.

Growling at lower back pains, Frank kicked his feet into his slippers and stepped out of his bedroom. He ducked through the hanging plastic sheets that kept his dining-room-turned-operating-room mostly sterile, and approached the front door. He leaned in, keeping quiet, and used the peephole. In that fisheye view of his front porch and patchy lawn, there stood a girl pacing from foot to foot, twenty to twenty-five, cracking her gum, looking over her shoulder three times in the couple seconds Frank stood watching her, estimating her, trying to think if he knew her.

He didn't open the door. He asked through it, "Can I help you?"

"Yeah, hey, I was told you take care of people here."

"I take care of my friends, that's true, but I don't know your face."

"I'm Simone Pescatelli." She didn't need to say more than her last name – and knew it.

He couldn't see her baby bump through the peephole since all of her looked so distorted then. But when he opened the front door he sure could.

She cracked her gum. "So, yeah, I'd like to not be knocked up anymore. My uncle says you patch up the boys so I was wondering if…you know, you do girls too."

Frank waved her in. She clicked onto his living room's hardwood floor on four-inch leopard-print pumps, leaving a trail of perfume that dragged a knife across his brain. His wife wore that. Wore it on their wedding day.

Before closing the door he surveyed the street, the row of little houses across from his. The cars parked there were all family-man minivans and Mexicans' pickup trucks with the Old English script of their fallen loved ones' names across the back glass. He was familiar with each of these vehicles; the only one out of place was the sky-blue Honda at the curb at the end of his walkway directly ahead.

"That yours?"

"Yeah," she said. Gum crack. "Ain't pretty, I know, but it's like a disguise you drive instead of wear. The Slavs don't know it."

"I see." Frank closed the door, threw all four deadbolts.

She stood in his living room watching the TV he'd left on all night for the company. Standing as she was, he got a good look at her in profile. Her baby bump was peeking out from under her thin, spaghetti-strap tank top. At a guess he'd say she was five months along, but wasn't sure, so he asked.

She shrugged tanned shoulders. "Dunno."

"When was your last period?"

She stopped chewing her gum. "Kinda personal, don't you think?"

"I won't be able to help you if you're past your first trimester." He stepped into the kitchen to get the coffee started. He lit a cigarette and stepped back into the small, bare-walled, low-ceilinged living room and sat on his stained Goodwill couch. "Have a seat."

She sat on the other end, eyes glued to the TV again. He shut it off. She blinked, and finally looked over at him, jaw working, denting her cheek in time with each slow grind. "What? I don't know, okay? It's not like I got a fucking journal for every time I bleed. Me and Joey started going without, you know, using rubbers and shit. He says he used to work around magnets a lot at the car-crusher place and he's shooting blanks because of it – but here we are, right? So, you gonna fix it or what?"

"I don't fix. I treat. And if you're past your first trimester, which it appears that you are, I won't be able to help you."

"Won't or can't? My uncle says you sometimes drive a hard bargain, so if that's what you're doing, you ain't gotta worry, I brought cash." She clicked open her leopard-print purse. A knot of dough the size of Frank's head could barely be held in her one hand, clutched hard with her eagle-talon nails the color of strawberries. "Name your price. I gotta be at the salon by noon, though."

The coffee maker chimed in the other room, full pot ready. He got up, trying not to let it show that he'd just about shat himself seeing that wad of money, and poured himself a cup. "You want some coffee?" he asked.

"Nah, I read online it's bad for your skin." Gum crack, a pause, slow blink, mulling something. "And if you're pregnant."

"Water?"

"I'm all right. So, we gonna haggle or what? I mean, I might've just had this one but I got my cousin's wedding this weekend and I don't want this fucking thing forcing me to have to get a new dress – I like the one I got. It's silk with this high slit on the side, kinda like you see them Oriental chicks wearing in the movies." She added with coquettish pride, "I'm the maid of honor." Gum crack.

Frank sat again, with coffee. She had laid the bundle of cash, nearly as big as a coffee can, on his end table. She wasn't even watching it or keeping it close by, she just laid it down in a stranger's house without even a thought – like it was something she idly plucked ripe off a branch on her drive over here.

"Five thousand," Frank said, starting higher than what felt polite – but she did wake him up, after all.

"Okay." She peeled a few bills, didn't bother counting twice, laid them on his coffee table, stood, and took off her shoes. "There you are. So, we doing this here or in there or what?" She paused, looking toward the plastic sheet dividing his makeshift operating room from the living room. "You ever help any of the Petroskys?"

That name rung something for Frank, but it wasn't anyone he'd ever treated. He knew all of those names by heart; part of his training, to always remember a patient's name without having to double-check their chart. Shows you care. Or at least gives the impression you do. "No," Frank said. "No Petroskys."

"Meaning you never fixed none of them before? Or that they've asked but you refused?"

"The first one. I've never treated anyone with that last name."

"Ever hear of them?"

"On the news." Maybe. Or somewhere.

"Well, color me glad – for your sake – you ain't never had them darken your doorstep because they're all pieces of shit, fucking Russians."

"I'll keep that in mind," Frank said. "But about your case, if we could focus on that a minute, you know that's way more than the clinic would've charged, if you'd gone in earlier."

"Fuck's *that* supposed to mean? I thought doctors were supposed to, you know, not get all judgey and shit."

"I apologize. In here, if you would." He held the plastic sheeting open for her to step through – and again caught a whiff of her perfume that dredged to the surface so much he both loved and hated to think about.

"Fucking say shit like that," she muttered under her breath. Gum crack. "And here I didn't say nothing about your ugly little house or nothing. Wanted to, but I didn't."

He let the plastic fall back and began washing his hands to the elbow. "If you want to remove your underwear and hop up on the table there, we'll get started."

Simone dropped her purse to the floor beside the table with a heavy *clunk*, like she was walking around with a lead brick in there.

As he scrubbed in at the cracked porcelain country sink he'd installed in the former dining room, Frank watched in the reflection of the glass-front medicine cabinet next to him as she wiggled and shimmied to draw a fire-engine-red thong down her legs, the delicate string hooked on a long, bejeweled finger. She kicked it aside and hopped up onto the table. She put her feet in the stirrups, looked up at the ceiling toward the light fixture that used to light the previous owners' dining room table, and cracked her gum.

He shook out two pills for her. "Need a glass of water?"

"What are they?"

"For the pain."

"Aren't they bad for the—?" she started, stopped. "Nah, I don't need no water. Thanks." She swallowed them dry and opened her mouth to flash her pierced tongue side to side and up and down. He didn't ask for her to prove she'd swallowed them, but smiled at the curious little display anyway.

Frank tied on his apron and when he turned, she giggled. "That doesn't look very doctorly."

Glancing down, he saw he'd put on the apron for his other job. JERRY'S ORGANIC GROCER & WINE SHOPPE. "If you don't mind," he said, "it's the only one I have clean right now."

"Long as you washed your hands, I don't care. You been doing this long?" she asked, hands folded on her belly and staring up at the ceiling, chest rising and falling.

"A little under a year." Frank got the tools he'd need from the disinfecting oven and arranged them on his wheel-about tray – a microwave stand he found at a garage sale, five bucks – and pulled it over toward his operating table.

"Uncle Robbie says you took real good care of my cousin Louie. Saved his life."

Frank gave his stool a couple cranks to bring it to the right height and sat. "Well, I do what I can." Louie Cassell had come in after a bar fight had resulted in a steak knife being stuck, to the wooden handle, in his shoulder. Three stitches and a sling. Robbie Pescatelli, with a handshake, passed him eight grand in hundreds and a friendly slap on the cheek for his trouble.

"So are you a for-real doctor?" Simone said. "Or did you just learn to do all this off the internet?"

He pulled on a pair of latex gloves. Last pair. Shit. "I went to school," he said. "Can you hold your skirt up for me?"

She did. Her dark pubic hair had been shaved into a heart shape.

He must've paused long enough for her to wonder what was going on and she sat up a little, peeking down at him over her rounded belly.

"Cute, right? My girl Becky does them."

"I'm Frank," he said, not sure why now would be a good time to introduce himself.

"I know. So, are we gonna do this thing or are you just gonna stare at my business? Because I know it's pretty and all, but...."

"Are you ready?"

She lay back. Gum crack. "Yep."

Frank did what he was getting paid to do.

"If you don't mind," she said when it was through, "could you put it somewhere I don't see it when I sit up?"

"Of course." He laid a cloth over the pan and set it, with care, in the sink.

When she tried getting off the table, her feet connected hard with the floor and she paused, head rolling loose on her shoulders. He took her by the arm and had her sit. "I'm feeling kinda weird. I don't do pills much."

"Just sit here a second. Take your time."

She glanced over toward the sink, closed her eyes, and whipped her face in a different direction, away. She remained that way, eyes squeezed shut, chin on her left shoulder, hands wringing together in her lap. He expected her to begin crying, as they sometimes do, but when she spoke her voice didn't quaver in the least. "I don't think I can drive," she said.

Frank pulled off his gloves and tossed them in the trash. "Can you call a cab? I actually have to get to work, I'm already late."

"But ain't this your work?" Her eyes were still closed but she started chewing her gum again. "Right, the grocery store. You said that already."

Using his body as a curtain so she wouldn't see, he brought over the garbage can to the sink and deposited the pan, with the child inside it, in with the used gloves, coffee grounds, and cigarette butts. A quick yank on the drawstrings and the bag was closed and the worst part over.

He set the garbage bag aside and stepped over to her. He put a hand on her shoulder; her skin was firm and cool to the touch. "I have to ask you to leave. There's a bus stop up the street. Nobody will steal your car in this neighborhood."

"It ain't just that," she said. "I don't really wanna go back. I mean, I know I have to. If I don't, Uncle Robbie will send everybody out to look for me, and I don't wanna make no drama, I just…need a minute, if that's okay. Maybe I could lay down on your sofa for a while, watch some TV, clear my head? They think I'm at the salon. I said I had an early appointment but it ain't really until noon. I'll go when it's time to get for the real appointment, okay?"

"I'm sorry, but you have to go now," Frank said. "I can't lose my other job because then I'll lose this one too – because I'll be in prison." Again.

"I won't steal nothing. I can even lock up when I go. I just need a little time." She pushed through the hanging plastic sheet and sat down, carefully, on his couch. "Where's your remote?"

Frank stepped out behind her with the garbage bag in hand. He noticed her look at it, hanging low at his side, when she sat.

She found the remote, and once the TV was back on, would stare at nothing else. He watched her raise her hand, slow, to bring it up alongside her face, blocking her view of what he had in his hand with her chipping red nails. "Five grand plus another two if you just let me sit here for a while. You can go to work. You do good shit for my family and I wouldn't fuck you over and mess that up. Please. It's eight now. I won't stay past ten, I promise."

"Fine. Just make sure you lock the door on your way out. Just use the one on the knob and pull it shut behind you." He snatched the money off the coffee table, with the additional two grand she'd peeled off from her massive roll. Frank left by the side door, went out to the garage, tossed the garbage bag in the back seat, backed his Lexus out, and left – not okay with having a stranger sitting in his home while he wasn't there. But what could he do? She was related to his most frequent flyer. Whatever she said, even in Frank's own house, became stone law.

Once he got to University Avenue, he dialed Mikey. "Hey, are you working today? Good. I need to drop something off." The garbage bag stared at him in the rearview mirror. "I'll be by in a minute."

Frank turned into the Taco Duck parking lot, bypassed the drive-thru lane, and went around behind the building where Mikey, with a face of acne like he'd caught a mouthful of buckshot, stood by the set of dumpsters in his work polo and visor with a mallard wearing a sombrero stitched onto its front. Pulling up close, Frank hummed down the back window. Mikey reached in, took the bag, tossed it in the trash and dropped the lid, gone. Frank rolled up the back window and lowered the passenger side and reached across to slap two hundred dollars in the teenager's soft hand.

"What was it this time, Mister Goode?"

"A fetus," Frank said, leaning to stuff his wallet back into his shorts pocket.

Mikey was laughing, then wasn't. "Wait, are you serious?"

"Just pulling your leg. See you around."

★   ★   ★

Amber Hawthorne was thrust out of dreams about Hawaii by a roiling stomach. And even though the bathroom door was closed and the hiss of a showerhead going, she burst in, dropped to her knees, and got *most* of the acid-hot deposit into the bowl.

Next to Amber still spitting and hacking – a long line of drool connecting her bottom lip to the toilet rim – the shower curtain rustled. Jolene asked through the shower spray, "Are you pregnant?"

"No," Amber croaked. "Just really fucking hungover."

"You hope anyway."

"Well, yeah." Spit. Flush. "Of course I hope not."

"You gonna be all right today?"

"What's today?" Amber dropped the toilet lid and sat, face in her hands. She had comets streaking her vision. She'd always been a violent puker, one of the few things she gave her all to. "What time is it, anyway?"

"It's almost noon. And we've got Mister Petrosky's funeral in an hour and then we got Mister Wicks and Missus Tamblyn getting dropped off tonight."

Amber stood, fought the bathroom floor that shifted side to side under her feet, and started brushing her teeth. She left her reflection hidden behind the fog on the mirror. She didn't want to look at herself right now. "Can I borrow those gray leggings of yours?" she asked around her toothbrush.

"Fine," Jolene said. With a squeak, the shower's hissing ended. Pipes rattled in the walls. "Do we have any clean towels?"

Amber turned around, surveying the towel racks – each empty.

Around the buzz of her electric toothbrush, she said, "Nuh-uh."

"Is it your week to do laundry?" Jolene said. One arm reached from behind the curtain to feel around the bathroom floor. Finding a dirty towel in the hamper, she pulled it back in with her – then a second to wrap around her hair. "I don't mean to nag, but...."

"You're not doing a very good job then," Amber said. She spat into the sink. Her toothpaste foam was brown. She twisted up her face, and killed her incoming queasiness by quickly looking away and running the tap for probably longer than necessary. "I can take a load tonight."

"The Laundromat closes at ten."

"I'm aware."

"We've got a lot of shit to do."

"I know. It'll get done."

The shower curtain's metal loops shrieked and Jolene stepped out, stood next to Amber, and got her glasses on. She paused, looking at the set of toothbrushes in their holder – and which one looked wet.

"Get me a new toothbrush while you're at it, if you would."

★    ★    ★

Jolene poured knock-off Cap'n Crunch – Admiral Tasty – into a coffee cup and added a splash of two percent milk that came in a bag. She took her breakfast into the office and sat in the wingback chair Amber's father had left when he'd signed the place over to his daughter before splitting for Hawaii, the same chair he'd done his business in for nearly thirty years. It was truly amazing to Jolene sometimes that in just a handful of years since taking over they'd nearly run the place into the ground. It was almost like something you'd have to work at, fucking up that routinely and universally bad each time, but they had certainly managed to do so.

She ignored the color-coordinated schedule filled with highlighter and colorful Post-its denoting funerals. At her elbow, there was a pile of screaming-pink envelopes, each marked

OVERDUE or FINAL NOTICE. All they could do was keep putting dead people in the ground and do the best they could to stay afloat, turn out good work with makeup and dressing them properly and doing their hair up nice. One day at a time.

⋆   ⋆   ⋆

'Ave Maria' was sung at the funeral, not very well.

At its conclusion, Jolene tapped her high-heeled shoe on the little lever and Ethan Petrosky was lowered into the ground. People cried. Missus Petrosky, as tan and fit as the eighties-idea-of-fit Mister Petrosky was, didn't jump onto the casket to ride into the void with her betrothed. She kept her composure.

Everyone else cried more than her, actually. Maybe it was a relief. Maybe they'd been having trouble. Maybe Ethan Petrosky was a handsome prick, as that is sometimes (okay, often) the case. Either way, Jolene watched from the back with Amber, both of them in their undertaker outfits – black on black and black on black. The family was now gathering around to toss flowers down onto their lost loved one.

Amber, in sunglasses, leaned over to whisper to Jolene. "You got this? I need a smoke."

"Can it wait? We're nearly done here."

"I didn't have time before getting in the shower. I haven't even had coffee yet."

"Coffee's typically a morning thing."

"I reject your dietary programming," Amber said.

"Well, if you wanted coffee maybe you should've thought about that before getting apocalyptically trashed last night," Jolene whispered back.

They were inches behind the funeral-goers. Though she'd raised her voice slightly above a whisper, apparently no one had heard.

Jolene cleared her throat. "Just wait. We're almost done. Could use one myself. And what's with the miniskirt? I thought you were going to borrow my leggings."

"I couldn't find them."

"They were in my dresser where they always are, second-to-bottom drawer."

"They were too small, okay? There. I said it."

"Maybe you should lay off the beer awhile?"

"And maybe *you* should try to not be such a bitch, huh?"

"You look like the Halloween costume version of a funeral director in that thing. Slutty Undertaker. Is that leather?"

"No, it's not. I love the animals. And for the record, I prefer Promiscuous Mortician. Nothing? Come on, that was good. Are you still mad? I said I'm sorry."

"You didn't, for the record, but forget it."

"Well, thirdly for the record: I'm sorry I look like a slutty undertaker, okay? Now I actually said it. This is where you say you forgive me and you love me and you're not mad at me anymore. I forgave you for calling me fat in that quietly cutting way you did."

"Be quiet."

The family was still tossing in flowers. The priest was coming over with the shovel for Missus Petrosky to drop in the first clump of dirt on her croaked beau.

Amber leaned over to Jolene again. "Is there spaghetti in the fridge at home still?"

"That depends. Did you see any of it in the toilet this morning?"

"Why're you being so pissy?"

"If someone has to ask that, then it should be pretty fucking obvious."

"Don't treat me like we're a couple. You know I hate that. Almost as much as I hate it when people are fucking vague. If you got something to fucking say, don't be a cunt and just fucking say it."

They weren't whispering anymore.

An old man turned over his shoulder to scowl at the undertakers.

"Sorry, sir."

Grunt.

Amber: "Solid save."

"Shut up," Jolene said. "Here comes Missus Petrosky. Pull your skirt down."

"Ladies," Missus Petrosky said, walking up, "could I maybe steal you away for a minute to have a word?"

"Certainly," Jolene said. The three of them stepped to one side as the other funeral-goers filed off to their cars, some still dabbing at their eyes.

Missus Petrosky glanced around. They were alone, just headstones. "Why did he look that way?"

"I'm sorry?" Jolene said.

"My husband. He looked like George Hamilton. Like you put him into the cremator a minute before remembering he was to be buried, not burnt."

Jolene turned to Amber. It felt bad to throw her under the bus, but sometimes, Jolene felt, Amber needed to be put on the spot for her to learn anything.

"I used powder that didn't match his skin tone," Amber said, pausing to swallow, "because I remember when you came in for the consultation you mentioned your husband enjoyed sailing. And I thought maybe giving him a light bronzed look might be nice."

"He looked irradiated," Missus Petrosky said.

"Missus Petrosky," Jolene said, "we're very sorry our services were not to your satisfaction. If there's any way we could—"

"I'll let you girls in on a little secret," Missus Petrosky cut in. "My husband and I have a lot of friends. Or, now that it's just me, I should say I have a lot of friends. And word gets around. A lot of us are getting up there in the years and are starting to make preparations in advance, since not many of us trust such an important thing to our children. I will not hesitate on giving them my full, honest opinion should any of them ask what I thought of how my husband was treated by the girls at the Hawthorne Funeral Home. But I won't go out of my way to tell them, either, because that feels somewhat tactless. I would – and this is just my two cents – if I were you, lean in a little closer and pay attention to what you are doing. This is your livelihood, isn't it? You two don't do anything else but this?"

Jolene and Amber shook their heads.

"So there's no excuse. This is what you do, so do it as well as you can. I admire your fib – Amber, was it? – about putting a darker shade on my husband. That fib took quick thinking. But, in the future, honesty is the best policy. Especially when dealing with senior citizens – in your line, I can't imagine many young people being brought to your door. Because old people may be slow, we may smell weird, we may drive slow and eat slow and bitch a lot, but we have experience with people. We lived in a time before all human contact and communication was done through texts and tweets and bleeps and clicks and what the fuck ever else. And I'm sure it's easy to lie using those means, but when it comes to eye-to-eye talk, real talk, between two people, us old farts know that and we can sniff out a lie a mile away. My point, and I have to get going here, my daughter's waiting for me, is this: if I hear about this mistreatment happening to any of my friends who come into your care or any of my friends' husbands, I will burn your establishment to the ground. Understand?"

Jolene's throat had dried to the point of cracking. She couldn't speak, so she only nodded.

Amber nodded too. "Yes, ma'am. Sorry, ma'am."

"Good. See you around." Missus Petrosky moved off, got into her daughter's waiting SUV, and left with several other attendees. When it was only Jolene and Amber, they both swore under their breath, collected the wreaths and flowers and the chairs, loaded up the hearse, and headed out, both of their minds buzzing from the old woman's threat that neither of them doubted she would make good on.

★   ★   ★

In Uptown, Frank parked his Lexus at the curb in front of Ted Beaumont's two-story house. Frank could've very well still been in his own neighborhood; the burbs look so similar, everywhere.

He stepped out into the clinging humidity – sweat pushing through across his brow immediately – and went up to the front door. It wasn't even ten yet and already it was likely pushing eighty.

Frank knocked.

Ted, six-four, black, and clean-cut, pulled open the door. "Well good *morning*, sunshine!"

"Hey."

"You all right, brother? You look like hammered shit."

"I feel like hammered shit."

"Well, come on in, I got the eggs in the pan. You're just in time."

Frank followed Ted through the living room, side-stepping action figures and Barbie dolls – all lying down and naked, like the aftermath of some gender war had left no survivors. The TV was on, morning talk bullshit at a low volume. The smell of breakfast hooked Frank under the nose and drew him along. His sour guts, for the moment, settled. He took off his sunglasses and sat at the kitchen table.

Ted set a full coffee mug in front of Frank. MY DAD IS THE BEST!

"Mind if I smoke in here, world's greatest dad?" Frank said.

"Rather you not, brother man," Ted said, back at the stove, scraping almost-burned eggs from the pan. "Nadine's on my ass to quit and if she smells it *in the house*, hooboy, watch out. You'll be finding yourself with a new roommate."

"How are you doing?"

"With the smoking? Down to three a day. One after breakfast, one after lunch, and one after dinner."

"Good for you." Frank looked around the kitchen. It was spotless and everything was painted in warm colors and there were pictures, professionally taken, of Ted and Nadine's kids in classy black and white. On the living room wall Ted had hung paintings of the African savannah. Lions lounging in the tall, golden grass and rhinoceroses standing unmovable. Wooden masks, empty eyed and staring. At home, Frank's walls were bare.

"What's a stay-at-home dad do when the kids are school aged?" Frank asked. He took his cup of coffee, went to the back door and stood halfway out, blowing his smoke across the backyard. There was a sandbox and more colorful toys all over – that red Playskool car with the yellow roof that seemed, to Frank, was assigned to your backyard when you had a kid, like it was a mandatory thing your little one required. Frank recalled putting together his kid's red car was a real pain in the ass. The wheel never turned right and Jessica kept getting stuck on things.

"Clean mostly," Ted said, scraping at the eggs like he was chipping ice from a windshield. "But I don't just keep the house and shuttle the kids back and forth. I work. You know I work."

"I know you do," Frank said.

"Amazing thing, the internet. Ten years back if I wanted to do what I do, I'd be sitting in a car, parked downtown, all fucking day long waiting on customers to come strolling by. Not no more. I sit my ass on *my couch* now, feet up, and just let the magic happen, one click-click of the mouse at a time." Ted turned with the two steaming plates of eggs. "Well, it's burnt to shit, but come and get it."

Frank stuck his cigarette butt in one of Ted's wife's potted plants and stepped back inside. The windows were open and someone in the neighborhood was mowing their lawn. Frank always hated that smell; the blood of plants.

"Simone Pescatelli rang my doorbell this morning," Frank said around a mouthful of egg.

"Simone Pescatelli," Ted echoed, picking a fleck of eggshell out of his teeth. "Remind me?"

"She's Big Robbie's niece."

"Shit. Somebody pop her?" Ted asked, daubing his triangle of toast around his plate.

Frank sipped his coffee. "No. I gave her an abortion."

Ted paused bringing the toast to his mouth. "Say that again?"

"I gave Simone Pescatelli an abortion this morning."

"Hold on. Run that by one more time."

"I gave Simone Pescatelli an abortion this morning." Frank didn't care for the internal rhyme in that.

"Good one. Hilarious, Frank." Ted's grin wilted. "Wait. You're serious."

Frank shrugged. "Yeah, I am. Why?"

"I hope you know that's playing with fire, friend of mine. Especially if the would-be-baby was sporting a dick."

"What's the big deal?"

"The big deal is that you assisted in fucking with Big Robbie's lineage."

"Simone's his niece."

"Doesn't matter. That's blood. Think how often the word *family* is said in gangster movies. That isn't by mistake. That isn't stereotyping. They *care* about that shit, capital C."

"I'd say it was her decision."

"How progressive. Did you tumble out of the one percent and land with a bleeding heart?"

Frank shrugged. "Wouldn't matter. Can't legally vote for another three years."

"Any money change hands?" Ted said.

"With Simone? Some, sure. I do run a business."

Ted was still holding his toast. "You gotta get your shit straight, Frank."

Frank counted in his head. Three, two, one.

"You shouldn't have done that for her," Ted said. "Even if she put a gun on you. You should've let her go squeal to Big Robbie and have him ask what she was trying to have done and then *he'd* straighten her out without you ever coming into it. But now that you've done what you did, you're right there in the fucking sauce pot with her, as an accomplice."

"I'm not going to lose sleep over it. Neither should you."

Ted finally bit his toast. "You suicidal or something, Frank?"

"Drop it. I'm sorry I even mentioned it now."

"Well, when Big Robbie sends his boys over to your place looking to put your dick in the business end of some bolt cutters, do me a favor: lose my number."

They were quiet a minute. Just the sound of a neighbor mowing his lawn drifting in through the window.

Ted sat back from his empty plate, folding his hands behind his head. "Noticed you're still driving the Lexus."

Frank swallowed his last forkful of eggs. Nothing tasted right with a hangover, but he was glad to have something in his belly to sop up the warzone going on down there. "No takers."

"You ain't gonna get the price you want for it." Ted picked something out of his teeth, eggshell maybe. "You should just sell it for whatever someone will take it for."

"I paid sixty-five thousand dollars for that car."

"And if you sell it, the thirty-five you *might* get for it will be thirty-five you don't have in your pocket currently. That fucker with the fat wallet is gone. Climb off him, Clooney, he's gone."

Frank said nothing. It was too bright in here. He put on his sunglasses again and pushed his plate back. "Thanks for breakfast. And sorry for insisting we meet this early."

"It's cool," Ted said. "Kids don't get home till one, Nadine's away on business. We couldn't have planned this better. Plus, who doesn't like doing their business over breakfast?"

"I would've preferred to do it over the phone, but that's just me."

"I know it sounds nutty, Frank, but sometimes paranoia, just sometimes, can keep your ass alive."

"Or turn you into a nervous wreck."

"I'll take my chances," Ted said, clipped. "You might consider finding yourself some paranoia, especially since you could be in hot water soon, killing unborn Pescatelli boys."

Frank ignored that. "I always hated morning meetings," he said. "I can't think straight until at least eleven."

"Oh, poor white boy. I bet you ain't never had to work first shift in your life."

"We're going to get into all that again?"

"No," Ted said with a chuckle. "We won't. I just mean you gotta learn to be adaptable is all. Working for yourself means living every single facet of that entrepreneurial lifestyle. There ain't part-time when you're your own boss – if you wanna keep the lights on."

"I'm aware," Frank said. His stomach, though full, started to sour again. He got up and got a glass of water for himself, knowing which cupboard to open.

Among Ted and Nadine's grown-up glasses were colorful plastic sippy cups – Frank remembered late nights scrubbing those with a special kind of dish soap and a brush wand, listening to the radio, while everyone else was upstairs asleep. It felt like someone else's memory. He filled the glass from the tap, sat again, and looked across the table and empty plates at Ted, who continued to wear this know-it-all smirk, hands clasped behind his head.

With his arms lifted, Frank noticed both armpits of Ted's thin cotton shirt had a dark dot of sweat.

"Something wrong with your AC?" Frank said.

"No. We started only using it at night. Bill was getting out of hand."

"Meaning you only get to be comfortable in your own house in the summer when your wife is home?"

Ted looked at him. "Why do you hate my wife, man?"

"I don't hate your wife," Frank said.

"Could've fooled me."

"I just think it's kind of fucked up that you have to sit in this hot house all day without AC – then she gets home and *that's* when it's allowed to come on, after you've spent all day burning to death in here." Frank pulled on the collar of his shirt a few times to push a breeze down his chest. It didn't help much. The eggs and coffee, hot in his stomach, made him feel like he'd swallowed a smoldering coal.

"It was my idea to only have it on at night," Ted said. "I do the budgeting and I don't mind the heat. I'm a Texas boy, remember. And it's not my house – it's Nadine's house as much as it is mine. That 'a man's house is his castle' bullshit doesn't fly here." Ted paused. "And if you was saying shit like that to Rachel, no small fucking wonder you two's divorced."

"I thought I was here so we could do business."

"Hold on. Let's finish this. I was getting somewhere. You're pissed off – on my behalf – because the air conditioner only comes on when my wife is home. You believe me, your friend, is being stiffed on the deal or neutered somehow. I got my home-life shit handled, brother. I don't need you to get riled for me, seeing me as some victim. I do appreciate the concern, even if it is coming from you projecting your ass off."

"All I meant was—"

"Let's not do that shit, man. It's too early for it."

"You fucking brought it up," Frank said.

"I did. But now I'm bringing it back down. Kelly Ripa is still talking in the other room. Minute her fine ass leaves my TV screen *then* we can talk about shit like that, if we must. Bad for digestion. And would you mind taking those off? It's disrespectful."

"I thought that 'a man's house is his castle' bullshit didn't fly here," Frank said, pulling off his shades again and setting them aside. He wanted another smoke already.

"It doesn't. Not with me and not with my wife, but I'm asking you to be polite to me, in my home, because that's just a plain matter of respect, man to man. But let's go back a second. I was getting to my point."

"Were you?"

Ted sat forward, broad shoulders settling over his elbows. Frank, instinctively, sat back. Ted may've noticed this shift in body language, or maybe not – he still grinned for a second before speaking.

"You gotta let all that shit go, man," Ted said. "That old life, that old you? He gone. That *life* is gone, wherever it was headed ain't where you is heading now. You're starting from the ground up. And, so far, I think you're doing a bang-up job, if you don't mind your old buddy giving you an assessment like that – that and I think one man complimenting another, on anything, is uncomfortable as fuck. But, to my point, I think you trying to make your old self cut alimony to the you now on account of you having gotten accustomed to a certain standard of living. And that, without a single solitary doubt, is what's gonna fuck you up faster than anything. You liked eating out every night. Who don't? You liked driving a nice car, seeing people at the light rubberneck at you in their shitty rust-eaten beaters all green-eyed full of envy and shit. Again, who don't? You liked going to the golf course gabbing about whatever white guys talk about – yogurt and camping or whatever. But that asshole fucked up, hard, and he, far as the you now should be concerned, is dead as fuck. The you now has to be realistic. And though it may stick it up your ego's ass a way that ain't particularly pleasant, it's what *has* to happen. I'm just saying this to you because I wanna continue to do business with you, man, and see to it we both have long, long, long, successful careers."

Frank stared at Ted. "You finished?"

Ted laughed. "Fuck you, man."

"Look," Frank said, taking his turn to lean forward on his elbows, "I went from pulling in a shit-ton of money every year to having no medical license, a huge red stamp on my permanent record that says *felon*, and having to work at a fucking grocery store for something to put down on taxes. But I think, if I may say so, I'm doing pretty well – relatively speaking."

"Work-wise, sure, relatively speaking," Ted said. "But I think you're not transitioning very well into this life – or even trying that hard to. Not as far as the important shit is concerned, anyway. But I get it, you're white and you come from money. Which is now all gone, yours and your daddy's, but look at it this way: if you didn't have that, your ass would still be sitting in prison. You're out, you're free, you're *not* sharing a cell with some gangbanger who sold his soul before the pacifier came out his mouth. Unlike a fuck-ton of brothers I know, you got a second chance."

"Fine, fuck it, okay?" Frank threw up his hands. "You're right, Ted, I'm out of prison and I should be clicking my fucking heels. It doesn't mean my prospects are all that great."

"Not to be a dick—"

"Here it comes."

"—but you only owe all of this, your station in life now, to *yourself*. Nobody else. Not a solitary fucking soul asked you to do what you were doing or twisted your arm to do it. Ain't nobody was breathing down your neck or putting the squeeze on you. It was you. That was *your* stupid idea to start doing that shit you were doing and it was *you* who got caught red-handed doing it."

"You don't think I know that?"

"I don't think you do, no. You wanna blame somebody, I know that for fucking goddamn sure. And for whatever reason you come in here with all this fire behind your eyes after I made you breakfast, gave you some of my coffee, and continued to put up with your fucking shitty attitude this early in the fucking day. You're lucky to have me in your corner, Frank. Because without me, where would you be? Huh?"

"All hail Ted, patron saint to fuck-ups." Frank feigned a deep bow.

"Damn straight. But since I'm just that much of a friendly motherfucker, I'm gonna do something extra special nice, as a friend, for you, right now. The morning is usually my time. I sit out back, have my coffee, read the news, after which I come in, take a shit, start the laundry, and put on another pot of coffee while I'm filling orders on the laptop. But because I am that aforementioned friendly motherfucker, I'm going to allow you *some* of that time to get shit off your chest. Because I don't believe anyone else has offered you the opportunity. And, just so we're clear, this is a thing I do *not* allow any other motherfucker to do in my home. Get your own shit straight, I usually say. But, since you are among my oldest of friends, and we are set to make each other some money, that inclines me to be a touch more generous and hospitable with you. So, with that said, please, I implore you: unfurl that shit you're holding on to and give it its much-needed air."

Frank blinked. "What exactly are you asking me to do here?"

"I'm asking," Ted said, "that before we get down to business – which requires a clear head – you vent. In this household, we share our feelings. We get shit off our chests. We do *not* bottle things up. We do not bury them neither, only to let them fucking fester and poison the groundwater and kill every other damn thing around them. Which, in the ecosystem that is Frank Goode, includes me. I don't want my grass to go yellow. I work hard on my lawn. So, tell me, what do you miss most about the old life? And don't say surface shit like your fucking office chair or the few fucking coworkers you happened to actually enjoy the company of and talked about whatever was on HBO last night with. I mean *the life*, what do you miss about *the life*? Big picture."

"Like work itself or…?"

"Whatever comes to mind first." Ted stood and brought the coffeepot over to the table, filled both their cups, and sat again. "Speak it. I'm here all ears. Think of this kitchen as your confessional, brother. Divulge, disclose, confess."

Frank sat back and folded his arms. He didn't have to think too hard.

"Honestly," he said, "it's having to worry about the equipment so much now. At the clinic, I never had to use the same scalpel twice. I don't even know what happened to them, if it was one and done or if they actually disinfected anything or just chucked them in the trash. Now, I obsess over my tools. Keep everything sharp, use the disinfecting oven you got me from when that tattoo shop went under."

"I recall it," Ted said, nodded. "Continue."

"And I guess it's all right, this way," Frank said. "Makes me appreciate what I have. I miss being able to just throw something down on the pan and let it be someone else's concern. I worry about keeping my O.R. clean, which was never my job at the old O.R. It's sort of like I'm the doc in some Western movie, one all-purpose room ready for whatever walks in bleeding."

"You sound like you like it this way."

"Well, it's mine. I have total ownership over it. I just wish I'd found something else for the on-the-books job than the grocery store. My boss just turned twenty, if you can believe it. Not old enough to drink yet, but he sure can tell me, somebody twenty-three years his senior, when I need to tuck in my shirt."

"You'll get there. Just gotta let word of mouth do its thing. I tell people about you. My cousin, who still runs with a crew. I guess they just do clean work since they never need a slug tweezed out of their asses."

"I hate wishing for more work now – even though putting food on the table depends on it."

"Why?"

"I never used to think about it at the clinic – people just came in and we treated them as we could – but I never stopped to think that our livelihoods depended entirely on the imperfect design of the human body. If it wasn't for shit failing inside them, I'd have nothing to do. And now, when I hope for more work, I'm hoping for suffering."

"Suffering that you get to fix," Ted said. "And I get to help keep you stocked up with supplies to make sure you can fix said suffering. We're doing good work, man. I don't think you see that. That whole shit about pre-existing conditions was one of the best things to happen to us."

Frank stared somewhere over Ted's right shoulder, lost in thought. "I didn't really care what was wrong with them when they came in. I just looked at them like problems that needed solving." Frank blinked, focusing again. "You get perspective on somebody's troubles when they're sleeping on your couch screaming 'Don't shoot me!' in the middle of the night."

"You were numb to it. Nothing wrong with feeling shit, even if you're just starting out now. Death is inevitable, for all of us, but it gives contrast to being alive, man. There's an ending we're all trying to stay ahead of."

Both men were quiet for a moment – the kind of quiet talking about death will often inspire, as all present minds wonder about how they will go, and when, and why, and what they'll leave behind other than a slab of rock with their name (hopefully spelled right) chiseled into it.

"You want some more coffee?" Ted said.

"I'm good. Think I might step out for a smoke though."

"I'll join you."

They stood out on the back porch, the morning sun warming their faces. Frank offered Ted the pack.

"Naw, I just meant I'd stand with you while you blackened your lungs. I had my breakfast smoke before you got here. Would've been happy to join you if you'd got here on time."

"Eventful morning." Frank added, "Not that I'm suggesting we return to that topic."

"Yeah, yeah. I made my point." Ted, careful of his back, sat on the porch swing. He rocked lazily forward and back, pushing off with one sandaled foot, slow and easy. "So, that all you miss?"

"Pretty much. Other than the obvious stuff, like Rachel and Jess. But that's sort of unrelated."

"They're part of it, the old life, sure. You had them when you were still practicing – legally, that is."

"Barely. I mean, I had Jess. But Rachel was halfway to the door, even then. Me getting sentenced just gave her that last shove."

"Say, have you two got that custody bullshit squared yet? I remember last time you were by you said something about a hearing."

"We haven't had it yet. We talk to a judge next month."

"How old's your girl now?"

"Sixteen. Seventeen in November."

"Goddamn."

"Tell me about it."

"Where does the time go? So, wait, she don't have any say who she stays with?"

"No."

"On account of you being an ex-con and all, huh?"

"Exactly."

"So you can't see her till y'all talk with the judge, at all?"

"I can see her. She works up at the Dairy Queen in the Mall of America. I swing by once in a while. Rachel doesn't know. She only lets the 'official visits' happen because it's court ordered and even then she makes it sound like she only lets me come over when she feels like I'm allowed, or *deserve* to or whatever. She knows it kills me." Frank flicked the gray ashes from his smoke over the porch railing to the green, green grass below. "I wanna call her heartless for it, but maybe I do deserve it. I can't imagine what Jess hears at school. Word travels. Couple of her friends' parents work at the clinic."

"What's that thing about 'sins of the father' or whatever?"

"Gee, thanks. That makes me feel real good, Ted. I appreciate your kind heart so very much."

"No, I just meant—" Ted started, laughed. "My bad. I take that back. But, hey, you did your time, right? Repaid your debt to society and all that. Breaking rocks in the hot sun, you fought the law and the law won?"

"You think teenagers give a shit about that? They just know Jessica Goode's dad did two years in prison. Some probably know more details than that; fucking clinic was about as bad as high school, all that gossip and shit-slinging everybody did."

"Fuck it. Fuck what kids say to other fucking kids. Doesn't mean nothing anyway. It's all *Minecraft* and fucking Littlest Petshop anyhow."

"For yours *now* it might be just toys and video games, but the twins are both in kindergarten. Just wait until they're in high school, man," Frank said. "Then shit, for the parents, gets *real* interesting. Boys and drugs and worrying some little bitch is going to put a picture of your kid on the internet – something that'll come back to bite your kid in the ass when she's applying for a job somewhere."

"Sure glad we didn't have the internet in school. Some of the shit we did, man? Yikes."

Frank drew in a deep breath, put his cigarette butt in the planter with the other he'd put there already, and sighed. "Mind if we get down to business?"

"Soon as you take those cigarette butts you're cramming in my wife's hydrangeas and walk them over to the garbage can by the garage there, sure."

Frank put his butts where they belonged and stepped back up onto the porch. "Care if we talk out here?"

"Not at all. So, what do you need?"

"You're not going to write this down?"

"Should I?"

"Busy weekend. Supplies got nearly wiped out. Used my last pair of latex gloves this morning. I also need about ten of the STD test kits."

"Ten?"

"The more hypochondriac-prone girls are seeing me twice a week."

"All right, ten blood-test kits, latex gloves. Fuck it, gimme a sec, I'll get a pen and paper."

Lighting another cigarette, Frank stood at the top of the stairs overlooking the yard. He could hear the highway from here, the low hum of commuters heading off to jobs they may or may not like, but most, if not all, were upstanding, over-the-table occupations, clean. He was here, when he should be at an office, feeling expelled from the great flow of having normal, upstanding purpose. The kind he could tell his kids about, brag about at dinner parties. Not anymore. But that was fine. He was rebuilding things, one day at a time. One pregnant prostitute who paid in food stamps. Or working bullets out of some kid's leg who couldn't have been a day older than Frank's daughter. But he was saving lives. And even if it wasn't work approved by the American Medical Association, he was doing what Frank felt he was meant to do.

The five grand he'd gotten this morning got cut in half but his truck was filled with gloves, various antibiotics and painkillers, IV tubing, bags, a new set of clamps, ten blood-test kits. You've got to spend money to make money.

With his Lexus's AC at full blast, windows up, Frank sat at a red light, smoked, drummed his fingers on the wheel, and waited.

This particular light always felt like it took longer to change than any other in town, so he had time to look around.

He used to drive this way to the clinic. Now, the only time he crossed through here was to go see Ted. So many things had changed, businesses had opened or closed, entire buildings gone and replaced with new, shinier ones.

He felt relatively the same, as a person, but his world, in a blink, had shifted. He adjusted the mirror to look at himself. He'd only had a little gray when he was sentenced. Now he looked like his dad. The stress of it all, he guessed, bleaching him from the inside. Maybe he had changed. But on good days, though they were few and far between now, inside, he felt fifteen still – until he looked in the mirror and was a little surprised, each and every time, that he sure as hell wasn't.

His phone thrummed in his pocket. It wasn't a number he recognized, so he let it go to voicemail, not in the mood to have anything threaten his mood, which was approaching what resembled feeling good now that his inventory situation was figured out. He had the day off from the grocery store too. No stocking fruits and vegetables only to return home with an aching back and a want to strangle his prepubescent manager to death and leave him lying among the expired bananas. Not today. Today was his.

The light changed and Frank went another block and stopped again at the next light – he always hated this stretch of town for this exact reason, all stop and go. He'd forgotten all about the caller when his phone beeped the voicemail beep.

He turned down the gale-force winds of the AC, watching for the light to change through his dark sunglasses.

Fuck. He couldn't not know. He brought the phone to his ear.

"I don't know if you remember me," the voice said, "but we bunked together a couple years back and you told me what you do and I thought maybe you still, you know, do some medical shit now you're out. See, thing is, I've got my cousin in the car and he's, well, he's fucked up real bad. I hope you're home, dude."

Hands and scalp going tingly, Frank rushed to call him back. He remembered the guy's voice but not his name. Young guy, young voice with just a drip of an Eastern European accent.

"Hey man, thanks for calling me back, I—"

"Whoa, whoa, hold on. What are you talking about?"

"Me and my cousin, we…well, we may or may not have run afoul of some not-friends of ours and he's got a nine-millimeter round in his leg. Up high, maybe in his junk."

In the background, someone squeaked, "*It fucking hurts, man. Really, really bad!*"

"And you're at my fucking house?" Frank said, beginning to sweat. His lower back felt like it was gluing permanently to the leather seat.

"Just about, I think. Okay, yeah. Is it this little green one on the corner with the red shutters? Three-ten Market Street? This you?"

"Do *not* park in my driveway. Keep driving. Take him to the ER."

"This is your house, though, right? Are you home? Is this your blue Honda?"

Frank's blood froze in his veins. The blue Honda was still there. *She* was still there.

"I'm waving, if you're home. That's me waving if you see a dude waving in the black Caddy."

"*How* do we know each other?" Frank said.

"Bryce Petrosky, dude. We bunked together in the pen, man. I know it was only for a couple months before they moved me but I remembered you told me you were a doctor and—"

"Not anymore."

The passenger on Bryce's end shrieked again. Bryce said, "Just keep pressure on it, man." Then, to Frank: "Look, word gets around. I know what you do. It's cool."

"It's not cool, Bryce. This isn't how I do business." The light changed. On the next block, he pulled into a fast-food parking lot to concentrate. "Keep driving. Take him to the ER."

"So, you're not home?"

Frank had no idea what would be the best thing to say at this juncture.

"Because we can wait, dude. I mean, he's bleeding but it's not like bad-bad."

From the background. "*It's not bad-bad? You get shot in the balls and see how fucking bad-bad you think it is!*"

Frank said, "I'm out of state. I'm on vacation. Very far away." He closed his eyes and wished it was true. It didn't work.

"There's ten grand in it for you, cash, if you get here in the next fifteen minutes. I got other sawbones in my contact list, man, but I figured you might want the business – word on the street is you're struggling. Also, did you mean to leave your garage open?"

Frank almost wanted to ask Bryce to repeat the price, but figured that'd show too much interest. He didn't like his clients to know how hungry he was – but evidently everyone already knew.

"Stay in your car. Don't play any loud music, my neighbors are old and they *will* call the police."

"That's cool. Quiet it is. Say, what are we talking on time? Because, my cuz here is actually looking kind of pale." Then, muffled: "I said keep pressure on it, dude. I know it hurts but just keep pushing down on it, you'll bleed to death." To Frank: "Fucking amateurs, right? So, think you'd be willing to cut short that *vacation* you're on?"

"I'll be there." Frank hung up, pitched his phone into the passenger seat. "Great."

# CHAPTER TWO

In the hearse the undertakers fired up cigarettes, got the radio going, turned on the AC, and merged with the early afternoon traffic on Hiawatha Avenue.

Jolene sat behind the wheel, cigarette forgotten between her fingers, waiting for the light to change. She kept hearing Missus Petrosky's threat.

A hiss of carbonation was freed, followed by a faint tang of citrus filling the car – and something else, something smoky. Amber's soda bottle didn't contain the impossible shade of green of Mountain Dew but something a few shades darker.

"Hair of the dog," Amber said. "Enough with the face, all right?"

"I didn't say anything."

"No, but you made a face."

"I made no face."

"But you did."

"I made a face. Sue me." Jolene squeezed her voice into Amber's higher register. "Do you love me still?"

"I don't talk like that."

"Oh, but you do. You sound like what's her name."

"Jennifer Tilly," Amber said with a sigh. "If I had a dime for every time I heard that, I'd put them all in a sock and beat the next person who said it to death with it."

"Kitty brings out the claws when she's hung over."

"Don't you forget it."

They were quiet for a while. The hearse's engine sounded like shit. The check engine light was on – and had been for weeks.

"You think she'd really do it?" Amber said.

Jolene didn't need to ask who she was talking about. "Yes, I do."

"She have ties to the mafia or something?"

"I've seen the Petroskys show up in the papers a few times, so maybe," Jolene said. "Racketeering, I think."

"What does that even mean?"

"Racketeering? No clue."

"I used to think it meant people were making knock-off tennis rackets."

"I don't think that's it."

"I know. I said *used* to."

Amber clicked away on her phone. She had a few friends from high school who still lived in the area. To Jolene, they were very annoying. Every one of them would never start a sentence without beginning with 'I' and when they were in a room together it was like they weren't speaking to one another, or even hearing one another, but just bleating thoughts at random. She hated how Amber got around them.

"Sorry. That was Susie. They're going to Vegas next week."

"I remember you mentioning that," Jolene said flatly. "And I can see you out of the corner of my eye: you can stop with the puppy dogs anytime you like. We can't afford it."

"Not to be a turd, but it would just be me going. Somebody needs to stay home."

"Exactly. Both of us do. I can't do this alone. And we need to talk about what the fuck you're doing with people's makeup. *Clownish* has been used, more than once. I let it slide because we got so much else going on, but after today…"

"That chick was scary."

"Yeah. She was. So next time…"

"I'll try better," Amber said, on a delay, still clicking away on her phone – texts going out and texts coming in, rapid fire. "They're going to stay in the Bellagio. Oh, can you drop me up here? I need to go see Slug."

"We're broke."

"I'm not going to get anything. I just need to talk to him."

"Do not ask a drug dealer for a loan so you can go to Vegas. I would think that'd be obvious."

"I'm not. I just wanna talk to him."

Jolene pulled up to the curb. "Laundry tonight, remember? That's on you."

"Yes, Mommy, I remember. I'll catch the bus back. You all right to bring in Missus Tamblyn and Mister Wicks when they get dropped off?"

"It doesn't seem like I have much of a choice."

"I just wanna talk to Slug for a minute. I haven't seen him in a while."

"You're not going to buy anything, right?"

"No, I said. I know we're strapped. It's fine."

"Please don't offer to blow him. Have that much respect for yourself."

"What? Gross, no."

"Oh, my God," Jolene said with delight. "*That's* why you wore the miniskirt. Isn't it?"

"*No.*"

"Because I'll tell you, it may've worked in *Basic Instinct,* but Slug won't just want a peek."

"Stop. We're talking about Slug here. *Slug.*"

"All right, well, don't become an after-school special."

"Fuck you. See you at home."

"Love you to pieces. Make good life choices, okay?"

Amber threw the door closed and watched Jolene pull off.

Once the broad back end of the hearse was out of sight, Amber turned and started down the sidewalk, texting while she walked. Her skirt restricted her legs quite a bit so she wound up doing this quick little shuffle with her knees always touching. She didn't mind. She was the best-looking one at the funeral today. She saw how some of those old men looked at her, their thoughts burbling up behind their eyes – those drifting gazes, nabbing peeks when they thought she wouldn't notice. Oh, she noticed.

A new text came in. Amber frowned. None of them were going to volunteer to pay her way to Vegas. Not that she'd ever asked them to. She was hurt, and shoved her phone in her purse after putting it on silent.

Amber clicked her way down the sidewalk with her restricted, short steps.

Slug, or Shawn Klegg as was his Christian name, lived in a two-story Craftsman he got for a song because it used to be a crack den. Not that it really changed much after it was signed over to him – just a different kind of crack den. She never used the bathroom or sat anywhere or touched anything other than the little baggies he handed her at the end of each transaction.

She went around the side of the house, careful of where she stepped to avoid the many piles of dog shit and sun-bleached trash blowing around, and knocked on the back door.

Inside there was a shout, a thunder roll of someone charging down some steps, another shout, saying there was someone at the door, and someone else shouting, "Then fucking answer it."

The door came open a crack. A little kid with a filthy face, no shirt, and shorts two sizes too big for him peeked out at her. He had that look all urban squalor kids have with the puffiness around the eyes like they sleep in an aquarium or something.

"Who're you?" the boy asked Amber's tits.

"Is Slug home, honey?"

"Who?"

"Shawn."

"Who?"

"Your daddy, sweetheart," Amber said through gritted teeth. The itch was on her and it was hot out here and she didn't have the patience for this.

"My daddy plays Xbox with Jesus and Uncle Bunk now. That's what my mommy—"

"Then your stepdaddy, honey," Amber cut in. "Is *he* home?"

"Yep. But he's pooping right now. Wanna come in?"

"I'll wait."

The kid remained standing in the doorway, staring at Amber's tits, mouth-breathing. Amber idly rearranged the apps on her phone, sighed a bunch. More martini glass emojis and yaas queen-ing continued as the Vegas preparations moved on without her. None of them seemed to notice she'd stopped contributing.

At last, Slug smacked the kid out of the way and let Amber in. "Sup, boo? What you here for?"

"I was wondering if you were holding."

"Sheeit, I *always* holding, girl. Come on in."

Slug was probably a buck thirty soaking wet. He was white as white comes, wore his hair in cornrows, weighted himself with a collar of gold necklaces, baggy everything save for a ketchup-dotted wife-beater over his thin hairless chest. On the inside of his forearm he had, no joke, *SHAWN aka SLUG* tattooed. Amber nearly died of laughter the first time he showed it to her.

"Why're you so dressed up?" Slug said, leading her through the kitchen with the overflowing sink full of dirty dishes and a bowl of milk and cereal left to congeal on the counter. Flies were in her ears and angling for her eyes behind her sunglasses.

"I worked this morning," Amber said, batting the flies away. "Could we maybe, you know, do business back outside?"

"Fuck that, hotter than a grilled cheese sandwich out there. We'll go up to my office."

Amber wanted a buzz more than she hated being in his house, she decided. Even though it was always full of the headache-making thrum of a thousand electronics going at once and always smelled faintly like cat pee and leaking industrial refrigerant.

"I was thinking you up and went AWOL on me," Slug said. "Forgot about your boy or found some new slinger to get your shit from."

"I couldn't possibly forget about you, Slug," Amber said.

"That's sweet. But I know it's because I'm your *numero uno* hook-up."

Amber smiled. She wouldn't hurt him lying to him more. They knew what they were to each other.

"Where's my manners? You want a drank or something? I got that purple soda."

"No purple soda. I wanna buy so I can get home."

"Aight, aight, sheeit, you in some kind of hurry?"

"It's laundry day and they close at ten."

Slug laughed. "Chill. It only but noon."

"Yes, but time loses all meaning for me when I'm here, Slug. It's always been that way with you. That one time senior year I thought I was at your parents' place for an afternoon, getting stoned in the basement, and it turned out to be three goddamn days."

"That wasn't my fault. That was the shit we were doing. Can't blame *me* for the time-altering ways of Oxy."

"See? And we're burning even more time talking about how we burned time. Can I make my purchase so I can fucking go home, Slug?" After this morning, with her morning puke still burning the back of her throat and all of the stress with work, Amber needed a pick-me-up the way fire needs air.

"Goddamn, girl. Bring yoself on upstairs then, if you is in such a damn rush."

Slug guided Amber up a creaking staircase with missing spindles and toys littered all over and a laundry basket heaped with dirty diapers, carpeted in flies. At the end of the hall, he threw out one sinewy arm for her. "Step into my office."

The windows were covered with tacked-up beach blankets. Posters for Insane Clown Posse were hung about the room along with pictures of topless chicks with enormous boobs brandishing machine guns and plenty of smeary ink-jet printouts of screen-grabs from *Scarface,* and a large swastika scrawled on the wall in purple marker.

Slug collapsed into a pleather recliner, cranked up the footrest, and gestured to a duplicate chair opposite. Between the chairs, on a milk crate, Amber noticed, was yet another overflowing ashtray, a roll of tinfoil, a pump-bottle of lotion, and a box of tissues. "Take a load off. Put your feet up."

Amber stared at the empty chair, wondering what sort of nightmares had been perpetrated upon its cracking fake leather seat. "I'm good." She hooked a finger into her purse for her money-clip. "I will take a gram, though."

Slug drew out a few feet of foil, tore it off, and produced a small plastic tube from over his ear and bit it between his teeth, smiling up at Amber, who by now had crossed her arms and was trying to ignore the smell of burnt cheese making her stomach turn. "Homeboy of mine swung past the crib last night with some Oxies," Slug said, grinning. "Care to partake, for the sake of old times?"

"No. I want a gram and I want to go. I've got laundry to do."

"You mentioned that. You really need to learn to chill." Slug used a *Boondock Saints* DVD case to grind the little orange pills into powder with his lighter. "You gotta kick back sometimes. *Actually* sit down when someone invites you to. Gotta learn to take it easy for reals, boo."

"If you were to ask Jolene," Amber allowed, "she'd probably tell you I take it a little too easy."

"Just because a girl has a sniff-sniff now and again don't mean nothing bad."

"I'll tell her you think so, Slug."

She watched him sprinkle the pale orange powder onto the little boat he'd made with the tinfoil. "Say, you remember Terrance Stephens?"

"No, but does he sell coke?"

"Naw, he works at Taco Duck now on the drive-thru. Remember in gym class that one time – wait, did you have that gym class with me or was that Jolene?" Sucking on the tube, Slug wiggled the lighter's flame under the tinfoil and vacuumed the thin trickle of smoke rising from the graying pill powder.

"Jolene didn't go to school with us. I met her in college."

"You sure?" Slug said, holding his hit. "Because we went to school with *some* Daria-looking chick."

"That was Natalie Rodriguez. She died on prom night in a car accident. You were driving."

"Oh, right. Anyways, I was just up here the other day, sitting right in this chair, thinking about that time Terrance Stephens shit his pants in gym class climbing the rope. You remember that? A big ol' glob of it slipped out his drawers and hit Mister Langford right on the shoulder, *bloop*, like Terrance was a fucking seagull or something. Man, I fucking miss high school. Being grown sucks."

Fanning the stink of burning pills away from herself, Amber looked around Slug's office – the décor, the trash everywhere, the jackoff-helping paraphernalia. "Things seem pretty much the same where I'm standing."

Slug burned and sucked another line. His eyes were getting glassy. Now was the time to get what was needed out of him before he fell into the haze and couldn't remember his own name, much less where he kept his stash.

"Slug. I'll say it again. One gram. Here's the money in my hand."

Slug tried twice to get his reaching fingers to go where his eyes were looking. He flicked through the bills once, then again. "We're a little light here, boo."

"Front me the last ten."

"How are you gonna do laundry?"

"What?"

"If this is all your cash, how are you gonna get quarters?"

"I'll busk outside the Laundromat playing a kazoo with my ass."

Slug exploded with laughter. "That's real fucking funny. You were always funny, Amber. Man, it's usually the fat bitches who have to have a sense of humor. But you got the whole package. You're like that one bitch, that one comedian bitch in that movie where she's a pussy doctor."

"A gynecologist."

"Naw, that ain't it. Starts with an M." Slug snapped his fingers over and over, glassy eyes searching the water-stained ceiling. "Fuck, what's her *name*. You know who I mean, right? The bitch with the dark hair and she kind of *talks like this*, you know, all lispy and shit?"

"The *coke*, Slug. Where is the fucking cocaine?"

"All right, all right."

There was a soft knock on the door. "Dad?"

Slug scrambled to put the cooler behind the recliner then wad the tinfoil and mash it, with the pale OxyContin powder, down deep within the chair. "What you want? Daddy's got friends over. We *talked* about this."

The door opened a hair, just enough for a nose and mouth to press themselves into the room. "Mom said you need to go down to the DMV so you can get the stickers for the Malibu. She said she already got pulled over once last week and the officer that pulled her over said if he pulled her over again and she didn't have the stickers updated on the Malibu she'd be in really big—"

"Tell her I'll get down there in a minute. Close the motherfucking door."

The door closed. Slug plunged a hand down into his chair to retrieve the crumpled knot of half-burned foil. He carefully unraveled it, the powder mashed into a little yellow pebble inside, a hillbilly heroin pearl inside a tinfoil oyster. "My bitch don't know I still do

Oxy. She thinks I just sling it. My ass would be grass and her the John fucking Deere if she found out, let me tell you. Her brother's doing ten for possession, so poor ol' Oxy kind of has a reputation in this house."

"Sure. Coke."

Slug reached under the recliner and drew out a shoebox. Under the lid were several small baggies, each wound tightly with a rubber band. Amber, for a moment, considered dealing with the repercussions of killing Slug and making off with what could be a several-month supply. He took one of the tiny baggies, of the several, and handed it to her.

"One gram, as the lady ordered."

It went right into Amber's purse. If there was no one at the bus stop in a minute, she might take a bump there or duck into a Starbucks bathroom. "It's been a pleasure, Slug, see you around."

The recliner made a metallic whine as Slug dropped the leg rest. "Hold up. Actually, I'm kind of glad you stopped by – I nearly forgot." He moved around her to stand in front of the door, his tone lowering and that annoying affectation of his falling away. "So, I was at my buddy's place last week and he says he wants to start getting out of smack and shit and move into a new bracket of sorts. I thought of you when he told me what he's fixing to start up with."

"I'm not going to mule shit up into Canada for you, Slug."

"No, no, no, not that. My boy's asking round for anybody who works in hospitals or morgues and shit if they can find him body parts – internal organs and eyeballs and shit."

Amber screwed up her face. "I sincerely hope, for your sake, you didn't give him my name."

"No, no, I wouldn't. It's just I knew you'd probably be by this week and I thought I'd talk it over with you some, maybe see if I could get a taste of the action – be like y'all's intermediary or something. Small percentage, small percentage. That is, if you were down with hollering at him about it."

"I'm not gonna start trafficking in human body parts, Slug. We're getting complaints about our makeup work so I don't think clients will be real pleased looking in the casket and seeing Grandma missing her whole fucking head."

"Won't be any of that. Take shit out of their insides – get me? – and then sew them back up again with a cut piece of Styrofoam or a pillow or some shit in there to, you know, fill them out some. Throw they clothes back on their asses again and nobody would ever know jack. And I mean if you take they eyes, who will know, right? How many people are buried with they eyes open? None I've ever seent and I've got a lot of homies in the ground."

"The answer's still no. Would you move so I can go?"

Slug remained in front of the door. "This shit helps people though. I mean, I was thinking of getting out of the drug game myself. Because I mean it's tight and all, but drugs are bad."

Amber put a hand to her chest. "They *are*?"

"Ha ha. I'm serious. But these parts, they go down to Mexico, down to fucking South America, up to Canada sometimes. Sick-asses get theyselves a new leg bone or a new, you know, wrist part or whatever. It *helps* people, it ain't poisoning them. Real shit, I kinda like the ring of that."

"Except, in my case, if I were to *ever* consider doing this, it would be parts taken from people who've paid me and Jolene to treat them with respect and dignity. And cutting pieces off of dead people, I dunno, Slug. That kind of has the ring of something that's the complete and total opposite of respect and dignity. Not to mention illegal *as fuck*."

"Okay, let me ask you this then. What do those dead-asses need them for? Huh? They dead, ain't they? They ain't using that shit. And do you know what one fucking eyeball goes for on the red market? Six stacks. Six thousand dollars, Amber. And that's just one eyeball, one peeper – singular. Blood, they pay a grand a *gallon* on that shit depending on the type. Hearts: eight hundred per. One kidney: two hundred thousand bucks. Intestines: five Benjamins per *fucking foot*. And speaking of feets – a good-sized pair of dude shoe-fillers go for nine hundred if they have all they toes. They pull the bones out or some shit."

"They probably take them for the tendons and veins for bypasses. A lot of capillaries in the feet and hands." The sounds of a slot machine avalanching a jangling golden jackpot into her lap rang in her mind. All of that money they were just throwing down holes all these years, all that money they could start having from now on. *What? No. Are you actually entertaining this idea?*

"See? You already know half this shit," Slug said. "You and Jo is *made* for this."

"And these aren't exaggerated numbers? Because you and math, if I recall, weren't exactly bosom buddies back in high school."

Slug raised empty hands. "Ask dude hisself. I can text you his digits right now. But I'm getting a finder's fee in this," he said as he thumbed around on his phone screen. "I made this connection between you and him. Remember that. I want you to mention me. I want you to say Slug introduced us, he's the big dick gee who *runs* St. Paul, Minnesota."

"I can comfortably say that I will never say that to anyone, Slug. Nor did I say I'm going to do this. Right now, I just want to hear the prices from the individual who'll be making good on them. I don't trust you with numbers."

Slug pocketed his phone. "Says the girl whom I just let ten dollars slide. I ain't gotta do nice guy shit like that. But since we go way back and we're cool and all...."

Amber's shoulders drooped – he had a point. "Okay, fair. I'll request you get a cut – *if* any deals get made. If. Big if. The biggest if. I still have to talk this over with Jolene."

"Thank you." He actually bowed. "I appreciate that. For real."

Her phoned dinged. She had a text from Slug, just a phone number. "This him?"

"That's him. Dude goes by Rhino."

"Rhino."

Slug nodded. "Yep. Rhino. Scary, right?"

"Scarier than Slug."

He shrugged. "Suits me."

★   ★   ★

The Lexus's tires chirped when Frank turned onto his street at forty-two miles per hour. He barreled up to his house, passing the sky-blue Honda at the curb, tires barking again as he fanned the wheel, turning into his driveway.

In front of the garage he'd left open, as Bryce had said, was a Cadillac Escalade, midnight black. A younger guy in a white T-shirt and fitted jeans stood leaning into the rolled-down rear passenger window, talking to the shot-up cousin if Frank had to assume. The kid noticed Frank arriving, stepped away from his SUV and waved, big and smiley.

Frank didn't return the gesture but sat behind his steering wheel a moment, looking at the side windows of his house – looking for shifting curtains. If her car was still here, he guessed Simone was still inside. Maybe she'd called her uncle, maybe not. At this moment, things seemed calm – besides the Russian kid bleeding in his driveway.

Frank got out of his car, approached, tore off his sunglasses, ignored the handshake offered by the guy he assumed was Bryce, and peeked into the open SUV window.

"You remember me, dude?" Bryce said.

"No. Move. Let me see him."

The second kid lay across the back seat, maybe twenty-three. A red hand clutched the crotch of his skinny jeans and the black leather interior all around him was shiny with blood. The kid raised his free hand and gave a limp wave, half-mast eyes blinking slowly. "Hey, man."

Bryce was at Frank's shoulder. "So, what're we thinking here? Want me to bring him and you can get started?"

"No." Frank pushed past Bryce to get to his house's side door. He paused before entering. "I need to prep. Wait out here. Tell him to keep pressure on it."

Frank stepped inside, locked the door behind him, and drew the blinds. He stepped into the kitchen and peeked into the living room. He flinched when Simone stepped out from the pantry door to his left, whisper-shouting, "Fucking liar. You said you never treated none of the Petroskys."

"I haven't."

"Then what are they doing here?"

"I don't know. I don't know how they knew to call me."

"Do they know I'm here?"

"I don't think so. Does your uncle know they're here?"

"What? He'd sooner poke his own eyes out before he had dealings with those Eastern European shitheads."

"No, I mean, did you call *anyone* when you saw who was in my driveway? And what the fuck are you still doing here?" He thrust a finger at the digital clock over the stove. "Your nail appointment was at noon, wasn't it?"

"I fell asleep. I was getting ready to go when I saw them pull in. I couldn't leave. I don't have your number and my cousins weren't answering my texts."

"What were you texting them about?"

"For *your number*, stupid, to tell you what's going on."

Frank's shirt was getting heavy with sweat. A dark ring around his neck was encroaching toward his belly. He stepped to the kitchen window and peeked out.

Bryce now had the back door of the SUV open and the second kid sitting with his legs hanging out – blood was dripping out of the kid's pantlegs and onto his driveway, a dozen red dots steadily doubling themselves. When Bryce leaned in past the bleeding kid for something inside the vehicle, Frank couldn't help but notice the grip of a handgun poking up out of the back of Bryce's designer jeans.

Simone stepped up next to Frank to peek. He didn't mean to use so much force, but pushed her back from sight.

"Hey!"

"You gotta hide. You can't leave until I deal with them."

"I ain't sharing air with those pieces of shit."

"Go in my bedroom, close the door, and don't make a fucking sound."

"I'm gonna tell Uncle Robbie you helped the Russians."

"Fine. Go fucking hide."

Once Simone had closed his bedroom door, Frank stepped back out into the blazing midday heat, smelling the kid's blood immediately. He held the door for Bryce to help the kid in – he groaned and grunted, painting red smears from his dangling legs across Frank's kitchen linoleum, his living room, and finally across the floor of his operating room. Together Frank and Bryce hoisted the kid onto the table and had him lie back.

"Pretty decent setup you got here," Bryce said, taking in his surroundings. "Almost like the real deal."

Frank washed his hands, barking over his shoulder, "Get his pants off." He swiped a finger into the box of latex gloves and remembered it was empty. "Scratch that. Take my keys, go out to my car, and bring in a box of gloves I have in the trunk. I'll take his pants off."

While Bryce was doing as told, Frank stepped over to the kid on the table. "What's your name?" he asked. As the kid blinked a few times, slow on the answer, Frank glanced out through the sheet of plastic to the hallway beyond. The bedroom door was still closed, but the sun coming in through that side of the house produced shifting shadows on the floor just outside – Simone was pacing in circles. But she wasn't clicking like before. Because her high heels were still in his living room. He just hoped nobody would notice.

"Vasily," the kid finally said. He had that youthful glimmer in his eyes, though right now it was dulled by blood loss, making him look faintly drunk.

"All right, Vasily, hold on. We're going to fix you up, okay?"

Frank used a pair of scissors to cut up along the kid's inseam. He pulled away the blood-sodden denim to reveal pale, skinny twig-legs. His entire crotch was a bloody mess, with the kid's hand barely holding with any strength, red lines drawing themselves down the side of Frank's table and forming dark red pools in valleys of the dropcloth.

The side door slammed shut and Bryce scrambled into the room with the box of gloves. Frank washed his hands again and when he was through told Bryce to do the same. Frank snapped on his gloves and slowly pried Vasily's fingers open. The bullet had entered at a downward trajectory just left of his penis – which had gotten nicked – and, if he didn't bleed to death, Vasily would have a small dick-notch the rest of his life. After taking a nibble out of his prick, the bullet had continued on its journey into his scrotum, detonated his left testicle, and burst out the sack's underside, whereupon it embedded itself in Vasily's left thigh. No exit wound.

"Holy shit," Bryce said stepping over to the table, and swallowed. "That looks...."

"Cousin. Is it bad?" Vasily said sleepily.

"Your balls are, like, exploded. That is so fucked."

"What?"

"Great bedside manner," Frank said. "Move."

"Is he serious? Are you playing joke, cousin? Tell me it's a joke."

Frank turned to his cabinets and began clanging the tools he'd need onto his cart. "Keep pressure on it for him, he can't do it himself anymore."

"With what?"

"With your hands, Bryce."

"But...that's his dick."

"Do you *want* him to die? Because those are your options."

"You better watch how you talk to me, man. I'm having a seriously shitty day. Fucking Vasily here gets shot, the day he's due to bury his father? Fucking sitting in the parking garage at the hotel and he's crying about it and out of nowhere someone fucking shoots at us? Don't those wops have any respect?"

Frank crashed the forceps onto the cart, stomped over to Bryce, took him by his narrow wrists, and guided his hands onto his cousin's crotch. "Shut up," he told him, slow and loud, "and keep pressure on the wound."

Vasily's head thumped back onto the table.

"Oh fuck!" Bryce shrieked. "Is he dead?"

Frank pressed two fingers under Vasily's jaw. "No. He's just unconscious. All your comforting words were a big help. Listen, we have to stop the bleeding. You are going to assist me. I need you to hold the hole open so I can get clamps in there."

"You want me to...what?"

"Like this. Use your fingers to spread the hole in his scrotum open."

"Just you saying that makes me feel fuzzy, dude...."

"Bryce. Open your eyes. Hold it open. Just like this. Now, I'm going to put a clamp in. Okay, all right, that's one. That was an artery. Take this flashlight, turn it on, and hold it right here and use this with your other hand and sop up the blood so I can see. Don't push down. Just dab. Lightly. You're giving a kitten a bath."

"I'm giving a kitten a bath."

"Exactly."

Vasily's left testicle was in pink chunks all around inside his nutsack. Frank had completed hundreds of surgeries in his time at the clinic and while he had seen a few grievous injuries to many a crotch, he could say with confidence he had never seen one quite like this.

"I'm feeling a little weird, dude," Bryce said.

"Just breathe. It's only meat. Same shit both of us have."

"Yeah, but ours aren't inside-out like his."

"Bryce, look at me. Breathe in, breathe out. It's just meat. Okay, now you can use that rag to keep applying pressure."

"But you said to stop pushing down."

"I thought you could stop but it looks like I need to get a better pinch on that artery. You can put down the flashlight, we don't need it right now. Do you know your blood type?"

"A-positive. We did this thing in high school biology where we took samples and—"

"Great story, Bryce, I'm sure, but do you know what Vasily's is?"

"A-positive too, I think. We took the same class."

"You think or you know? It could kill him if you're wrong."

"Ain't blood just blood?"

"No. Blood isn't just blood. Think. Are you both A-positive?"

"Yeah." Bryce paused, nodded. "Yeah. We are."

"You're going to give your cousin some of your blood. See that machine over there? Wheel it over here. Have you ever shot up before?"

"Once or twice. Only socially though."

"Go in that drawer there, take out some of that clear tubing – not that one, the roll next to it – okay, good, now connect it to the side of the machine. Now, screw the needle into the tube and get the needle in your arm. All right, now switch the machine on. It'll start to fill up that container on the side while I get the other end in him." Frank spiked Vasily's arm. "All right, he's ready. Come over here and keep putting pressure on him, otherwise it's just gonna leak right back out of him. Bryce, can you handle this?"

"It's only meat."

"Exactly. Now, if you start to feel light-headed again: say something. Don't be a tough guy. Tell me, got it?"

"Okay, Frank."

"But you're doing great, Bryce. Your cousin will probably live."

"Really?"

"Probably. We still have to get the bullet out of his leg." Frank checked Vasily's pulse again. Weak but maintaining. "We're not out of the weeds yet."

As Frank turned around to get a pair of tweezers from the cabinet, with his back to Bryce, he glanced up the hall again. No sign that anyone was in there. Closed door, dead quiet. Of course, with everything going on in this room Simone could've been screaming her head off and Bryce probably wouldn't have noticed. Frank looked at how Bryce was staring down at his cousin. He was genuinely worried. His eyes were watering and with one hand keeping pressure on his wound, he stroked his cousin's cheek with his other – until his hand started to slip off and Bryce began teetering on his feet. When Bryce collapsed, away came the rag and a gout of red erupted out of Vasily's punctured scrotum and drew a sloppy line up the wall and across the ceiling.

"Fuck."

The needle had torn out of Bryce's arm when he fell. Frank got the bloody rag pressed onto the wound again and, nearly dislocating his shoulder, bent down to retrieve the needle off the floor. Flopping the plastic tube over his shoulder, he reached out with his left hand, right still on Vasily's junk, and felt for a pulse. It was very slow and very weak.

Frank glanced at the container on the side of the transfusion pump. Empty. Vasily's heart had already sucked up every drop. Frank pulled the tube, draped over his shoulder, and caught the end with the needle. A bead of Bryce's blood hung on its tip. Frank let go of Vasily's wound long enough to slap his own forearm twice – and jam the needle in.

Frank looked over his shoulder at Bryce lying slumped against the wall, spit bubbling on his lips and eyes looking in different directions. "Didn't I tell you to *say* something?" He looked at the needle jammed in his own arm. "Well, I hope you were clean."

The container filled, the new blood was pushed into Vasily, and in a few seconds his pulse started to perk up a little, its tempo climbing with each soft thump against Frank's fingers. Having to work against the clock of his own draining blood supply, Frank fed a pair of tweezers to the puckered hole into Vasily's thigh, pushing deeper until he heard the muffled clink of metal touching metal.

★   ★   ★

Jolene sat in the funeral home office, holding the phone and listening to the muted puttering of it ringing, thinking that halfway across the country, in a familiar kitchen, a phone was ringing and her parents were looking at each other, debating who was going to answer it. Maybe they drew straws. Maybe like Amber and Jolene did sometimes, they played a quick game of rock paper scissors. Either way, it wasn't until the tenth ring that Mom finally answered.

"Hey, Mom, it's Jo."

"I know. I saw the number on the little screen thing here. What do you want?"

"Nothing, nothing. So, uh, how are you? How's Dad? I heard you guys were getting some pretty serious rain out that way last week."

"What do you want, Jolene?"

Jolene's eyes moved to the pile of unpaid bills standing in a column on the desk. "So we recently hit kind of a snag here and I was wondering if—"

"Last time you called to ask for money I told you no. Then you went behind my back and called your father at work. You should know an answer from one of us is an answer from both of us."

"I'm sorry, Mom. We were really in a fix and—"

"I bet you were hoping your father answered, weren't you? Sorry to disappoint, sweetheart."

"No, no. I love talking to you, Mom, I do. Sorry it's been a little while, I've been super-busy, but I've been meaning to call."

"It's been a little while since you needed money, too, I suppose. So you might as well start your sales pitch."

"Mom, I think we're in a lot of trouble here."

Her mother sighed. "I know we've talked about this, but nobody asked you to move in with that girl."

"I know, but—"

"Nobody asked you to try and help her. If the business – *her* family's business – is going under, you should just cut ties with her and start over somewhere else. Let her drive it into the ground herself. They say being a mortician is one of the most reliable jobs you can ever hope to have and I'm sure, somewhere else, they're hiring. Think of where you are now as just you gaining experience for a place that'll treat you better, a stepping stone."

"But it isn't just Amber's business, Mom, it's mine too. We're partners. I can't just flake on her. I owe her."

"One misstep in college she helped you with does *not* mean you owe her your entire life," her mom said. "She did a nice thing for you by driving you to the hospital. But I think it's kind of hurtful that you forget you lived with us for almost a year after that. Who paid for the ER visit? Who drove you to your meetings so you could…figure things out, Jolene? It wasn't Amber. It was your father and I. But it's us who's getting the short end of the stick, even after all that. All she did was drive you to the hospital. She didn't even visit you when you were in there. But your father and I never left your side."

"I know, Mom, and I really appreciate what you and Daddy did for me—"

"Don't do that. That may've worked when you were six, but don't do it now."

"I didn't mean to, Mom. I just…I just miss you guys. Mom? Are you there?"

A long hesitation. "I want to bring something to your attention, Jolene. You may say you and this girl are partners now but any other time you call – when it's not to beg for money – it's you crying about how she's not pulling her weight or spending all the money on booze and going out and everything else. You hitched your wagon to the wrong horse and I don't know when you'll learn that. That girl is—"

"Mom, stop. She's my friend."

"Let me finish, Jolene. Until you learn she is *not* really your friend and you don't actually owe her anything, I don't think there's anything more we can do. I'm sorry to do this, honey, but we really can't afford to give you anything more without your father taking on more hours and then he, technically, won't be retired anymore and he'll lose his benefits. So, I'm sorry, but it's sink-or-swim time, baby. But I really hope you figure this out. I love you, Jo-Jo. Goodbye."

"Mom? Mom. *Fuck.*" Jolene had a nice quiet meltdown.

In her bedroom, lifting the lid on her jewelry box, Jolene felt a spike of shame rise in her heart as she looked at her grandmother's necklaces and earrings.

They'd pawned things before. A few of the old things Amber's parents had left behind because they couldn't take them to Hawaii without the shipping costing an arm and a leg.

They didn't have a TV anymore because that was currently hanging on the wall among the many others at the Pawn America across town.

Jolene's fingers were coiling around the three gold necklaces – one of which her grandmother had worn the day of her wedding – and was about to make herself pick them up to take across town to join her TV, when across the house, she heard the doorbell.

She closed the lid on the jewelry box, wiped her eyes, and padded on bare feet up the hall. The house was divided between the living quarters and what the customers would see. Connecting them was the display room with all of the sample caskets and their hardware option boards, fabric swatches and pillows a client could try out to see if, when dead, they'd enjoy resting on that particular model for the rest of eternity. Jolene passed through the display room and into the reception area, going around the check-in counter to check the CCTV giving her the view of the front steps and the garage door around back.

And at her front door, in grainy black and white, Jolene saw Cornelius standing with a dozen roses and the ever-present trilby sitting cocked on his tiny, misshapen head.

She pulled open the door. "Go away."

Cornelius smiled. "Hello, Miss Morris. Lovely day, isn't it? Warm but not too warm."

"What's with the flowers?"

"Oh, these are for you. A dozen red roses. When I saw them, I immediately thought of—"

"Shove them up your ass. Answer's still no, weirdo."

She could've just closed the door in his face, but sometimes, like today, trying to see him struggling, yet again, to convince her to let him in could be mildly entertaining. So she remained leaning on the doorjamb, letting him dig a hole for himself.

"I see you're still a tough customer," he said with a giggle. "You're sticking to your guns, that's good, I like that, an easy sale is no challenge for the salesman. It doesn't feel like a true victory then." The snaggletooth grin plastered on his face didn't budge. Setting the flowers on the porch railing, he adjusted his black silk tie and straightened the lapel of his suit, the color of butter. "Do you like my new suit? I received it in the mail, special order, just this morning. In Japan they call suits like these, roughly translated, 'bossman suits' because wearing them they're meant to instill an air of—"

"You can put it in a new package but you still look like the same sick fuck to me."

His smile still wouldn't come loose. "All right then. Well, if I may steal a moment of your time, Miss Morris, I will begin detailing the latest draft of my proposition to you – I think I might finally get through and have you see my side of things."

"I seriously doubt that."

"Well, if I may, after I say my piece I'll be on my merry way to let you consider what I've said."

Jolene said nothing.

"I take your silence as a stoic yes. Ahem."

As he began his rap, Jolene considered that, if nothing else, she was glad to see someone other than her in this world was being routinely denied simple happiness – though she didn't feel so bad Cornelius wasn't getting what he wanted. But, end goals aside, it was comforting to know she wasn't alone in the uphill battle. It made her feel even worse about herself, in a way, too. Here he was, chasing after this dream of his without any sign of giving up. This – and only this – is what he wanted and he'd try again and again to obtain it. As he spoke, she stared at his round pink face, his oddly tiny teeth. She'd missed most of what he'd said.

"—and so, in conclusion, you'll never know I was here." Cornelius counted on his fingers. "I will be quiet, I will be quick, I will treat whomever you appoint to me with absolute respect, and mostly importantly I will be immeasurably discreet. No one else need ever know of this exchange and what wonderfulness you have permitted this humble man standing before you to experience. So, today, with that said, my offer is one thousand dollars, cash on the barrelhead, right now. What do you say, Miss Morris? Do we have ourselves a deal or do we have ourselves a deal?"

"Fuck off," Jolene said and slammed the door in his face.

She would pawn her grandmother's jewelry and everything she owned before she'd allow that to happen. And, of course, she could've always called the cops on him. But there was something nice about having such stark abhorrence arrive on your doorstep and you get to be the thing to keep it at bay. Jolene didn't feel good about the way her life was going, nor did she really feel that proud of much she'd accomplished in her thirty-two years on this planet, but getting to tell Cornelius to go away once a week, if nothing else, felt like something she had done and done well each and every time.

She had barely sat down in the kitchen when the doorbell rang again. Normally Cornelius only required one tell-off to get the hint. When she ripped open the front door she had a few choice words ready in the chamber – but faltered, seeing it was the handsome EMT with his ambulance parked in the driveway.

"Hey," he said. "Got two for you in the bus. Sign here?"

She scribbled her signature. "I'll meet you around back."

She stepped out into the garage, where the heat felt bottled and worse than in the house, then she side-stepped around the hearse and hit the garage door button and listened to it judder and squeak as it struggled to hoist the overhead door – everything in her life was a little broken, it seemed. They backed the ambulance up and the two EMTs carted in the bodies, one then the other, in their black body bags. Without even being asked, they volunteered to slot each body into a refrigerator drawer in the workroom. She thanked them and she stood in the driveway, watching them go. The ambulance barely cleared the driveway when another large vehicle turned in, a white panel van with Rent-a-Center's logo on the side.

She met them at the truck before they had even gotten out. "We still have one more month. I called and asked for an extension."

One burly mover checked his tablet and said, "Says here today's the day, ma'am."

"Maybe you can just take some of it? We need the couches in the entryway for our clients. The room will be completely empty otherwise."

"It looks like it's not just the couches."

"Come on, guys. Could you call your boss?"

"Sorry, ma'am. Today's the day."

"Yeah, you said that."

"Could you please let us in so we can get started?" asked the second man with the hand-dolly ready.

Jolene sighed and waved her hand toward the house. "Go ahead. Front door's unlocked." She remained in the front yard, which was looking pretty overgrown, she noticed. She couldn't remember the last time she mowed. The Hawthorne Funeral Home sign looked faded from the sun, two of the letters missing. Shithead kids. She watched the movers step in through the front door, close it behind them, kind of hoping they would just take the whole goddamn place, foundation and all. With nothing left, she'd have no choice but to start over. But no, there were always specks left to sweep together with her hands, enough to keep her there.

She turned, seeing Amber coming up the street with a skip in her step. She had her earbuds in, swinging her arms as she walked, occasionally taking a slurp from the green straw of her Starbucks cup, sunglasses on, a smile on her face.

"What's shaking, bacon?" Amber said. "Why are you standing out in the yard?"

Jolene thumbed over her shoulder at the Rent-a-Center van. "We're getting repoed. That's what's *shaking*."

Amber tore her earbuds out. "But I thought you called."

"I did."

"I thought we got an extension."

"I thought so too. But it looks like they changed their mind."

"What are they taking? Not our beds, I hope. Were those rented?"

"Yep. Same as all of the entryway furniture for the clients to sit on, the entertainment center, the coffee table, everything but your dad's desk in the office and our kitchen dining set."

Crossing her arms, Jolene watched the front door to see what would come rolling out of their home first. It was one of their beds, the mattress, stripped of its sheet.

"Why did we rent everything anyway?" Amber said.

"It was your idea! You said you didn't want any ugly cheap furniture. So we rented the nice stuff. Now, it's leaving on a truck."

Amber slurped her Frappuccino. "Say, do we still have the sleeping bags in the basement?"

"I think so."

"Okay, well, at least there's that."

"At least there's that," Jolene echoed flatly.

Amber leaned in close to Jolene's ear. "When we get a minute, I got something I want to talk over with you."

Jolene faced Amber, but kept her arms crossed. "This better be good."

"It is, yeah."

Jolene raised a hand to block the sun from her eyes. "Well? Don't leave me in suspense."

"Not out here. Once they're gone, we'll talk."

"This isn't some fucking scheme Slug dreamed up, is it?"

"It involves him but no, it wasn't his idea."

"What is it?"

"All I can say is this: I think we're gonna be okay."

"That doesn't answer my question, Amber."

"I know. But trust me, we're gonna be okay. All it will take is for you to keep a very open mind."

"I don't like the sound of that at all," Jolene said.

"Could you fucking *try*? I'm trying to get us out of this, Jo."

Jolene watched the two men negotiate a second mattress through their front door. "Okay, I'll try to keep an open mind."

# CHAPTER THREE

Once Vasily had been pulled back from death's door and Frank had gotten him wrapped in a thick diaper of bandages, gauze, and tape, the ex-doctor tore off his latex gloves, gave one peek up the hall to his bedroom door – the shadows had stopped moving around inside, maybe Simone was lying down – and stepped into the living room, where Bryce sat slumped deep into the couch with blood on his clothes and new freckles of it dry on his face, staring at the TV that wasn't currently on, his handgun on the cushion beside him.

"When I woke up you were working on him," Bryce murmured, slow-blinking toward the TV, "and you were giving him your blood. I thought you said the wrong blood could kill him."

"I'm O-negative," Frank said. "Universal donor."

"Oh. That's cool." Bryce cleared his throat, tried to sit up, couldn't. "I will kill them," he murmured. "It was his dad's funeral today and they couldn't even put shit aside for *one day* and let him have that. Fucking animals, all of them."

Frank stepped into the kitchen, got a beer from the fridge, used the corner of his counter to snap off the cap, and collapsed into his easy chair. "Get out. You can pick him up tomorrow."

Bryce remained looking like he'd melted into the couch cushions, turned his head, close-shorn hair still beaded with sweat, and zeroed his small blue eyes on Frank. "You ever fix any of them, Frank? You ever let those wops on your slab, man?"

"Don't get wound up. You'll pass out." Frank bottomed-up his bottle and drained it by half. "Be careful driving home. See you tomorrow. Let's say no earlier than noon."

Bryce sat up again, elbows on knees, head lolling. He was still pale, his eyes drifting every time he tried focusing on anything.

Even sitting up too fast made him look like he was about to face-plant into the floor. "Do you ever fix any wops, Frank? Hey, asshole, I'm *asking you* if you ever fix any—"

"I *treat* patients, Bryce. You fix cars, you fix leaky faucets."

The young man slow-blinked at the beer in Frank's hand. "Can I have one of those?"

"No, because you'll be asleep on my couch after one sip. We worked on Vasily for three hours and I'd like to have some me-time now if you wouldn't mind." Frank put his feet up and clicked on the TV. "Door's over there. I'll watch him tonight."

"You into drag, dude?"

Frank changed channels, then again. "What?"

"Those shoes over there."

Frank's heart turned to cement in his chest. Simone's animal-print pumps lay where she'd kicked them off by the front door.

"Thought maybe they were your wife's or something," Bryce was saying, "but I don't see any other feminine touches in this place. Just those shoes. So you're either married, got a girlfriend, had a visit from a real forgetful pro...or you like to dress up like a chick."

"They're my ex-wife's," Frank said. "I take them down out of the attic sometimes and sniff them when I miss her."

Bryce stared over at Frank, partly grinning. "I don't know if you're fucking with me or...."

"Oh I'm not fucking with you, Bryce. After three hours of working side by side to save your cousin, I feel like we've really developed a bond. Surgeons get that sometimes, especially after really harrowing touch-and-go cases – like ours today, with Vasily. But you and me, man, we're as close-knit as two men can get now." Frank stifled a belch, changed the channels again. "So I feel I can share with you who I really am, the man inside, in here. So, I told you one of my secrets. Give me one of yours. Make it a juicy one or I'll be offended, Bryce."

"Why are you being so weird? You get turned in the pen when I wasn't paying attention?"

*I'm doing this because you're not focused on the shoes across the room anymore.* "This isn't weird, it's just not what you're used to," Frank said. "This is what total honesty feels like, what brotherhood feels like. I mean, we shared a cell for a while and tonight we shared a needle, Bryce. Name a way two people can get closer than that."

"I got a brother," Bryce said. "And it don't feel like this."

"Tell me something. *Share* with me. Don't feel you need to rush, give it a minute. Think. Something you've never told anybody, just like with me and my wife's shoes."

"You never told anybody that before?"

"Not a soul. Now it's your turn. Think. Pretend we're back in the cell together except now there's no one around to eavesdrop on us."

They sat watching TV together. When it went to commercials, Bryce said, "I....I sometimes stood on my bed and peed out the window at night when I was a kid."

"Why?" Frank said, having not looked over at Bryce for any of this. Next channel, next channel. He settled on some home-remodeling show. *Nice kitchen. Oh, that's the before?*

"Because I didn't want to go to the bathroom."

"Why didn't you want to go to the bathroom?"

"It was dark in the hallway."

"I see." Frank finished his beer, set the dead soldier aside. "Now wasn't that liberating?"

"I guess."

"So you could say we trust each other now, right?" Frank finally looked at Bryce. "*Do* you trust me, Bryce?"

"I guess. You're not gonna try and kiss me, are you?"

"No, Bryce. I think you're a nice young man but I don't feel that way about you. But, maybe since we trust each other so much, you'll believe me when I say I'm dead fucking tired and I really need some sleep. Everyone in this house lost some blood today." Including the woman waiting in the bedroom who Bryce didn't know was there, and who Frank was still surprised hadn't let her presence be known in some really easy-to-avoid manner.

"Think I could crash here?"

"Afraid not, buddy. I can't sleep when there are other people in the house."

"But Vasily is staying."

"Yes, but he's on so many drugs he's basically furniture right now. Please leave, Bryce. And don't forget your gun."

"Fine, Jesus, okay, I'll go." Bryce struggled to his feet and stuffed his gun in the back of his pants. He wobbled his way over to the front door. "I'll be by tomorrow. Need me to call or anything before I pull into the driveway or—?"

"Nope. Bye."

The front door closed and Frank was on his feet in a second, crossing through the blood-spattered O.R., swatting aside the plastic sheet, and thumping down the hall to his bedroom. Simone lay asleep, curled on her side on top of the covers. Frank clicked on the bedside lamp and she made a small grunt and rolled onto her other side. "Turn it off."

"Coast is clear," Frank said, "you're free to go."

Simone sat up, squinted around the room. Her eyeliner was smeared down her cheek and on his pillowcase, a blurry black checkmark. "Did the borscht brain make it?"

"Yeah."

"Huh. Shame."

Frank picked her purse up off the floor, wondering at its surprising weight, and handed it to her. "What the hell is going on between your families?"

Simone shrugged. "War's on, I hear. Somebody popped somebody early last month. Dunno. Uncle Robbie don't tell me much."

Frank pointed out the door. "Your uncle shot that kid on the day of his father's funeral. Did you know that?"

Simone scoffed. "I highly doubt it was Uncle Robbie who did it. His big ass is on his third replacement knee, him and 'moving around quick' aren't on the best of terms. But maybe he did – again, I'm not involved in that part of the business. I sit in my little tiny office behind the goddamn shoe store and call my uncle when the police come around asking for him and that's all I do." She spread open hands. "I don't know nothing about nothing about *nobody* getting shot today, yesterday, tomorrow, or when the fuck ever."

Frank peeked out the window. Bryce's SUV was gone. The streetlights were coming on and the crickets had started up. Frank listened for an idling engine, for any sign Bryce had just moved his vehicle out of sight. Nothing. "All right, he's gone. Take off."

When he turned around, Simone wasn't in the bed – and the pillow with the eyeliner smear on it was gone.

Frank rushed down the hall and had barely pushed through the hanging sheet before he heard the muffled *fwap*.

Simone stepped back from what she'd done and put the small chrome pistol in her purse.

Feathers rained about the room. The pillow over Vasily's head quickly grew a bright red circle, further blood dribbling out from underneath, collecting with what was already spilled there trying to save his life.

Frank pressed on the sides of his head with his hands. "What did you just do?"

Simone snorted. "I shot him? Fuck were you?"

"You just said not two seconds ago you don't *know nothing* about anybody getting shot – and then you shoot him, right here in my house?"

"Yep, that's about the size of it."

Frank let his hands drop to his sides and stared at Vasily as feathers landed in the blood puddles about the room, wicking up the red.

The smoke drifted, a rotten egg smell that stung his nose.

"I put three hours into him. I saved him and you just walk in here and fucking kill him."

Simone stepped out of the room and turned into the kitchen. Frank followed, dragging his feet; the sting of losing patients was nothing new to him. But this wasn't lasering a tumor out of a child's brain so they might grow up to do good things. This was sticking fingers in a leaky dam, a dam that *wanted* to break. Pointless. These fucking people.

As Simone ducked to peer into his fridge, Frank collapsed into a chair at the kitchen table. His hands shook as he lit a cigarette. "Why not do that when I first brought him in? Why wait until after I'd saved him to kill him?"

"Because I'm not that great of a shot," Simone said, selecting one of Frank's Tupperware bowls and prying up the corner of the lid to peek inside before putting it back. "If I had shot Bryce and he got away, well, then you'd be fucked – so I didn't, because after this morning, even though money changed hands, I still feel like I owe you one."

"Owe me one?! How is killing a man – or anyone – in any way *helpful* to me?"

"Quit screaming. Jesus. I'm talking hypothetical. I didn't shoot Bryce, here, because if he lived he'd squeal on you and you'd get in a heap of shit with them thinking you was in cahoots with me and my family. So I held off, and only offed the cousin instead. Who was not a very nice boy, for those at home keeping score."

"I can't believe this is happening." Frank could imagine the rattling of a cell door shutting behind him again. This was murder. And without his family's money around to shoehorn him out of trouble again, this would stick. Not to mention if there was one Petrosky in prison with him before, who was to say there wouldn't be another next time? Or more than one. And this time they wouldn't be trying to make friends with him.

Simone pulled open drawers until she found a fork and stood leaning on the counter harpooning olives out of a jar. "Ain't nothing like this ever happened here before?"

"No, nothing like this has ever fucking happened before."

"Don't whine. It ain't manly." She bit another olive off the fork tines, scraping teeth on metal. "Look at it this way, as far as the Petroskys are concerned, Vasily just died in his sleep."

"Oh? Correct me if I'm wrong but in my personal experience, people's brains don't tend to fly out of their head when they sleep."

"Don't interrupt. Look at it this way. You got a blank canvas in front of you right now, paint what you want on it. Tell whatever story you want to tell. Something like, I dunno, you thought you saved him but forgot to button up some blood vessel or something and he up and fucking croaked anyhow. Best intentions and shit." She returned her focus to the olives. "They'll get over it."

"He got shot in *the balls*. And now there's a bullet in his head? How am I going to explain this to them? Huh? They're coming back tomorrow morning to pick him up – and they're expecting him alive."

"Get the fucking gum out of your ears. I just told you. Shit, tell them he left. Snuck out in the night when you was sleeping. They'll go off on their wild goose chase and you'll be in the free and clear."

Before he might pass out, Frank put his head between his knees. "Unbelievable," he told the kitchen floor.

"Okay, you know what? I kind of fucked up," Simone said. "A little bit. I fucked up a little bit. I'll give you that."

"You fucking *think*?!"

"Hey, be nice. I'm trying to help you here. You gonna be nice?"

Head between his legs, Frank just laughed.

"I was just gonna say, if you want, I can help you lug him wherever you usually dump your stiffs. I ain't got anything going on tonight. Already missed my appointment at the salon."

"I don't have a place where I take bodies," Frank said as he quickly sat up, comets streaking before his eyes, "because I've never lost a patient. Not here, anyway. They've all walked out on their own two feet."

"Not nobody never?"

"No."

"Huh. Good job, doc."

"Do you have somebody? Someone your uncle uses?"

Simone was busy angling her fork down into the jar where the more stubborn olives kept dodging her attempts. "Somebody to do what?"

"Somebody *who gets rid of bodies*, Simone. Jesus Christ."

"See, my uncle *does* have a guy, but I'd have to call my uncle to get in touch with him. And I'm not real over the moon about doing that because, see, I'm not supposed to be involved in this side of things – bumping off the competition and whatnot. That's boy work. And the few times in the past I've done shit like this they got all bent out of shape about it. Like it requires a dick shooting somebody. They definitely would this time since they tried doing Vasily earlier today, apparently, and failed. If they hear I did it, Shoe Store Simone? Nah. No, thanks. Thanksgiving is awkward enough."

Frank took three deep breaths. "So you're not going to call your guy because it'll hurt the feelings of the men in your family? You're willing to sell me up the river if it means protecting their fucking *pride*?"

"You don't need to shout at me, I'm standing right here. And ain't nobody being sold up no fucking river neither. Relax."

Through gritted teeth he said, "I'm sorry, Simone. But this is kind of a big deal. There is a dead man in my house who the Petroskys are going to expect to *not* be dead. I can tell them he snuck out, maybe that'll work, but in order for there to not be a Vasily in the other room to make that story convincing, we need to get rid of him. He isn't a goldfish we can just flush down the toilet."

"I understand he ain't a fucking goldfish, Frank." She set the olives aside. "You ain't gotta talk to me like I'm a fucking retard, okay? I grew up in shit like this. Seen this shit all my goddamn life."

"Then *help me*. I'm begging you. Fucking help me."

"I really can't. Wish I could, but I think this is out of my depth. Sorry. Anyhoo, I should scoot. Seen my shoes?"

"You think you're just going to *leave*? No. You're helping me." Frank grabbed her by the arm – and in one smooth motion she twisted, pulling him along, and ran him into the floor, his collarbone banging on the hardwood. She turned his arm back against itself, wrenching his elbow toward the back of his head.

"Stop, stop!"

"You don't wanna touch me. Joey gets slappy with me sometimes, and if I don't take it from my boyfriend I sure as shit ain't gonna take it from you. Now look, this has been a fucked up day. They happen. You gonna try grabbing me again if I let you go?"

"No, no, no."

"Good."

When she released him, Frank held his arm, sitting in the doorway of the kitchen. He watched Simone snatch her shoes off the floor, pause at the mirror mounted next to the front door to touch at the eyeliner smudge on her cheek, and step outside. The screen door screeched shut and Frank, alone with the dead body, heard the beleaguered engine of the Honda start up and drive away. Stepping into his O.R., clutching his wrist, Frank looked at the dead body – and the fire-engine-red thong lying in a twist in the corner, covered in blood and feathers. Vasily's blood. Bryce's blood. Some of Frank's, too.

Frank took his phone out, dialed in Ted's number, hesitated

longer than he did when he'd stuck a used needle in his arm, and hit CALL.

Blaring, bouncy cartoon music was playing in the background when Ted answered, two little voices singing along shrilly. "Hey, can you guys turn that down? Daddy's on the phone. Hello?"

"Ted, it's Frank."

"Hey, what's going on, brother? You sound kinda stressed."

"I am stressed. I have...."

"I'll take that hesitation to be you have something of a *sensitive nature* you wish to discuss with me."

"You could say that." Frank stood in the doorway of the O.R. looking at Vasily's dead arm hanging limp and gray off the side of the table. The pillow was still leaking feathers, each heavy with blood, hitting the floor without a sound.

"I'm gonna ask you what it is," Ted said, quickly adding, "I have not asked yet, mind you. But when I do, your answer must be worded *very* carefully. Gimme a sec."

Waiting, Frank listened to the cartoon music coming through on Ted's end fade, then the creak of a door. When Ted spoke again, it had an echo to it, like he'd gone into the bathroom.

"Okay, go, what is it?"

"Rover died."

"Uh, a little less cryptic maybe?"

"My *dog* died, Ted. One of *my dogs* died."

"Well, uh, okay, did Rover come over to play with a doggy friend who might be able to help you take your furry friend somewhere? Is there a name on Rover's collar?"

"No. Rover's alone. No collar. But his dog buddies are going to expect him to be able to play fetch with them tomorrow morning."

"How did dear old Rover, uh...? Fucking dog metaphor. This is so fucking dumb."

"He got *Old Yeller*ed, Ted."

"Holy shit, Frank. By you?"

"No, not by me. Christ. I spent three hours trying to save his life. I gave him two pints of my own blood."

"Let's keep it cool here, Frank. Remember we're just talking about *dogs*."

"Okay, okay. Sorry."

"It's all right. Now, was Rover the type of dog inclined to bum around with a pack of mean junkyard-type dogs?"

"Very much so."

"And you say he got *put down?*"

"Yeah."

"By his pack?"

"No, a dog from another pack."

"Just now?"

"Yes."

"In your house?"

"Yes, in my house, Ted. I'm looking right at…Rover, as we speak."

"So you want him taken to the special farm in the sky, is what you're saying?"

"*Yes,* Ted. Do you have somebody?"

"Well, a buddy of mine said he just made a new friend. They haven't used them before, but this might be a way for them to get a try-out."

"I don't want somebody who's brand new to this shit, man. I need somebody who knows what they're doing. Don't you have a cleaner or somebody who specializes in dead…dogs?"

"I have a cleaner, yes, but he is currently on vacation in the Keys with his grandkids."

"That doesn't help me much."

"No, it does not. All right, here, I got their address; I'll text it to you. Hawthorne Funeral Home. Ask for Amber."

"Wait. A funeral home will take care of a dead dog?" Frank said, pulling the phone away from his ear a second to check the screen. The text Ted had sent had the address. A neighborhood across town, not far from where Frank used to live with his wife.

"According to my buddy," Ted said, "they've hit hard times and they're looking for a side hustle."

"So they're first-timers?"

"Would you prefer to bury Rover in your backyard?"

"Okay, so what do I do? Just drive it over to this Amber person in my car, or what?"

"Well, you could try emailing it to her but, forgive my doubting nature, I don't think that'll work real good."

Frank knuckled his forehead. His arm still hurt. All he could smell was alcohol swabs, blood, and gunpowder, filling each breath. "They'll take it no questions asked?"

"According to my guy, yeah. Should be as easy as returning a video to the video store. Chick he said he talked to apparently sounded real enthusiastic about starting ASAP."

"Should be easy as that? *Should* be? I don't like should, Ted."

"What do you want me to do about it, Frank? I can't leave. I got the kids here. Nadine's still in Cedar Rapids."

"Have you at least met this funeral home chick, this Amber person?"

"I haven't, no."

"What if I get there and she freaks out and changes her mind? What then?"

"Let's pause a second, Frank, and discuss your options as they presently stand in front of you. You have a dead dog in your house and you don't want Rover's friends to be disappointed tomorrow morning finding out he's dead, because they might get mad at you and bite you a little – or a lot. With it currently…nine thirty-six now, that leaves you only a handful of hours to decide what you wanna do. You can take Rover to the funeral home and risk her potential freak out or you can sit there and get rabies tomorrow morning wishing you'd taken the chance and gone."

"What do I do with Rover if she changes her mind?"

Ted sighed. "That I don't know, Frank. You'll just have to bury him somewhere, I guess, and hope they find him long after *you've* gone up to the special farm in the sky following a long, happy life."

★   ★   ★

There were dents in the carpet where their rented furniture used to stand. Amber and Jolene shouted at each other, their voices echoing in the empty reception area of the funeral home.

"Do you have any idea how illegal that is?" Jolene was saying.

"I know it's illegal. It's *super* illegal. But think about what kind of money we could make. The dude I talked to said he pays a thousand dollars per gallon of blood, if it's O-negative. Think about that. We probably dump hundreds of gallons into the waste tank every year. We were flushing money down the toilet, Jolene. And two hundred thousand dollars for one kidney! Nobody will know if we take one stupid little kidney from somebody. Who'll check?"

"But you haven't met this Rhino guy. You've only texted with him. Anyone can sound trustworthy through text messages. What if it's some kind of, you know, *sting* or something? It's almost worse if he *is* legit. Then we're in some kind of criminal underworld, in people's favor and shit. I don't want that. I just wanna run a regular business, doing what we do, and not have to worry about the police kicking down our door because we're trafficking human body parts."

"I kind of thought you'd be more receptive to this idea," Amber said. "I mean, I knew you'd pitch a fit at first but…you made a lot of good points." She winced.

Jolene's hands went numb. "What?"

"Thing is, I already agreed to it."

The color ran out of Jolene's face. "You *what*?"

"I told Rhino we'd start parting up bodies. They want something by the end of the week."

Jolene held her stomach. "Don't say that. Don't say *parting up*. God, even the lingo is fucking horrifying."

Amber led Jolene over to the reception desk and had her sit in the office chair. Setting aside her glasses, Jolene sat with her face in her hands. "We should've just went bankrupt, got regular jobs, called it when things started getting rough the first time."

Amber knelt in front of Jolene, hands resting on her friend's knees. "Look, I know this is scary. I don't know about you, but I can't work for anybody but myself. Call me spoiled, call me a bad employee or whatever, but I only wanna work with you, J-Bird. We don't have to do this forever. Just enough to get us out of the hole. Three drop-offs to Rhino, max, I swear. After that we can discuss whether or not we want to keep going with it."

"I don't want to discuss us keeping going with it. I want to discuss whether we should start *at all*, Amber. Why the hell did you tell them we'd do it before you talked to me? This is my business too. I know my name's not on the sign but I work here, I live here. This fucks with not only my job, but my home too. We *live* here."

"I know we live here, I know. And this is drastic. This is a big change, for sure. But I made a huge decision I knew you wouldn't follow me on. Sometimes people need a push. Sometimes *you* need a push. And if this works out well and we start doing really good, we can maybe sell this place off and go move somewhere warm, say fuck you to Minnesota winters once and for all. This can be not only what pulls us out of the hole – Jolene, look at me – maybe this won't just *pull* us out of the hole, but *launch* us out of it. We can be done working altogether. Think about that. Not working for ourselves, not for anybody. Isn't that the dream? We can be retired before we're forty."

"I still don't like this."

Amber's knees started to hurt from kneeling so she sat on the desk next to Jolene. She reached out and took Jolene's hands and held them cupped in hers. "You said something to me once that really freaked me out. I'm pretty sure you know what I'm talking about."

"Yeah."

"I came to your dorm one night and your roommate said you had gone to the showers. I thought that was weird because you've always been a morning shower person – and you still are. But I went down to the bathroom and I found you with both your wrists cut and an entire bottle of aspirin in your belly. And when I tried pulling you out of that bathroom stall, do you remember what you said to me?"

"Leave me," Jolene said.

"Yes. You wanted to just close the door and act like I never saw you in there."

"I wasn't doing very well."

"Well, not to make excuses for you but, I mean, it was the first time you were away from your family. You didn't know anybody in Minnesota. But you met me, right? And we hung out, we watched movies, we played video games down in the common room, we smoked pot, we hooked up with guys, we *shared* a guy that one time I don't think you like to think about…"

Jolene closed her eyes. "Could we maybe not…?"

"We had a blast, as you're supposed to in college. My point is, you wanted me to leave you to bleed to death in that bathroom. But I wouldn't. We weren't really close then, but we are now and I think we owe a lot of our friendship, and who we are as a team, to that night. And when I say this, I'm not meaning to make you feel bad, but sometimes, *sometimes* I have to drag you toward things that, at first blush, may not *seem* like the right decision. And with this, today, this could possibly be—"

"No, no, no, you can stop right there. I was trying to kill myself and you convinced me to go to the hospital because you couldn't bear the thought of having left me there to die."

"What?"

"I've been thinking about that night. And I think you're right, we do owe a lot of our friendship to that night – how we work as a team, like you said. But you've been holding that over my head for years how you saved my life. You tell anybody who'll listen about that night. Every time we go to the bar you tell somebody that fucking story. Oh, I saved Jolene's life, Oh, Jolene was so depressed but she's sitting here right beside me now because of me, aren't I so great?"

Amber let go of Jolene's hands. "Would you have preferred I left you?"

"I asked you to, didn't I?"

"Oh don't get all fucking emo about it," Amber said, sneering. "Do you still wanna kill yourself?"

"No, I don't. I took the lessons, did the workbooks, got on and off medication, and I don't wanna kill myself – *but* I don't want to get *murdered* either, Amber. And that's the likely result if we start messing around with fucking criminals. I don't know shit about that world, or how to act, or any of the code words or even if there *are* code words. You may've saved my life once, twelve years ago, but you're threatening it now, by getting us involved in this. Do you see that?"

"Nobody wants to kill anybody. As long as we don't fuck things up and don't strike up a conversation about it with the first cop we see, we'll be fine. We will figure it out. Feel our way through it, same as us taking over this place. Baby steps."

Jolene shook her head until Amber shut up. "I can't do this, Amber," she said. "This is where I draw the line. Either you text them back and say you changed your mind, you won't do it, or I'm gonna go pack my shit and leave."

"You'd seriously just go?"

"Yes."

"Of course. Minute I finally found a way for us to fucking survive this shit-storm, you want to give up. I swear you *want* to be fucking depressed."

"I'm not who I was. And you're not who you were anymore either. We were going to start our own funeral home, have no ties with your dad. But when he handed you this place, you saw it as a free ride. You didn't have to do anything but let me do all the work while you do makeup, badly, and try to drink yourself to death. And I was fine doing most of the heavy lifting; I felt I owed you. But I don't feel I do anymore. We're square."

"Fine," Amber said, face reddening. "Go then, bitch. Fucking *leave*. Go back to Mommy and Daddy and kill yourself in *their* bathroom. See if they bother taking their thirty-year-old loser daughter to the hospital. Maybe if you ask them they'll just leave you like I should've."

Jolene stood. "Take that back." Her hands balled into fists at her sides.

"Go pack your shit, like said you were gonna, and go. Do it. Go."

"I really want to hit you right now."

"Then do it. Commit to something. You keep saying a bunch of shit, follow through. Go ahead. I'll close my eyes and you really wind up and hit me right here in the fucking—"

The doorbell rang.

The room emptied of air.

Amber and Jolene stood facing each other in their empty reception room, all anger falling from their faces.

Amber whispered, "Did the doorbell just ring or am I having a stroke?"

"If you are, then I'm having one too."

They scrambled around the reception desk and peered into the CCTV screens. No one was at the back garage door, but out front a middle-aged guy in cargo shorts, sneakers, and a dark T-shirt was standing on their porch. They watched him reach forward and press the doorbell again, then knock, then shift from foot to foot, and ring the bell a third time.

"Who the fuck is that?" Amber whispered.

"I don't know." Jolene glanced up over the CCTV screen to look at the front door, where he stood just on the other side. "Could it be Rhino?"

"You're so smart. I didn't even think of that. Should we just answer it and ask?"

"This is your thing," Jolene said. "I don't know what's protocol."

"What if he's a cop?"

"He's not dressed like a cop."

"Doesn't mean he isn't one."

"True," Amber said. "So what do we do?"

"I have no idea. Answer it?"

"Look, if that *is* a cop and this is, you know, the end," Amber said, "I'm really sorry for all that shit I said a second ago, I—"

"Stop, it's fine. We have to deal with this guy. He's not going away."

"Let's turn off all the lights," Amber said, "and pretend we're not home."

"Because that'll work. That won't be obvious at all."

The bell rang again.

"Okay," Amber said, "I think I'm gonna just answer it."

"Don't."

"Why?"

"I don't know!" Jolene whisper-shouted. "Fuck, this is so fucked up."

"Come with me. We'll answer the door together."

"Because we're *so* intimidating, right? Us in our Dollar Store flip-flops."

"Come over here. Come on. We'll answer it together. Ready? You do the talking."

"What? No! This is your deal. *You* do the talking."

"Fine, fine, fine, okay. Ready?"

Jolene swallowed, nodded. "Okay."

Amber pulled open the door an inch and peered out at the guy in the shorts standing on their front steps. She dropped her voice low and narrowed her eyes, though she was about ready to piss herself. "Who're you?"

"Hi. I was told to come here if, uh, I had something to drop off." Amber noticed the man's hair was wet and freshly combed. He smelled like shampoo. But under his fingernails, each had a dark red something. He must've seen her notice and put his hands in his pockets.

"Is this a test?" she said. "Are you Rhino?"

He frowned. "Am I a rhino?"

"Not *a* rhino, *the* Rhino. Is your name Rhino?"

"No. It's not. I was told to come here if I had something to drop off." His gray-blue eyes moved between Amber and Jolene. "Is one of you Amber?"

"How do you know my name?" Amber said, noticing the Band-Aid on the inside of his left elbow, the faint red dot in the center. Either a junkie or gave blood today. Something.

"Our mutual friend, I guess you'd call him, told me to come here and ask for Amber. Said if I had something like I have with me, out in my car, I was to bring it here and you'd take care of it." He glanced back, toward the funeral home sign in the front yard, half-buried under weeds. "I suppose you cremate them, huh?"

"We don't do cremations anymore," Amber said. "You need all kinds of expensive permits and stuff for that. Hey. Look at me, guy. Who said you could drop things off here?"

"He's a friend of mine, he's my supplier." He withdrew his hands from his pockets to press them out flat toward Amber and Jolene, in surrender. "Listen, I don't want a hard time. I just really need something out of my possession before the end of the night. It's kind of an emergency. They said you were new to this, well, so am I. I've never done anything like this before in my life."

He seemed sincere enough. Amber decided he wasn't bullshitting and opened the door the rest of the way. "Come in."

They let him in and quickly closed the door. Amber watched him carefully as he ran his eyes around the reception area, the bare wood-paneled walls and the lighter sections of the carpet where the furniture had stood up until earlier today.

Amber moved to stand in front of the door.

Jolene, clearly not sure what to do with her hands, stood far off to the side, staring holes into Amber, her forehead shiny with sweat.

"Hot one tonight, isn't it?" the guy said.

"Yeah," Jolene said. "High nineties tomorrow."

"Is that right? Jeez."

"Good for Fourth of July though," Jolene said. "Supposed to be clear too."

The guy was nodding. "Cool."

Amber rolled her eyes.

"What?" Jolene said.

"Nothing."

The guy turned around to face them again. "So should I just back in to the driveway? I don't mean to rush this, but I really need to get home."

"What's your name?" Amber said. "You know mine so I think it's only fair."

He hesitated before saying, "Frank Goode."

"I'm Jolene," Jolene said.

"Hi," Frank said.

"Hello. How are you?"

"I've been better."

"I know what you mean."

"Jesus Christ," Amber said.

Frank said, "So, uh, is money supposed to be exchanged here or something? Because I didn't think to bring any with me, if that's the case. I could go to the ATM. Or are you supposed to pay me, maybe? I don't know how this works."

"I think we're supposed to pay you," Amber said. "They didn't say. But we're currently strapped at the moment too. Can we maybe work that out later?"

"Sure, yeah, that'd be fine." Frank drew his keys from his pocket. "So I'll go out and back my car in, okay?"

"Wait." Amber kept her back pressed to the door, blocking his way. "Are you, uh, a cop or something? I have to ask."

"No," Frank said. "You know that whole thing about them having to tell you they're a cop if you ask if they're a cop isn't real, right?"

"Not helping your case much, buddy."

"Again," he said, "I am not a cop. Are *you* a cop?"

"No," Amber said. "And neither is she."

"Nope, not a cop," Jolene said. "My uncle was a sheriff for a few years though. He said it sucked. Small town. Nothing ever happened. Fished a couple drunks out of the river, but that's about it."

Frank nodded. "So none of us are cops. Swell. I'll go back in my car now."

"I can't do this," Jolene said.

"Keep it together, Jo," Amber said.

"This is so *wrong*. He probably has a dead kid out there or something. Fuck, did you kill somebody?" Jolene shouted at him. "Is that what's happening here right now? Oh, God. Are we destroying evidence for murderers?"

Amber hissed, "Keep your shit together, Jo." She smiled at Frank. "Sorry. Stressful day."

"I didn't kill anybody," Frank said to Jolene, then looked at Amber. "He was killed, that much is true, but not by me."

"That isn't better!" Jolene shouted.

"Maybe I should leave," Frank said.

"Yes, that's a good idea," Jolene screamed. "Take your murder victim and go, murderer!"

Amber grabbed Jolene by the shoulders. "What the fuck is the matter with you? Be cool."

"Be cool? There's a murder victim in his car!"

Frank ran out the front door, leaving it open. Amber watched him bounding across the front yard with the maximum velocity his dad bod could hope to achieve and get in his car. She threw the door shut and whipped around to face Jolene, who was running through the house screaming unintelligible noise and tearing at her hair.

"You need to calm the fuck down," Amber said, following her from room to room. Through the arranged display caskets, the viewing room, the dining hall, then the reception area again before going through the caskets again. "We have neighbors, you know."

"All our furniture's gone and we got people bringing dead bodies to the house now? What the fuck even *is* our life?"

"They've always brought dead bodies to this house," Amber said, still following. "It's kinda what goes on here, if you haven't been paying attention."

"Yeah, but, you know, through the right channels," Jolene said. "Legally. Not stuffed in the fucking trunk of some middle-aged guy's car."

"Okay, so the maiden voyage was a bust. That's fine. We can work with this. Next time, I'll manage the drop-off. Hey, where are you going?"

"I'm doing like I said. I'm packing my shit and I'm leaving."

"Wait, I thought we fixed all that. I said I was sorry."

Jolene's dresser had gone with everything else, leaving her clothes in a heap on the floor where the bed used to stand. She pulled a suitcase down from the overhead shelf in the closet and began throwing fistfuls of clothes into it.

Amber stood in the door, watching Jolene try to mash her suitcase so it would zip all the way around. "I need your help."

"You should've thought of that before you agreed to let people drop murder victims on our front step."

Amber stepped into the room and knelt beside Jolene. "I've fucked up. A bunch. This place, without you, would not have survived a year. You've worked your ass off. If this place was yours and I had no involvement with it, it'd be doing great now. I know it."

Jolene kept pressing down on her suitcase. "If you're expecting me to tell you you're wrong, I'm not going to."

"I don't want you to tell me I'm wrong. I don't want that and I don't want you to think you owe me anything, J-Bird. But I'm asking you, as my best friend, the Jay-Z to my Beyoncé, just one more time, to be my ride or die. We have two bodies down in the basement. Their funerals are tomorrow morning and the next day. I can't do it alone. I'm not asking you to help me cut them up. I'll do that."

Jolene gave up on ever getting her suitcase to close. She swept the hair out of her face and finally looked over at Amber kneeling next to her. "With what, exactly?"

"I'll need to buy a saw. Rhino recommended one."

"We're broke."

"I have one credit card that hasn't been maxed out yet."

"This feels so awful."

"I know. It is awful. And I know this probably isn't the best time to tell you this, but…."

"Oh, God. There's *more*?"

"The bank's been calling. We have two weeks to pay what we owe or they're going to foreclose."

"Goddamn it, Amber. I'm *through* with this. *So* fucking through."

"I know you are. I know. But I don't have anywhere else to go. Dad left this place to me and took off. He won't return my calls. I think he changed his phone number. He doesn't care. And your parents, well, we tapped that vein too many times. This is on us. We need to be grown-ass adults and this is the only way I can see us getting out of this, in the time required to do it in. I need your help to keep the funerals going while I tend to the side stuff. I'm trying to make up for all my years fucking around. We can do this. Please."

The doorbell rang.

Jolene violently flinched. "What did I *do* in a previous life?"

"Come on, let's go see what that is. Together."

They returned to the reception area again and went behind the desk. The CCTV showed no one on the front porch. But the second screen, giving a downward angle of the driveway, right in front of the garage door, showed a lump lying pressed near the house. The camera's quality wasn't great and to them it looked like an impossibly large black cocoon.

Amber rushed to the front door. She saw a silver Lexus tear out of her driveway, barking tires as it flew around the corner, and speed away. Across the street, she saw the neighbor's upstairs lights come on. She ran outside around the house, across the side yard, hopped through the overgrown flower bed, and slapped on bare feet down the driveway. The motion light clicked on, and as if on stage under a spotlight, there lay a body wrapped in a rug, just like in the movies.

The garage door shuddered open, Jolene standing inside as it rose. Amber watched her stare at the body from behind her smudged glasses, hike her shoulders and sigh. She dragged her eyes up to Amber's, standing on the other side of the body. "Get the shoulders, I'll get the feet."

# CHAPTER FOUR

"Thank you." Amber tried leaning over the body toward Jolene. "Seriously, thank you. Hug me."

Jolene batted her away. "Get the shoulders. The sun will be up soon."

As they hoisted the body off the ground, it peeled away from the cement with a wet sound. Tottering backward, Amber maneuvered the corpse alongside the hearse, pressed the button to drop the garage door, and they waddled it into the workroom, counted to three, then swung it up onto the stainless-steel slab. Upon impact, a puff of white shot out the end of the rolled carpet, each feather seesawing through the air to land on the bleached, tiled floor.

"Think it was a pillow fight turned fatal?" Amber said. "What? Don't tell me we're not in the exact kind of situation that all but *demands* some comic relief."

"I'm really afraid to see what's inside this thing."

"Whoever they are, they don't smell," Amber said, lifting a corner of the rug wrapping the body. "Which is good, because Rhino said we can't bring him anything that's been harvested from someone who's been dead longer than a day. Oh, and none of it can have been embalmed. We have to take everything out of them first. He suggests packing peanuts, to bulk that back up. And when we get the saw, we need to get those coolers that can hold a six-pack, some plastic wrap, and dry ice. He won't accept deliveries in anything else. We need to get their approximate age, gender, and blood type if we can. He really stressed the blood-type thing. He *also* said—"

"Let's just see what we're working with," Jolene said. "And start there."

"Do you want your radio on?" Amber asked.

"Sure."

Once they found some light classic rock station to help bring some levity to the room, they snapped on latex gloves, donned plastic face-shields, and opened the rug.

Inside was a man, probably somewhere around their age, maybe a little younger, close-shorn hair, skinny, and naked. His bloodied face had feathers stuck all over it. He had two bullet wounds in him – one between his pale blue eyes and another in his crotch. The latter wound seemed older, the crust black around the wound, and his legs from groin to his socks, the only clothing he was wearing, were brown with dry blood. Amber couldn't help staring at his massacred scrotum; she didn't have testicles, but still winced sympathetically seeing the disaster that'd been made of his.

"What's the story here you think?" Amber said. "They blew up his junk."

Jolene's mouth was a thin, bloodless line as she surveyed the corpse, hands on her hips, shaking her head. "Some kind of mafia thing maybe."

With her gloved hand, Amber lifted the guy's arm by the wrist. "Rigor mortis hasn't set in. He's still kind of warm too."

On the inside of his left arm there was a small puncture wound. Since it was the only one, he either was a first-time user of intravenous drugs or he'd had an IV put in. On his bicep was a tattoo that looked relatively new; it was still peeling. Russian characters, a string of ten in all.

"You suppose anybody's looking for this guy?" Jolene said.

"Maybe. Better to get this over with soon."

"He's so young," Jolene said. "It's kinda sad."

"We should get to the store. Let's get him in a drawer and go before rush hour starts." Amber tore off her gloves.

Pinching them by the toes, Jolene peeled off the dead guy's socks and stood at the corpse's pale feet, her face a matching bloodless shade.

"What's wrong?" Amber said, turning off the radio.

"I want to stick around."

"Okay, honey. I was never gonna kick you out. Did you think that?"

"No. I didn't think that. But I wanna stay. We can make this work, I think." She looked down at the corpse again. "This isn't what we talked about doing in college. But it's still working for ourselves." She lifted her eyes to meet Amber's again. "Do you feel good about this?"

"I will, once we get paid. It's not like we're selling crack on the street corner. This guy won't miss any of this."

Jolene nodded, small. "Hey, I'm really sorry I said what I said before."

"I'm sorry too. We're cool, you know that, right?"

"Yeah. I do. Okay, let's go get a saw."

★　★　★

Maybe it was muscle memory, but Frank spun the wheel of his Lexus onto 146th and cruised down the empty, dark street. It was tree-lined as it had been before, all the familiar houses. Nothing much looked different. He slowed to a crawl when he came to house 121. The shades were drawn, curtains closed, and he was sure the keys on his keychain wouldn't work in the locks anymore. Not that he would do that. Though they'd said some terrible shit to each other in therapy, then in court when therapy wasn't getting them anywhere, Frank wouldn't become one of those crazy ex-husbands. He still thought about Rachel all the time. The day they met in school. The first time they kissed, in her parents' basement listening to Bob Dylan after feeding the koi fish they kept in a kiddie pool down there so they wouldn't freeze in the little pond out behind the house. The first time they had sex, just a few feet from where they first kissed; the washer and dryer rumbling away helped mask any sound they made from her parents right upstairs. The little gasp she made the third time they had sex, when it worked the way it should've. Then the thousands of times after, and how about year four of marriage it started to taper off and taper off. Hours at the clinic, a million bloody faces. And the faces he wanted to see, those of his wife and daughter, in his memory of those years, were so few and far between until soon, it was waking up at the hospital, working all day, then spending the night there again. Coming home to argue, happy to have his pager go off, giving his daughter a kiss on the forehead as she stared into a computer screen moving little monsters around and her saying 'I love you' like she had no tongue because she was so distracted and probably, now, had a hard time remembering his face because he was never there. A smear of color in her life, the occasional word or two. Or maybe those were just dads she saw on TV.

The lights were on in the house. He could tell by the way the curtains glowed. Only the downstairs ones, though. The upper right window on the second floor was Jessica's room. It was dark. Maybe she was at work or with friends. She sent him a friend request on some social media thing but Frank couldn't ever get his brain wrapped around how it worked so only occasionally checked it. Jessica didn't have Frank in one of her 'inner circles' so he didn't see a lot of what she wrote, only pictures of meals she'd had and the occasional video clip of some singer she liked – Michele something-or-other, some French guy.

Frank pressed the accelerator and left the neighborhood. Back on the highway, having it mostly to himself, he floored it. Away from the funeral home, away from that corpse he didn't make but still had to deal with, away from his old house where he probably wasn't even remembered as having set foot in – he could barely remember living there himself.

*　　*　　*

It was only an hour's drive home but Frank smoked an entire pack of cigarettes in that time, leaving a trail of orange filters across Minneapolis and into St. Paul. The sun was coming up and his car told him the outside temp was already seventy-one degrees. He felt none of it. He kept the air conditioner cranked, only feeling the humidity coming down like a blanket over the city when he tossed out another cigarette butt. The car was full of fog by the time he pulled into his driveway. Missus Shulman, who lived next door, was standing on her side of the hedge with her gardening gloves on, even at this hour, looking at his driveway. She didn't acknowledge him having pulled into the garage until he said, "Good morning, Missus Shulman."

"What's all that there?" she said, pointing with her little hand-rake at the black dots and dark smears on his driveway – a blood trail leading to the side door of his house.

More blood on the doorknob, on the jamb.

It didn't look so bad in the dark when he'd left.

"I barbecued steaks last night," Frank said, blurting it. "Accidentally dropped a few." Before she could look behind him, into the garage, where his grill sat under a coat of dust, he tapped the garage door button to close it.

"Harold and I like to grill out," Missus Shulman said. "Why didn't you invite us over? We were home. Watching TV. Not doing anything. You could've had us over. We would've come."

"It was friends from work. Trying to impress the new boss."

"I thought you were a bag boy at that hippie grocery store."

Frank shrugged, tried smiling amiably. "I'm chasing after a promotion and the best way to a man's heart, I've always heard, is through his stomach."

"Are you trying to impress him or fuck him?"

"Is there anything else I can help you with, Missus Shulman?"

"No. You should clean that up before it attracts flies. If you use dish soap and—"

Frank closed his blood-spattered door behind him and stopped in his kitchen. In the cold light of day coming in through the back window, the blood almost seemed to glow. It had darkened and dried and cracked in places, but in others it still sat pooled bright red and shiny-wet. It smelled like a slaughterhouse. Frank tried not to step in any of it as he moved into the living room and turned to look into the O.R. where the plastic curtain remained pinned back. As Missus Shulman warned, there were flies. More blood. All over his operating table, smeared on every handle of his supply cabinet, all over the sink, the mirror. And the exclamation point, Vasily's artery had come loose and sprayed up the wall and arced across the ceiling.

Frank got out the bleach and the kitchen gloves and got to work on hands and knees. He scraped the most indictable thing, all the bloody feathers everywhere, into small piles and flicked them off the glove fingers into the trash bag. He scrubbed and mopped and sprayed and wiped. He needed some of it left behind, though, because having it *too* clean would tip the Petroskys off. Frank considered how much blood a man shot in the nuts would produce, trying to remember what the O.R. looked like before Simone had shot Vasily. He left some, enough, and took the bag of bloody feathers out to the garage and flung it in the garbage can. He came back inside, set up an oscillating fan to kick some of the stink out of the house, and checked the time on his phone.

It was nearly nine.

He hadn't eaten since breakfast at Ted's the day before and hadn't slept in longer. He had a headache that'd settled across the top of his skull sometime yesterday and had remained bolted there, crushing his brain. He washed his hands to the elbow twice, had a glass of water, started the coffee, scraped the green off two pieces of bread and put them in the toaster.

He was due for the afternoon shift at the grocery store but he was considering calling in sick. He didn't know what time Bryce would be by looking for Vasily and how long it'd take to explain what supposedly had happened. As Frank watched the coils inside the toaster begin to glow orange, he ran through everything he'd need to say to keep himself alive.

"I woke up and he was gone. I didn't hear him leave. I checked on him before I lay down and he was stabilized for the time being. No. I woke up and he was just…gone. I remember I set an alarm for three a.m. and when it went off, I got up and he was just…gone. I thought about calling you guys but I didn't have a number."

He nodded to himself, liking how it sounded. Maybe make it a little more frantic and apologetic, stammer some. Like Simone said, they wouldn't suspect him of killing Vasily after he'd proven himself working so hard to keep him alive. He had that much at least. Frank watched the two slices of wheat bread in the toaster begin to darken, the crusts shriveling away from the heat. He didn't like the idea of trusting total strangers to do whatever they would do with Vasily to purge him from the face of the earth. Frank always liked doing things himself, seeing a job through on his own to know it was done right. He had removed everything he'd put on Vasily, every bandage and piece of tape he'd used. He didn't touch him at any point without gloves on so there was no chance of fingerprints, which Frank had heard were always difficult to lift, accurately, from skin anyway. So other than maybe the odd hair or eyelash, there was nothing on Vasily that could possibly link Frank to him – *oh, fuck.*

Nothing except for the two pints of *your own goddamn blood* you shoved into his veins, you fucking dumbass.

When the toaster sprang, Frank's arm involuntarily delivered a punch to the toaster, spilling charred crumbs everywhere as it clattered loudly onto the bloody kitchen floor. He stood, now with broken skin across his knuckles, mind racing. He had to know. He had to go and see those two women again and ask what they do. He had to know there'd be nothing to link Vasily to him.

He heard a car door close in his driveway. Then a second, then a third, a fourth.

Frank took three deep breaths and started toward the front door before they had a chance to knock. And when they did knock, three hard booms, he didn't answer right away. That'd seem too eager. Bryce stood smiling at Frank with two large men in leather jackets and fitted jeans – perhaps that was Russian mafia enforcer chic – and a small silver-haired woman in a satin tracksuit and both wrists heavy with thick gold jewelry. She had the same pale blue eyes as Vasily.

"Morning, Frank," Bryce said. "This is my aunt Tasha Petrosky and my cousins Oskar and Vlad. We're here to pick up Vasily, if he's ready."

"And discuss your reward for the kindness you showed my son," the small woman with the sharp features and searching eyes said. "Bryce tells me you gave him some of your own blood to keep him alive. You are a true hero, Mister Goode."

All four were smiling politely until Frank said, "Actually, I've been trying to get a hold of you all night, Bryce. Come in."

Bryce, first in, cut through Frank's living room and paused at the pinned-back plastic wall. He turned around, eyes wide in shock. "Where is he, Frank?"

The door closed. One giant, bearded cousin remained near it while the other passed into the kitchen, glancing around, one hand on his belt. He nodded to the first cousin, then to Tasha, who had a seat on Frank's couch and crossed her legs. She looked at him, her face giving nothing, seemingly calm as could be like she knew to expect this.

"Frank, where *the fuck* is Vasily?" Bryce said.

"He was here last night. When I woke up, he was just...gone. I only nodded off for a couple hours. I ran outside to look for him but he was gone. He left his clothes. I would've thought the cops would've seen him and picked him up or taken him to the hospital. I didn't know how to reach you." And the Oscar for Best Actor goes to...

Bryce pulled out his phone and held it to his ear, his eyes glued onto Frank. A half-breath later, 'Dark Eyes' started playing in the next room. Bryce tried avoiding the puddles of blood in the O.R., knelt, and fished a small white cell phone out from under the operating table. He brought it into the living room and put it in Tasha's papery hand, who sat waiting with it open, palm up. She continued to wear the small, sharp smile despite having just heard her son was missing. She thumbed around through his phone, then with both hands and seemingly very little effort, cracked the device in half and set the pieces on Frank's coffee table.

The silence was thick. The oscillating fan shook its head at them, at Frank, blowing the stuffy air around that smelled vaguely like a poorly maintained deli.

"I don't know what happened," Frank said. "I'm really sorry, Missus Petrosky, but he just wandered out in the middle of the night. I know it's my fault, but I really tried to take good care of him. He had enough drugs in him so he'd sleep through the night. I never would've thought he'd wake up in the middle of night, let alone get up and walk out of the house."

Tasha Petrosky sat with her veiny hands in her lap, her large blue eyes touring the room, peering into the operating room, then into the kitchen, then following the blood trails across the floor, then Frank a moment, then to Bryce, the cousins, then at Frank's handful of stale-smelling old furniture.

Bryce cleared his throat. "Aunt Tasha, what should we do?"

Tasha dipped a hand into the front pocket of her tracksuit jacket, took out a cough drop, unrolled it, popped it between her lips, and clicked it around her teeth a few times before answering. "We heard nothing from the police about anyone finding Vasily. He is still missing. It's only been a few hours. Let's not get wound up."

Bryce ran a hand through his hair. "I bet it was the fucking Pescatellis. I'd bet my fucking *life* on it." Bryce balled a fist, looked around the room with it raised, apparently found nothing worthy of destroying, and lowered it. "Goddamn it."

"I'm really sorry about all this," Frank said, trying to keep a balance between slathering it on too thick and not showing *enough* remorse. He wanted to just say it was Simone Pescatelli but had no idea what kind of domino effect that would set in motion and if the war between the two families would eventually circle back around and crush him too or if they'd just snuff each other out. And if word got around he gave up Simone, then he'd have the Pescatellis after him with Simone, at any moment, to turn the whole thing back on Frank with her own brothers and cousins ready to do their *boy work* on him. So it was best to just be Switzerland in this situation, the innocent ex-doctor who just lost track of a ball-shot thug who, as far as the story went, wandered off into the night in his diaper made of gauze.

"Regardless of what happens today," Tasha said, "that can never take away what you did last night, Mister Goode. I would like it if you gave me an estimate on what you feel is owed to you." With a snap of her long fingers, Cousin Number One by the front door produced a billfold and brought it over to his aunt, bending for her to finger through the thick pile of bills crammed within. She looked at Frank, who was currently trying not to let it show he had no idea what to do with his hands. "Well? Please give me a figure – and don't be humble."

Bryce was shaking his head. "This is bullshit. He lost him, Aunt Tasha. He let him walk out of his fucking house, bleeding from the balls, in the middle of the night. And you're gonna *pay* this asshole?"

"I am. Because do you think, if Mister Goode hadn't done what he did to save your cousin's life, he would've been able to walk out of this house at all? No. He wouldn't have been able because he would've been dead. But I can see it in your face, Bryce, that you're just feigning to be upset he's gone. With your uncle and now your oldest cousin out of the picture, that leaves you. But the reins aren't yours yet. We will find Vasily and you will go back to being his second-in-command." She smiled a little more. "Okay, sweetheart?"

"Fine."

"Mister Goode. We need to go begin searching for Vasily. Your fee, if you would."

Frank swallowed. "Fifty thousand."

Tasha's wrinkled brow folded. "I say don't be humble, not greedy."

"Sorry. Ten?"

From the billfold the cousin was holding open, Tasha pinched out the entire wad and put it on the coffee table next to the halves of Vasily's broken phone. As the cousin helped her to her feet, Bryce stomped over and snatched the money away.

"Fuck this. If he was involved in Vasily going missing then you just funded his escape," Bryce shouted at his aunt.

Her face didn't move. "Put that money back on the table and let's go. Mister Goode, we will be back later in the evening to search your home. Please be home. Bryce, get Mister Goode's telephone number so we can reach him if we find Vasily."

Bryce shook the stack of cash in his aunt's face. She didn't blink. "I'm not letting you give him this," he said. "Even if he didn't have nothing to do with Vasily vanishing, we scared the shit outta him. He's gonna run even if he's guilty or not. Weren't you, Frank? That was your plan, wasn't it, asshole?"

"I think I liked you better when you were passed out from blood loss," Frank said. It just fell out of his mouth. Maybe it was exhaustion, maybe it was because he hadn't eaten in over twenty-four hours, maybe at this point Frank Goode *truly* didn't care if he lived or died.

"What did you say to me?"

"I put three hours into him. You were there, Bryce. I gave him two pints, you gave him two of your own. I don't know if it's something from being a doctor for so long or what, but even with you threatening me, I still care about Vasily. I didn't know him before yesterday. I don't know what his voice sounds like when he isn't screaming. But he was my patient and I have an interest in making sure he lives, even if he doesn't owe me a thing." He nodded down at the money in Bryce's hand. "Take that. I don't want that money anywhere near me until I see it for myself that he's alive."

A moment. Frank's heart was about to pop. His feet were sweating.

"That is a very honorable gesture, Mister Goode," Tasha said. "But I have a parrot at home that also repeats things I want to hear. Your ex-wife's name is Rachel, right? She has her maiden name again, isn't that right? Burke, yes?"

Frank's bowels liquefied. "Yes. That's her."

"And you two had a daughter together, seventeen now, named Jessica. She works part-time at the Dairy Queen in the Mall of America, yes?"

Frank nodded. "Yes."

"Due to start her senior year soon."

"Yes."

"All right. I just wanted to make sure I had my facts straight." Tasha took one giant nephew by the arm. "Boys, let's go home. We'll tell everybody what's happened and we'll begin calling hospitals and police stations. Thank you again, Mister Goode, we'll see you tonight."

Bryce shoved the money into his jacket pocket. "Yeah, see you tonight, Frank."

"Get out of my house."

Bryce turned to follow his aunt and cousins. "Go sniff your ex-wife's shoes, *bryet*."

"Piss out a window, idiot."

Tasha Petrosky had a single blood-stained feather stuck to the back of her tracksuit. Upon seeing it, Frank felt all the blood in his body rush toward his feet. Just as Tasha was stepping outside, Frank, feigning to hold the door for them, reached out and pinched the feather from her. Bryce noticed Frank rushing up, all smiles, and sneered at him. A spark of suspicion, but nothing more.

They left.

Frank approached the kitchen sink and calmly vomited. There was nothing to bring up but stringy yellow bile. His toaster was on the floor. The two burned slices, dotted with flies, were sponging up the blood he'd left, just enough, to make it look like a man had walked, nut-shot, out of his house. Whether he was successful, only time would tell.

Once he'd recovered, he stepped into the operating room and surveyed the state of it from the doorway. He noticed his Jerry's

Organic Grocer apron hanging on the wall by the sink. Maybe some time away from this would do him some good. Clear his head with the mindless work of arranging pears and apples in neat little pyramids. He gathered up Vasily's shredded jeans, peeled Simone's panties up off the floor, tossed those into a trash bag with the phone he still wasn't sure why Tasha had snapped in two, set the bag by the door, went to the bedroom, changed out of his shorts and T-shirt, got on his work-issue polo and khaki pants, snatched up his work apron, keys, phone, sunglasses, and the trash bag, and stepped out into the sickening heat.

"Who were those people?" Missus Shulman asked, still at the same spot at the hedge.

The startle made Frank jump like he'd been shot at, his arm pinwheeling sending the plastic bag, weighed by bloody clothes, undergarments, and a broken phone, whipping over his head, snapping back around, and slapping him on the back. "Jesus."

"Guilty conscience? Is that why you're so flinchy, Frank?"

"No, I just figured you'd be inside. It's getting awfully hot out."

"You're up to something," she said. "Those people looked like hoodlums. Except that old broad, she seemed nice. I liked her hair. Do you have them bring old folks over so you can do nasty shit to them against their will? I heard about things like that on the news. That's why the wife leave you? Me and the girls still can't figure that one out. Alice has thirty down saying you're a pedophile."

"Goodbye, Missus Shulman," Frank said, backed his car over the blood-smeared driveway, and began the trek across town to the grocery store.

★   ★   ★

Amber and Jolene sat in the front of the hearse watching the doors of the Mega Deluxo Super Store, waiting for ten o'clock to roll around. The combination grocery store, department store, auto body, liquor store, and fireworks outlet occupied, in cinderblock, a square quarter-mile. To stand in front of it, one could not take in its entire width straight-on with human eyes. But of all the items available at such low, low prices, Amber and Jolene were only interested in a select few, marked on a piece of torn notebook paper, the things Rhino had said they'd need.

"He seemed really nice," Amber said. "Like he knew I was just starting out and wanted to make sure I got the right stuff. He named a few brands for us to look out for, especially when it came to the power tools."

Jolene crushed her cigarette out in the hearse's console ashtray. "Well, I'm very happy for you that you like your new friend. It's ten, let's get this over with."

Amber and Jolene traded the hearse for a golf cart once they were inside the store. The little red electronic buggy had a basket on either side and a red button on the dash for any time you needed assistance. They'd ping the individual cart and dispatch a Mega Deluxo team member on a Segway immediately. Keeping their sunglasses on since it was about as bright inside under the fluorescent lights as it was outside, they hummed through shoes, furniture, sporting goods, and electronics before coming to the home and garden section.

"This is why every other country hates us," Jolene said, watching row after row of specially priced junk slide past her side of the cart.

Leaning out, Amber snatched a four-pack of cigarette lighters and tossed them into her basket. "What? We need them."

They parked at the hedge trimmers and chainsaws and got out of the cart. They took turns lifting the display-model power tools off their racks — each one kept tethered by a long black wire. None of them had their chains on them, or gas in them, so it was impossible to say how much they'd weigh when being used.

"We'll probably be doing this inside," Amber said, holding a chainsaw with a three-foot blade on it out in front of her, "so we should probably go electric. Plus I think they'd be quieter."

"Do we really want to use chainsaws?" Jolene said. The thought of the back-spray when cutting up a body with the thing Amber was currently holding made her stomach pull a twitchy, gurgling somersault. "Because wouldn't that be sort of crude and imprecise? It'll just chew things up."

Amber looked over each shoulder before saying anything more. They were alone in the aisle. "Buyers want the full limb because most of the time it's what's *inside* it they actually want, so the cuts can be crude. They just want the whole thing because the bigger the chunk, the longer decomposition takes."

"That's it," Jolene said, nodding to herself, "I have discovered the ideal diet. It's discussing this shit. Yep. I will never eat again."

"Here we go. This is the one Rhino recommended. The BranchBuster 9000."

"That thing looks nasty," Jolene said. For a garden-care tool it had an angry appearance to it, housed in hard red plastic and its blade cruelly curved like an overly large skinning knife.

"The BranchBuster Compact Chainsaw with patented QuickNibble tooth technology," Amber read from the box, "is perfect for trimming off smaller tree limbs of hardwood variety trees without ever any worry of damaging surrounding bark or foliage. Its narrower blade helps to get into hard-to-reach places and is perfect for dead limbs." Amber paused. "I'm serious. That's what it says, right there. Perfect for dead limbs."

Jolene sighed. "I believe you."

Amber continued reading: "It can use gas or go full electric (at a lower RPM – extension cord not included) and has a lifetime money-back guarantee. Includes chain, oil, and carrying case. Regularly eighty-five ninety-nine, down this week for Summer Deluxo Days to sixty-two bucks. Nice. We'll need an extension cord though."

Into the cart's side basket it went, along with the twenty-foot orange extension cord once they found the aisle that was hiding in. Then the set of plastic painter suits. And a little further down at housewares, two rubber mallets and a set of chisels. Amber read the how-to line of texts from Rhino as they hummed down the store's main thoroughfare, which painted to look like a two-lane highway: "Getting the joints to cooperate sometimes will require a chisel – I suggest one with a sharp point, not that flat tip. Insert tip and hammer it in, wiggle it, then hammer it in a little more until you hear it pop."

"Jesus," Jolene said.

"That's what it says," Amber said. "This is Rhino's instruction, not mine."

"Don't you find it weird how helpful he's being? I mean, you've never even met him face-to-face and he's trusting you to not just turn all these texts over to the cops."

"We took care of that. In every text he makes sure to mention I'm his new employee at his butcher shop and this is just cow parts we're talking about."

They paused their talk while passing other customers in their carts going the other way. They were encountering other shoppers more frequently as they approached the grocery side of the store.

"I still don't like this," Jolene said once they were alone on Deluxo Boulevard again.

"How is it different from what we've been doing?"

"Well, for one, we were never selling their body parts. Or cutting them up. We drain them, put in the embalming fluid, get them dressed, get their eyes glued, get their makeup on—"

"I know the process, Jo," Amber said. "I just mean, sure, this is gonna be a little more invasive than what we've done before but it's still dealing with the dead. The shock of seeing a dead body, to us, is long gone. It's kinda what makes us perfect for this, a clean transition."

"It's still people we're selling."

"Again, they aren't going to miss it. And again, we're helping others by doing this. Remember that."

They hummed along in the cart for a few seconds, silent, passing the tire department and the auto body supplies, then the quarter-mile of wall space made up of nothing but TV after TV after TV all blaring the same thing at once, slightly out of sync with each other.

"It's also sad that people have to get help this way, that it takes getting what they need through the black market just to live."

"Well, be rich and white and you can be top of the list to get your needed organ. Be a senator, be a mayor, be the guy who owns the golf course. See? We're like a couple of Robin Hoods – except we're even better than him because we're not taking from nobody who will miss what we steal."

"The real Robin Hood didn't steal from the rich. He stole from anybody. And it was all to fund his revolution. He was basically a 1600s terrorist."

"You really know how to suck the fun out of a thing, don't

you?" Amber said. "Keep going straight here, we need coolers and dry ice next."

Ten minutes of driving later and they were at the back corner of the store where the camping supply goods were. There they got three Coleman lunch pail–style ice chests. In the section with toilet paper, paper towels, and garbage bags, they threw into the side-basket of their golf cart four rolls of double-thickness and strength Saran Wrap. And up at party supplies (they had to press the red button on the dash to get directions) they got four gallons of dry ice and two pairs of the special insulated gloves required by law to be purchased with any sale of dry ice.

Only four of the one hundred seventy-five check lanes the store had were open. Jolene angled their soft rubber bumper into the swarm of golf carts and put it in park to wait. She noticed a round-faced boy in a baby seat clamped to the top of another golf cart eyeballing them as he contemplatively nursed on a popsicle. Jolene glanced next to her, where the kid was looking, into the side-basket of their cart.

She leaned over close to Amber to whisper, "Is it wise to be buying all this in one go like this?"

Amber put away her phone. "What do you mean?"

"Look at what we're buying. We basically have the dismember-a-human-body-at-home kit in our basket right now. Anyone with half a brain could look at this and put together what we're up to."

"So?"

"So it looks bad, Amber."

"Let me ask you, did you ever work retail?"

The line moved, Jolene inched them forward. "Yeah, at Kmart, in high school. What's that got to do with anything?"

"So I guarantee you we could add a couple of shovels and a bottle of bleach to what we already have in our basket," Amber said, "and nobody who works here would bat an eye. These people get paid minimum wage, which means minimum give-a-shit."

"Maybe you're right. But we still should've found a way to pay in cash," Jolene said. "A credit card leaves a trail. And that still leaves the question, does that have enough room on it for all this?"

"It'll be approved. And, yes, if we had cash, that would've been the better approach, true, but we don't so we can't. Don't get weird when we get up there, okay? We're apprentice butchers. That's the cover, should we need one."

"Okay, okay. Apprentice butchers."

The family ahead of them buying twelve cases of hot dogs and *only* twelve cases of hot dogs finally paid and moved on. The teller stepped out of his little booth with his scanner gun ready in his holster, khaki pants and green vest on – and paused.

Jolene and Amber, in the front seat of their golf cart, also paused.

"Miss Morris, Miss Hawthorne," Cornelius said, "what a pleasant surprise."

The undertakers couldn't put together a word between them. Cornelius came around to Jolene's side and began zapping barcodes. "Coolers, huh? Planning on doing some tailgating this Fourth of July weekend? Looks like you got some plastic wrap for the leftovers too…and a chainsaw."

Amber leaned across Jolene and whispered through her teeth, "Say a fucking word, Cornelius, and I only have to shout three words of my own and your job here is toast."

Moving around to the other side, Cornelius continued zapping barcodes, a line of sweat running out of his high hairline. "Whatever do you mean? I just see two young ladies preparing for a weekend barbecue. Got your dry ice here for making fun drinks and painter's suits to…clean up after your guests. What's out of the ordinary here?"

"I'm serious. 'He's a necrophile.' That's all I gotta shout."

"Perhaps we could come to some sort of arrangement. Consider my silence a favor that you two may be inclined to repay, maybe?"

"We have *you* by the balls here," Amber said, "not the other way around. Is that not evident?"

"Gossip is just gossip," Cornelius said, zapping the chainsaw's barcode. "I can find a new job. But if what I think you two are planning to do later today is accurate, given the items you're purchasing at such low, low prices.…"

"Listen to me, and listen good—" Amber started to say.

"I have your total when you're ready." Cornelius stepped behind his booth and swiveled the screen out so they could see their total. He smiled, holding out the card scanner for them in two hands as if presenting frankincense. "That'll be three hundred and eighty-nine dollars and twenty-two cents. Will that be debit or credit?"

"Credit." Amber swiped the card, and crossed her fingers.

Ten awful seconds passed before the screen flashed green, approved.

"Have a good day, ladies, and thank you for shopping at Mega Deluxo," Cornelius said with the receipt out for them to take. "Would tomorrow be okay for me to swing by for a visit?"

Amber and Jolene exchanged a look and Amber snatched the receipt from him. "Fine."

Outside, they filled the back of the hearse with their purchases, got in, Jolene volunteering to drive this time, lit up smokes, turned on the radio, and headed for home.

"Are we really gonna let him?" Jolene said.

Amber dropped the glove box and shook some powder out onto it. "We'll cross that bridge when we get to it. Do you have a dollar?"

"No. And when did you buy that, might I ask?"

"Yesterday," Amber said and scooped some coke with her pinkie nail and snorted it that way.

"The day you said, straight to my face, that you weren't buying anything from Slug."

"Yes, I know, I know, I *know*, but listen, after tonight none of this piddly little shit is gonna matter. We'll be out of the hole and probably with money to spare, if our Russian friend back home has two good kidneys. If all of him is good, we're looking at close to a million."

"I don't want to talk about that," Jolene said. "I just want it done and over with."

"Want some of this?"

Jolene, at the next red light, glanced over. "Just a pinch."

But before she could hook her fingernail under the little pile to take some, Amber slammed the glove box shut – nearly with Jolene's finger inside – throwing a puff of scattering white everywhere.

"What the fuck? That *Pretty Woman* shit isn't funny." Jolene said, until she saw Amber was staring at the side mirror. "What is it?"

Jolene tried angling her rearview mirror around, looking past the heaps of bags in the back of the hearse, through the rearmost windows. Just cars, every windshield blaring morning light at her eyes.

"There's a cop back there," Amber said, "next lane over, like five cars back."

Jolene couldn't angle her mirror around to see what Amber was talking about, but still believed her. "Do you think Cornelius called them when we left?"

"Maybe. Fucking *shit*, I'll kill that pervert."

"Shit, Amber, look," Jolene said, having angled her rearview mirror the other way.

"What?"

"The silver car, on my side. It's that guy."

"What guy? What're you talking about?"

"Don't *look*. But…you know, look. Over there. The Lexus."

Amber leaned, pulled her sunglasses down the bridge of her nose and squinted over them. "Holy shit, it *is* him. Roll down your window."

"No."

"I wanna discuss his rudeness with him." Amber beat a fist on the horn, the hearse sounding a half-hearted *blat*. The drivers next to them and ahead of them all glanced their way, but not the guy in the Lexus. He was holding the wheel in both hands, staring straight ahead, talking to himself or maybe singing a slow, sad song.

"Roll down your window," Amber said.

"There is a *cop* back there, Amber," Jolene said.

"Roll down your window."

"No."

The light changed.

"Follow him."

Jolene groaned. She knew there was no point in arguing. She threw on her blinker and wedged the hearse over a lane, then another, settling in behind the Lexus. The cop, Jolene saw in her mirror, turned off. False alarm.

They followed the Lexus through a few intersections, into the part of St. Paul where it became nothing but fast-food joints and bookstores – catering mostly to the university students. It was a neighborhood Jolene and Amber both knew well; it was where they'd gone to school, around where Slug lived too. It was one of the few sections of the Twin Cities Jolene knew like the back of her hand. Confidence gaining, and also wanting to have a chat with the man who dumped a dead Russian in their driveway before speeding off, Jolene pressed the accelerator to swarm up large in the Lexus driver's mirrors. The hearse made its rattling and pealing sound being put through the paces like this, but Jolene wouldn't let him evade them – plus chasing some random guy around the city meant more time before having to help Amber disassemble a dead body back home. Little wins.

The Lexus pulled into the parking lot of a strip mall and settled itself into a spot in front of Jerry's Organic Grocer & Wine Shoppe. Though it was a handicapped spot, Jolene swung the hearse in and rolled down her window just as the guy, who apparently hadn't noticed them following him, was getting on a baseball cap and frowning at himself in the rearview mirror."Hey," Amber said, loud, deafening Jolene. "Hey, prick, look over here." She tore the gum out of her mouth and lobbed it out the window where it smacked onto his, and held.

He glanced around, spotted Jolene and Amber mashed into the same window of the car next to him, and went wide eyed. He hummed down his passenger window, the gum going down into the door with it. "What are you two doing here? How'd you know where I—"

"I don't think so, asshole," Amber said, "we're gonna ask the questions right now. What was with last night? We never agreed to take him."

"Look, I'm really sorry about that. But I had to. I had to have him out of my house."

"We would've taken him," Amber said, "but we had to discuss it first, between us. Patience is a virtue, you know. In ten minutes we would've gladly taken him."

He glanced between Amber and Jolene, Jolene unable to keep steady eye contact with him.

"She doesn't look like she believes that," he said. "And last night it looked like, to me, she was on the verge of freaking out and doing something stupid."

"Hey," Jolene said, "I'm new to this, okay?"

"I apologize," he said, "but I had to get out of there. Did you, uh...get rid of it? I was planning on coming back today to apologize, I swear."

"No, we haven't done it yet," Amber said. "We were too busy discussing what it might be worth to you. And now with added interest, for assholery."

"I would pay you whatever you asked," he said, "I really would, but it might have to wait. My money situation hasn't changed since last night. I don't have any money. Can we talk about this later? I have to get to work."

Amber dropped the glove box open again – everything inside now dusted slightly – and snatched out one of the Hawthorne Funeral Home business cards and flicked it across the empty space between the cars. "Call us. And we'll pay you."

He stared at them, holding the business card. "What *are* you two?"

"We're entrepreneurs," Jolene said, dropped the hearse into reverse and pulled them out of the spot. They rejoined the morning rush hour and wove their way through the side streets, what she hoped were shortcuts, back toward the funeral home.

"Why did you say we'd pay him for the body?" Jolene asked.

"If we get what Rhino says we'll get for the Russian," Amber said, "then we'll have enough to spare."

"We hope. I mean, really, Amber, you're counting on a lot of people staying true to their word."

"What choice do I have? It's this or the bank takes the house. And, though it's sorta fucked up to say, I'd trust a total stranger who I only know through their text messages more than the fucking bank at this point."

"All right, all right, but what about paying Frank for the body?"

"It's like my dad used to say. Whatever a person is to you, if you put money in their hand, they become your friend. No, it doesn't *always* work, but I can tell that guy's a lot like us – he's new to this. And if we throw him a couple bucks, he'll remember that. People are a lot more likely to fuck someone over whom they've *given* money to, *lost* money to. We're buying him, in a matter of speaking."

Jolene lit a cigarette. "How much for a kidney again?"

"Two hundred thousand dollars."

"For the set?"

"No. Each."

Jolene sighed out her drag. "Okay."

★   ★   ★

Amber and Jolene, covered head to toe in plastic suits, goggles, and booties, crunched over plastic sheets they had laid down on the floor.

As was custom, Amber said, "On three," and lifted the Russian off the drawer, onto a gurney, and then on a second count of three from the gurney to the slab. Amber found an available outlet for the extension cord and Jolene stood ready with the cling-wrap and a cooler, a look on her face like her mind had abandoned the warm cradle of her skull for a faraway destination.

"So where do you think we should start?" Amber said, muffled behind her paper mask. Her blue eyes, brought out by the white-white painter's suit, flicked over to Jolene. "Or should we both go try to barf again first?"

"I don't think I have anything left," Jolene said, staring at the corpse. The cooler felt very heavy in her hand and her heart was in her throat. "What does Rhino say to start with?"

"He didn't," Amber said, setting aside the saw to thumb through her text chain. "He just says 'drain the cow, bottle the blood, and get it down to thirty-five degrees, then begin taking the cow apart.' That's all."

"We did the blood," Jolene said, motioning toward the refrigerator drawer with the three milk jugs they'd dug out of the recycling, now filled to the brim with Russian red with the digital thermometer punched down through the cap of one. "So do we just hack his legs off or...? Fuck, I can't believe I just heard myself say that."

Amber pulled off her goggles and mask, a red line pressed in across the bridge of her nose and both cheeks, and said, "Maybe you should leave this to me, like we previously agreed."

"I want to help."

"I know you do, Jo, but we still have two funerals – one tomorrow morning and one on Sunday. We need to get those started. So let's say we just go to our separate corners of the workroom and do our own thing. We'll break for lunch – if we can stomach the idea – and maybe if I'm running behind you can help me in the afternoon. Sound like a plan?"

Jolene nodded. "Yeah, I like that. I'm really sorry, but…I just can't. Not yet."

"It's fine. Go get some coffee started." Amber picked up the chainsaw and engaged its electric motor with the thumb switch. The machine numbed her hands with its idling putter and grumbled a nasty, hungry note, ready to be fed. "I got this."

Jolene took off her goggles and mask and paced out of the room in her plastic booties covering her sneakers. She closed the door behind her, crossed through the display room, every empty casket open and waiting, and into the kitchen. She poured coffee beans into the grinder and started it, blowing every other sound away. But when she stopped, the crunching and sharp whine of the electronic motor continued, ringing in her ears, coming through the walls a few rooms over. She bolted to the bathroom, only *thinking* she didn't have any more to throw up.

# CHAPTER FIVE

Frank wheeled the boxes of apples and pears over to the display case, under its cosmetic lighting, and began arranging them two at a time into a neat pyramid. The store was quiet today. Most of his coworkers were his daughter's age. They chatted to each other about movies and music, and often hushed and pretended to act busy when Frank came wheeling by with a fresh box of produce to put away. He was probably thought of as the weird old guy, but he was fine with this. He wanted to focus on this simple task now and think about nothing else. Two apples on the pyramid, two more, two more. Careful of knocking the entire thing over, he completed the apples and started in on the pears. He heard footsteps approaching from behind him and his hands paused, pears in both fists. He closed his eyes, expecting the next thing he heard to be a gunshot – then oblivion.

"Francis," a young male voice said, "can we talk a minute?"

Frank faced his boss, floppy hair in his eyes and a lip ring that'd click against his soda-stained teeth whenever he issued an F- or M-sound from his dopey face.

"Sure. What's up?"

"You punched in late this morning. You were on for ten, not ten-oh-three."

"You're going to write me up for three minutes, Jeremy?"

"It's Mister Ward, Francis."

"Frank. It's right here on my nametag." Every time the automatic doors whooshed open and someone entered out of the blazing heat and into the store, backlit by the sun, Frank held his breath – this time, just a young hippie couple padding in on Birkenstocks and matching dreadlocks.

"Want another one for insubordination?" Jeremy said.

Frank sighed. "No, Jeremy, I don't."

"Look, bro. I know this is uncomfortable for you. It's weird for me too. You're as old as my grandfather but I'm still your manager, bro, so treat me with some respect, cool?"

"Grandfather? How old do you think I am?"

"It doesn't matter. Just buckle down and fly straight, dude. This isn't coming entirely from me. It's my boss who's pushing me to keep an eye on you dudes we get through the release program. I gotta do it. I'll let the insubordination thing go, but you can't be late anymore, man. Work with me here."

The automatic doors whooshed apart and all three hundred pounds of Robbie Pescatelli strode in wearing penny loafers, crisp-pressed black slacks, and a floral-print Hawaiian shirt. He paused in the entryway of the store, ignored the peon trying to shove a coupon book at him, and lifted his aviator sunglasses to scan his surroundings. His heavy face and dark-ringed eyes latched on to Frank and a smile grew, spreading his heavy bulldog jowls wide.

Jeremy was saying, "Because, dude, even if you are like a hundred years old, I still think you can do this job. They probably had you working your ass off in the pen pressing license plates or whatever so I know you can work hard, so, for my sake—"

Robbie stepped up between Frank and Jeremy, a cloud of Brut and menthols catching up after his heavy steps. "Hey, kid. I gotta talk to my pal here so why don't you go get a haircut or something? Looks like you could use one."

Jeremy sneered. "Frank, is this guy a friend of yours? Because you can talk to your buddies on your break, not while you're doing restock."

Robbie swung his prominent gut, swelling his shirt out – much like his niece's had yesterday morning – and aimed it toward Jeremy. "Piss off, kid. Run along and count your pubes or something. Tell you what, if you come back and tell me you got more than two, there's a shiny nickel in it for you."

Jeremy backed away, turned, and ran the length of the store, back to the safety of his tiny manager's office.

Frank felt sweat run out of his armpits and down his sides, two lines racing each other for his belt. "Hey, Robbie, uh, what brings you in?"

"I like that all-natural coconut milk."

"I can't tell if you're kidding, Robbie."

"I am. When's the last time you saw tits on a coconut? I'm here to talk to you," Robbie said. "See, my niece stopped by the house last night and told me she came and paid you a visit and you done a real good thing." He clapped Frank on the shoulder, his hand heavy and hot. "I wanted to come down in person and thank you."

"How'd you know I work here?" Frank said. A quick peek over his shoulder and Frank saw every employee had stopped to stare. "And could we maybe talk about this some other time?"

"My niece said she saw this embarrassing thing they make you wear, hanging in your house," Robbie said, giving Frank's apron string a flick. "I tried calling you but you didn't answer."

"They make us keep our phones in our lockers."

"Ah, well, anyways, about that thing Simone said you did...I want you to keep doing it, every chance you get, understand?"

"I didn't want to do it. But Simone made it sound like it'd be a one-time thing. She said she has a wedding to go to and...." Frank trailed off, unsure what to say. Especially with all of his coworkers listening just a few yards away. Muzak played from speakers above and Frank hoped it drowned out most of what was being said. Subjecting himself to a lungful of Brut, Frank leaned in close to Robbie and said, "She paid me five thousand for it."

"She should've paid you more than that," Robbie said, "and that's why I'm here. Keep up, Frank. You offed that little shit and when she told me, I was over the moon about it. Here I was, thinking you only had the balls for patching up us fellas, not doing in Slavs too."

Frank's mind ground gears. "Hold on, I don't think we're talking about the same thing here."

Robbie looked around them. "Can you take a coffee break or something? All these kids you work with staring at us is giving me the heebies. Fucking *Village of the Damned* over here."

Frank untied his apron and followed Big Robbie out into the wall of heat that rushed in to assault them as the automatic doors parted.

"I'm over here," Robbie said.

His Jaguar sat glimmering like a wet stone off on its own, parked diagonally across four spots.

Frank, as he followed Robbie's labored breaths, glanced around to make sure the two undertakers in their rust-eaten hearse were gone. They were.

"Get in."

Frank let the Jaguar's leather seat hug him. Robbie, on his side, had some difficulty wedging himself back in behind the wheel. After pulling the door shut, he sat staring out the windshield a moment as hippies came and got their Fourth of July tofu and bundles of organic leeks. Realizing they were being observed, the couple with the matching multicolored dreadlocks, in unison, presented two fingers toward Robbie and Frank in the Jaguar. Frank, in return, lifted only one finger.

"Is there gonna be another Woodstock or something? What *planet* is this?"

"It's an organic grocery store," Frank said. "So, what exactly did Simone say I did for her?"

"She said one of the Petrosky boys came in all shot up, at your place. That was Louie who done that to him, FYI. He's a shit shot, I keep telling him, but he says he wants the work so I send him – anyway, evidently Vasily Petrosky ended up at your place, huh?"

Frank swallowed dryly. "He did."

"And Simone says she was at your place too, hiding in your bedroom."

"I told her to hide," Frank said, adding, "nothing happened before that, I swear."

"Except something *did* happen, Frank. You wanna tell me about *that*, huh? That little favor you did her? We'll put the Vasily Petrosky discussion on pause a minute."

"What did she say I did for her?"

"She says you gave her something for her back. This being with her knowing we got a pharmacist in the family. But she goes to an outside associate to get her pills? And I mean this ain't none of your fault, you don't know who's a friend of ours and who ain't. But I just wanna tell you something right now if I may: don't give her no more pills, Frank. Get it? She needs something, she can come to me and I can send her to our guy. And if you gotta give her something, give her diet pills. She's too young to be going to fat – she ain't even married off yet."

"Okay," was all Frank could say, as his brain was too preoccupied trying to turn itself inside-out.

Robbie nodded. "Good, good. Glad to hear it. Real glad. Now, on to Vasily Petrosky. She says she was hiding in your bedroom when those two Slavs came busting up into your house demanding you help them. And you did, just to get Bryce outta the house and then you – and I still can't believe you did this, it tickles me like nothing else – you go and ice Vasily before Bryce is even outta your driveway! I mean, Jesus Christ," Robbie squealed with delight, "I didn't even know you owned a piece, Frank. And you blast him right in the head? You're all right, Frankie, you are *all fucking right.*"

Frank put one hand on his knee to keep it from shaking. "I just did what I thought was right."

"Well, you did more than what was right, Frankie, you did what was fricking awesome. I wanna put you on a retainer. You only see my boys from now on, okay? We can discuss terms since I know you gotta get back to work at this…place you work, but, hey, how's tonight grab you? I can send a car for you, we can go get something nice to eat, sit down, somewhere private, throw some numbers back and forth?" Robbie elbowed Frank in the side. "Eh? I already told the other off-the-book sawboneses I got to go take a fucking hike because I got the only one I need right fucking here!"

"Tonight's no good," Frank said. "I'm busy tonight." The Petroskys were coming over, again, to see if Vasily had turned up. He had to be there. If he was gone, then it would be obvious he had bolted.

Robbie wasn't pleased. "I'm *talking* about giving you a hundred grand a month whether I need to send somebody your way or not, Frank. And you're just gonna brush me off like that? What do you have going on that's so goddamn important you can't come have dinner with me and the boys, huh? A *free* meal at that."

"I'm making dinner for my daughter," Frank said. And he had to admit, given the half-second he had to come up with that, it wasn't bad. "I only get to see her a couple times a month."

"All right," Robbie said, "I can respect that. Family comes first. We'll arrange something."

"Sounds good," Frank said, a mote of relief drifting into the whirlpool of shit that was his life currently. "But, one small thing. About what you said earlier about you wanting me to 'keep doing it'...."

"Right," Robbie said and snapped his thick fingers. "I said I want you to see my boys and only my boys but – but – I also want you to let the Petroskys in too. But just each time you do see one of them, do like you did before and ice them. They'll never see it coming. I got a guy who can come and pick up the stiffs after you're through. It's like a fucking trap, you know. They walk right in, jabbering that Slav shit they talk, thinking they's gonna get their boo-boo looked at and *bam!* Here comes Doctor Frankie the Badass, Doctor Bullets, Doctor motherfucking Murder, bringing that bad medicine down on them Ukrainian shitbags!"

Frank tried to make himself laugh, too, but it came out sounding like a hiccup. "Yeah. That's me."

"So what do you say, huh? You got it in you to blow away some more vodka-swilling commies for us? Gonna be a whole bunch of them coming your way soon if I got anything to say about it – if I don't kill them outright. Well, the ones you do get will be ones Louie was told to take care of, let's say that. I know how to shoot."

"I think I'd prefer to make that...thing I did a one-time thing."

"See, you say that, but it's only because you work for yourself. I get it. You wanna be sovereign. You work at this hippie-dippie bullshit place as a cover, for the taxman, and it's smart – nobody wants to go down like Capone because it's fucking embarrassing. But, I ain't gonna make you turn away them poor folks you take care of. Keep seeing the blacks and hookers if it gives you the warm and fuzzies, but just set aside the Slavs into the 'okay to bump off' pile, get me?" Robbie filled the car with booming laughter. It wound down to a *hee-hee-hee* and he took a deep breath and sighed powerfully. "Shame it's all gonna be over before long. Wars never last. Hits summer, when the conditions are right for both sides to give it their all and, foof, one nutty week and it's over until the next generation's old enough to start their own hubbub. Gonna miss it. This'll probably be my last one."

"How'd this one get started?" Frank said. From where he stood it all seemed pretty pointless. Shooting each other in parking garages and sneaking up on one another when they were at the mall with their families. Retaliation after retaliation with the inciting offense long forgotten by all.

"You gonna think we're low as dogs, Frankie," Robbie said, "that we're kicking them while they're down – and maybe we are – but the Petrosky patriarch kicked the bucket last week, leaving all those sons and cousins and nephews scrambling to see who's gonna be the new top dog, top Siberian husky so to speak. Bryce is the oldest son, but he's got no spine. Vasily was up for it, but he's dead now, as you know. And Tasha, old Roman's wife, well, she's getting up there in years and word around the campfire is she's got a head full of the Old Timers."

Frank nodded, understanding. But the idea of gossip spreading, with news of one family's activities and personal drama spreading to the other, scared him. "Nobody can talk about Vasily being dead, Robbie. I mean that. They think he's missing."

Robbie turned his large head to look over at Frank. "They don't know he's dead? I mean, I just figured you dumped him and they put two and two together."

"I did dump him – and before you ask, I have people for that – but the Petroskys think Vasily walked out of my house on his own, wandered off in the night while I was sleeping. They're looking for him and I think they suspect I did it."

"That'd make sense since you did do it," Robbie said. "*Didn't* you? Don't tell me Simone got her facts screwy. I swear if she's killed somebody else and tried lying to say somebody else done it, I'll wring that girl's fucking neck."

"She told you the truth. I did do it, I, uh, killed the shit out of him, absolutely, but…I don't want *them* to know I did." *Why lie for her? She didn't deserve protecting; she got you into this whole mess.* But Frank thought he had a plan – and the sound of being put on a retainer, even if it meant with Pescatellis – did appeal to him. "Right now," Frank continued, "nobody thinks *anybody* killed Vasily because they think he's missing, wandering around the Twin Cities with his balls blown off. And to *keep* them thinking that, I can't have you or any of your guys talking about how I did anything to anybody. Don't brag me up. That's all I'm asking."

Plus, if he could convince the Petroskys Vasily did, in fact, wander off, maybe split town to start over or something, trying to use getting ball-shot to fake his own death or something, then maybe Tasha might make Bryce give back the money she originally offered Frank for his services. There was a way to win this. It just took staying a few steps ahead and being prepared for every unexpected turn. Frank Goode was confident he could turn this shitshow into a fortune, if he made every move perfectly. He could get paid twice for one job. And then maybe, finally, he could get ahead. He could maybe even stand a chance in court next month. Maybe Jessica could move in with him, stay at his place on weekends when she went to school. Maybe every birthday he missed being on call at the clinic could soon be erased.

"So what're you saying to me here exactly, Frankie?" Robbie said, indignant. "You don't think we can protect you, is that it? Because I got guys, guys *for days*, any of them will watch your back – even when you're here, stacking pomegranates at this waste of a storefront, if you want."

"I know you got guys. And I appreciate the offer. But for now, keep clear of my place. Don't even be in my neighborhood. Don't send anybody to watch out for me. Let me handle this."

"You know, if your place is the last place they seen they boy, Frankie, you can bet your ass they ain't gonna stop looking for him there. It's like losing your keys: look the last place you saw them first. But, when you can't find them, you might need to cut open the dog – since he was the only one home – to look for them in there, if you catch my meaning."

"I know. But trust me when I say I have it all under control. I'll be fine and no harm will come your way either, I swear."

"So you's got a plan."

"I do. Let me handle it. I just need a few days."

"All right. I'll trust you – especially since you're clearly overflowing with surprises already. Anyways, Doctor Killer, I'm gonna let you get back. Say, me and the boys are still going out tonight if you wanna swing by after seeing your girl. We'll be at Tony Russo's Taste of Sicily in St. Paul. Know that joint?"

"Yeah."

"Good. Call me, Frankie. This could be real good for you."

Frank got out and watched Robbie's Jaguar scream from the lot and out of his life, for the time being. Returning inside the cool air of the organic grocer, Jeremy was standing where Frank had been arranging pears, scribbling something on his clipboard. Tearing it free, he pressed the slip of paper with a pathetic dollar amount printed on it to Frank's chest.

"You're done here, bro."

★   ★   ★

Frank got in his car and sat there for a while, looking at the place where he worked up until three minutes ago, thinking about how he desperately needed a legitimate, on-the-books nine-to-five for tax time. So now, on top of everything else, he'd have to go job hunting. But updating his resume and suffering the question of: "So between this date and this date you were doing what exactly…?" would have to wait. He left the strip mall parking lot, taking note of the time – just past one in the afternoon – unsure of what time the Petroskys would be coming by. He had to come up with something to say to them, too. He got on the highway, westbound, but called Ted to make sure it'd be okay if he came by.

Frank parked on the curb and noticed Ted's Buick was sharing the driveway with a second car, a 1984 Coupe de Ville, bronze, lifted on massive, ornate rims.

Ted didn't mention his wife had returned from her business trip – and having met her, he doubted Nadine would drive a monstrosity like that. Frank wasn't sure what Ted would prefer in this situation so he remained in the Lexus and dialed Ted from the curb.

"I'm outside," Frank said.

Ted peeked out the front window, holding his phone to his ear. Frank watched Ted's mouth move and then, on delay, heard him say, "Come on in, I'm just wrapping some shit up with another client."

Frank watched the curtain fall back. And he heard, as he held the phone to his ear, about to hang up, Ted say, muted, "Naw, it's just this dude I sell supplies to. He doesn't know this side of it. Don't be a dumbass and let nothing slip, though, okay? You're just another back alley surgeon like him, far as he needs to be concerned."

He hadn't hung up. Frank wondered how long he could sit in the car listening, with Ted's phone still on the call in his pocket, before he noticed Frank hadn't come inside like he'd asked. Frank hung up, unsure what more he wanted to hear. He just knew whoever he was about to meet wasn't going to be what they introduced themselves as.

Ted's twins, Chiffon and Darryl, were playing on the front porch pushing toy cars around on a square of carpet made to look like a town with little streets and houses and schools and churches. "Hi, Mister Goode," they said together. "Daddy's inside."

"Thanks, kiddos," Frank said and let himself in. There was a slight whiff of marijuana slithering through the house. Frank didn't see anyone in the living room or the kitchen straight ahead, and moved to the open windows over the sink giving a view of the backyard. Out back, by the gate leading to the alley behind the property, standing by the swing set, was Ted and some young white guy with his sandy-colored hair in cornrows, drowning in a white T-shirt multiple times too big for him, and a pair of low-slung jeans. When Ted brought him over to Frank, the kid – maybe thirty at the oldest – smiled a mouth full of metal at him. It was incredibly distracting.

"'Sup, dude, I'm also a sawbones," the kid said, throwing out his hand.

Frank took it, shook it, and gave the kid a hard squeeze. "Frank Goode."

"Shawn Klegg. Everybody calls me Slug. Good handshake on you, man."

They released hands. "How long have you known Ted here?"

"A while," the kid said, flat. "Say, how's bidness on your block? Heard shit's gotten kinda rocky for your ass lately."

"Where'd you go to school?" Frank said. "If you don't mind me asking."

"You know, up north. Medical school up north. Did all four years."

"Four?"

"Right, I was just talking pre-med. The stuff before the real shit.

I didn't want to toot my own horn. But I did all those years, man. *So much reading, right?"*

"Up north. So Duluth, then?"

"Naw, naw, up in Canada. Up there somewhere, near Montreal." Frank noticed Ted was giving him the stink-eye – as much as he could, with Ted's eyes both glassy and bloodshot. The smell of marijuana was stronger here, hanging heavy on the warm afternoon air.

"So," Ted said, having a seat on the rim of his raised flower bed, "what brings you out here, Frank? Said you had a bit of a pickle you're needing help with. Let's hear it."

Frank glanced over at this kid Shawn before meeting eyes with Ted again.

"He's cool," Ted said.

"Yeah, man," Slug said. "I'm in the know. Heard you went by my bitches' crib last night to do a drop-off." Slug sat next to Ted. "You ought be thanking my ass, dude. I brought them into the network myself. You wouldn't have had a place to take your shit otherwise."

Frank waited until Slug was done making noises and looked at Ted. "I can't handle this kid, man."

"Beat it, Slug. I'll call you later," Ted said, standing.

"But we wasn't finished discussing the trip."

"We'll talk it over later. I need to talk to my buddy here."

"But *I'm* your buddy, Teddy Bear."

Ted raised one arm – and pointed toward the front gate. "Go, Slug. Before I get pissed."

"Aight, aight, damn," Slug said and waddled off, pants nearly around his knees. Frank waited until he heard the rumble of the Coupe de Ville start, and fade, before saying anything else to Ted.

"Who's the trailer trash?"

"An associate. Just because you and I are friends doesn't mean you gotta know everything, Frank. I keep all this secret from my wife. Do you expect to get to know more than she does?"

Frank nodded down to Ted's hip pocket. "You might want to end that call before you run up the bill."

Ted took out his phone, cursed, and hit the red button to end the call. "All right. How much did you hear?"

"That I was not to know who or what 'Slug' actually is to you."

"You met him. He runs his mouth. There's some shit that we have on the back burner right now that doesn't need to be brought to the front – or have anyone even know there *is* a back burner. Speaking of which, if you have any trouble starting Monday of next week you're gonna have to figure it out yourself. I have a trip coming up. Which means Nadine will be here with the twins – and she is not to be bothered about where I am or what I'm up to. Understand?"

"Fine, whatever, I'll keep my distance. I need your help with something, right now, though. Or are you too busy?"

"Don't get like that. Don't be a clingy ex-girlfriend, Frank." Ted lit a cigarette. "What're you at my home for? Speak."

"I don't think those girls know what they're doing."

"Of course they don't. They're brand new to the network, man. But Rhino says he's walking them through it, nice and easy."

"Who is Rhino, anyway? The one girl mentioned that name, asked *me* if I'm Rhino."

"Rhino's just Rhino," Ted said. "He is an associate of mine, a distant associate of yours, and a friend thrice removed of Slug's, through me. And Rhino was happy to arrange it that you could drop off *what you had to drop off* at Slug's friend's place. If I had his address, I'd give it to you so you could send him a thank-you card. He really saved your ass and he don't usually trust new recruits that quick neither, so consider yourself one lucky duck." He paused. "I assume since you were able to drive your ass over here that means the Petroskys are still in the dark?"

"For now. They're coming by my house tonight."

"What for? Did you tell them Vasily wandered off?"

"I did but I don't think they buy it."

"You saved his life. Why would you turn around and kill him? Speaking on what *they* should be thinking here, I mean."

"It's hard to explain but if you'd been there you would've seen it: they suspect something. The old lady, Tasha, not so much. Or maybe she does. She's unreadable. It's like looking at a wall with her. But Bryce, the little moron, seems convinced I had something to do with it – he just can't prove it yet and isn't willing to act prematurely on any theories. That, more likely, his aunt has him on a short leash. Saw it in his face he wanted to kill me right then and there."

"You thinking about running, then?"

"Can't. They did their homework on me. They know where Rachel lives, where Jessica works, where she goes to school, everything."

"Ah, fuck all that worry-wart shit," Ted said, waving a dismissive hand at him. "If you're on Facebook and left your shit public then you've volunteered all that shit to be known. They're just trying to freak your ass out."

"But I'm not on Facebook," Frank said.

"I bet your kid is. Or your ex. Or both of them. Practically every chick I know's on there. Nadine, all her sisters and all her friends from college and grammar school and shit, all her aunties. It's like if you wanna know what a bitch do or say, just punch in her name and click on the selfie they put on there that looks like them and *boom*, you got they whole fucking life – even when they 'checking in' at a place where they eat, after taking a goddamn picture of it, of course. Like anybody fucking cares. Anyway, now, far as your case goes, if the Petroskys had suspected you were up to anything nefarious they would've said it when they dropped in on you. Gangs do the same shit as cops, they won't out-and-out accuse you of shit because it's much more advantageous to them if you spill the beans your own damn self. Kind of like Slug only maintaining that guise I told him to take on for approximately twelve seconds. Anyway, you say they is swinging back to your place tonight to try it again. That being the case, if they'd *known* shit they would've *done* shit – definitely by now. And they wouldn't have penciled in a visit, give you any lead-time. They would've found you and done you without announcing one word preceding the fact."

"Oh, but it gets even better," Frank said. "Today, at work, none other than Big Robbie comes walking in, wanting to put me on a retainer because – get this – fucking Simone told him *I* killed Vasily. And Robbie's all giddy about it, having another Russian-killer in his Rolodex, and I'm saying not to spread that shit around because if it gets back to Tasha and Bryce that Vasily is dead then I'm dead too."

"But fucking Italians talk," Ted said. "A lot."

"I know. So, there's that."

"Ain't no hushing up the grapevine, brother man."

"I'm aware."

"Just saying. So what do you want me to do about it?"

The gate screeched open across the yard, nearly giving Frank a heart attack. But it was only Chiffon and Darryl running over to Ted, asking if he could put the wheel back on their ambulance. Chiffon explained to Frank as Ted did the repairs, "People who are hurt need to get where they can get help so they can be happy again. Right now there's a lot of sad people in the city and none of them know who to call because the ambulance man's wheel fell off."

"I see," Frank said.

"Here you go," Ted said as the twins raced off with the mended ambulance. "You two need to get inside soon and wash up for dinner."

"Okay!" came in stereo.

Ted turned back to Frank, his fatherly voice dropping away. "I get the impression you didn't come here to just give me the 'last time on Frank Goode's fucked-up life' update, did you?"

Frank shook his head. "Any ideas?"

"Well, I assume you didn't just tell Big Robbie the truth about who killed Vasily because that'd erase the clout you have with the Pescatellis, right?"

"Yeah. That and if his niece says I'm lying, I'm guessing Robbie will be inclined to take her word over mine. And making the guy who's pleased with believing you killed somebody suddenly doubt who did it and why...that can't lead anywhere but straight to disaster. It's safe this way, as things are. He likes me. The Petroskys don't. No reason to piss *everybody* off at once."

"You should get in contact with that crazy bitch and see what she thinks she can do."

"Simone? No. I don't want anything more to do with her."

"Let's hold on a second, man. I don't think you're telling me this straight." Ted thumbed his chin and squinted at Frank. "Now, correct me if I'm wrong, but I think you're trying to finagle something here. You're trying to weasel them, aren't you? Get them to run against each other?"

"I wasn't planning it but it's just sort of happening that way. All I know is I can't keep having them visiting me because eventually they're going to end up meeting on the sidewalk."

"Sure, I get that, but there's something you're not saying here. So, come on, share with your boy. Tell me what you've got on *your* back burner."

"Fine. I stand to benefit by keeping this balancing act going."

"But how? I'm lost, go back."

"Number one. Big Robbie thinks I killed Vasily. He wants to put me on a retainer of a hundred thousand a month even on months I don't lift a finger to patch anybody. I can still practice helping anyone I want who's unaffiliated with any crime body, which is extra money and I'm not just sitting around all day waiting. Number two. Tasha Petrosky is willing to pay me up to sixty thousand dollars for saving her nephew's life. If I can convince her – and Bryce – that Vasily walked out of my house on his own, I can get that money."

"Which means producing some proof of life – which is gonna be tough, obviously. Plus you *know* they're never gonna stop looking for him."

"Right," Frank said, "which brings us to the matter of the body itself. I don't trust those girls to have done a good job, Ted. They also visited me at work today—"

"You need to find a new fucking job, man. Sounds like everybody knows where Frank Goode is five days a week."

"Not anymore. I got fired. Which, when I go in to check with my parole officer for my quarterly update, might be tough to explain. So if you know of any *legal* gigs, let me know. Anyway, the girls came up – in their fucking hearse no less – and said they're going to pay *me* for the body even after I was under the assumption *I* was paying *them* to get rid of it. But they won't have any money until they get paid, which somehow, I don't know why, sounded like they were going to be using Vasily's body to do so. Not that I care. I just want it gone – completely gone."

"They *are* gonna use it to make money," Ted said, "from Rhino. They don't get rid of the bodies at the funeral home, they part them up and sell them on the red market."

"Bullshit," Frank said. "That's just an urban legend, like that fucking guy who wakes up in a bathtub full of ice with his kidney gone."

"That one's bullshit, yes, because they don't bother keeping people alive – the ones that do business like that, which is not me, for the record. I work with people who get their stuff off the dead, people who died naturally or in car accidents and shit. We benefit from murder but we don't keep murder in our toolbox. Them's Rhino's rules and I tend to agree that's for the best. It's clean. Well, clean*er*."

"And that's what Rhino is, the boss of all this?"

"He ain't the boss, but he's high up. He sets up 'funnels' – as in he probes a city's mid-level dealers and convinces them to hang up slinging to find people who can get him bodies. Then once they get him said bodies, he moves the bodies wherever they go, to quacks like you who do transplants and shit, and then he packs up and moves to a new town and does it all over again. Cool dude, despite what you might think given his type of work."

Frank had his arm partway up, pointing the way Slug had gone when he'd left. "Is that kid Snail part of this?"

"Slug. And yes, Slug was one of those dealers Rhino transmogrified into a red market 'sourcer' as they're called. Slug pegged your hearse girls to start as his sub-sourcer and your Vasily was their very first 'strip', to throw yet another industry term at you. If and when you talk to them again, it'd be in your interest not to mention who that body belonged to. Keeping a buffer between the layers can't not be smart. Otherwise someone might try to take advantage and ask you how much it's worth to you this body disappears, blah, blah, blah, and then that tends to spread and fucks things up for everybody up and down the line."

"Holy shit, Ted," Frank said, "I thought you just sold medical tubing and gauze out of your garage."

"What you and I do is just but one string in the quilt, Frank. There is a lot of layers, a lot of players, and a lot of money flying every damn which way. Thus," he knitted his fingers together, "the network."

"Does that mean I'm a part of this now, now that you've told me all this?"

"I gave you no names or addresses, so no. I gave you a peek, that's all. Shit, I hardly know anything – most of what I just said might be bullshit somebody told me and bullshit somebody told them. There may not even be a Rhino. Might be a buncha Japanese chicks on laptops all crowded in a basement somewhere for all I know and they just hired some brother to sound all intimidating on the phone to do the deals."

Frank checked the time on his phone. "I should get back. I don't know when they'll be there."

"You got a story ready? Because I was gonna say, you could tell them Vasily called you to say he's hiding and that he was afraid to call anybody else thinking he was being listened in on and—"

"Don't mean to cut you off, but that's no good," Frank said. "They found his phone at my place and broke it."

"They broke his phone?"

"Is that bad? I thought that was kind of strange."

"They know he's dead. They just need proof now. That's what that means."

"Fuck. You really think so?"

Ted nodded. "You should run. I got a guy who can get you a passport."

"No. I can handle this. I can come up with something and send them back out looking for Vasily again. After that, I can tell Big Robbie everything – well, not everything – and maybe get him to do something. And even if they were trying to scare me saying they know Rachel and Jessica, that doesn't mean they won't use that knowledge. I can't risk them."

Ted was shaking his head. "You're playing with fire with this shit, man. If I were you and I knew me, I'd be asking me for that passport I just offered. I'm going out of town and I'm going off the grid, like, totally off the grid. So if you want something, you best say something now – because I know I'm your only contact to shit like this."

"I have to get back to the house."

"You're asking for it, man. I'm telling you. Those hearse girls are gonna be cutting up another body and I'm sure they'll recognize this new one."

Frank started back across the yard. "Call me when you're back in town."

"See you around, Frank," Ted called from where he remained sitting on the edge of the raised flower bed. "Been nice knowing you."

★    ★    ★

Amber used her elbow to slide open the workroom door, stepped out, closed it behind her, and slipped and slapped across the hardwood floor to the kitchen. She laid down an old newspaper before sitting. Her suit felt like it was sticking to her – wet on both sides, sweaty inside and bloody outside. She felt shrink-wrapped. Jolene was at the stove, with her back turned, pushing around pieces of bologna in a frying pan with one hand, smoking with the other.

"I did it," Amber finally said. "He's taken apart."

Jolene turned around. "God, what did you do?"

"I followed Rhino's instructions," Amber said, red head to toe. "Can I bum a smoke?"

"Go take a bath first."

"Take a drag and blow it in my face," Amber said. "I'm too tired to move."

Jolene stepped over to the bloody mess sitting at the kitchen table and held the cigarette for Amber to take a drag.

"God, I didn't realize how much *work* would be involved. I had to bend his fucking knee backward until his toes were touching his hip before the thing finally gave. It sounded like a gunshot when the cartilage...."

Amber paused, watching Jolene take the frying pan off the burner and scrape the bologna into the trash.

"Sorry."

Amber stared in the general direction of the refrigerator, her bloody arms resting on her bloody knees. One strand of hair that had fallen loose from her painter suit's hood hung glued to her cheek. "Rhino asked us to use a marker to write on the plastic wrap what their blood type was. Do you think he'll be pissed we didn't know our guy's?"

"I'm sure he has a way of figuring it out," Jolene said, filling the sink with hot water. She started scraping the pan. "Would you please go take that shit off? I can smell you."

"Do I stink?"

"Yes, like you just cut up a Russian guy."

"Did you get the two others done and ready for their showings? Because I was kind of in the zone in there. I was taking off his head and I said something to you, looked up, and you were gone."

"I finished them. They're in their drawers ready to be moved over into their boxes. I got those moved by the door so we can just drop them in tomorrow morning and the day after."

"Shit, I just realized I never did laundry," Amber said. "Can I borrow something of yours for the funeral tomorrow?"

"Before you ask, the leggings don't fit you."

"They probably do now. I feel like I sweated off fifty pounds in this thing. Oops." Lifting her arms, a long strip of something unidentifiable peeled off from Amber's arm and splatted, loud as a clap, to the kitchen floor.

The undertakers stared at it.

"What do we do with what you can't pack?" Jolene said. "There has to be leftover shit they can't use, right?"

"A few things. Ribcage and stomach are no good. I was thinking we'd just put them in the cremator."

"We haven't turned that on in years."

"Yeah but it's not like the gas has gotten turned off."

"Yet."

"Yes, smartass, but what I mean is it probably still works. I figure we just throw in the shit we can't pack for Rhino and torch it, dust it out after, and toss the ashes in the toilet."

"Who do you think he was?"

"No. I spent the last four hours kicking back that question. We've got to look at this like we're farmers or something. We start giving things names, our constitution for it will never hold out."

She had a point. Jolene stepped over the piece of mystery meat on the floor and sat across from Amber. She butted out her smoke in the ashtray. "I'm sorry I didn't help."

"It's fine, you had the other two to do. I was kind of sad when I saw you had gotten them drained and were starting the embalming pump. And before you say anything, no, I didn't cut them up after you left. They can't use stuff in that condition, after it's been chemically treated. I just mean if we took a few extra things with us, maybe Rhino would take them."

"That's being greedy," Jolene said.

"I know but that's the thing. I keep looking at everything now with price tags on it. Like the whole time we were at Mega Deluxo, I kept looking at the other people shopping there thinking, oh, she's got two kidneys, that guy's got two lungs. We're all just money bags walking around."

Jolene inclined her head. "I hope you know how psychotic that sounds."

"I wouldn't actually do it. Jesus. I just mean, I think I found my ambition again."

"Great."

"What?"

"Nothing. I just wish you could've found it a few years ago, back when we still had a chance of pulling ourselves out of the hole without having to become criminals to do it, but whatever, that's just my two cents."

"Jo. Please. I've had a very long day."

"And I've had several *years* of long days. Where's my reprieve?"

"Do we have any beer left?"

"Yes. But don't change the subject."

"If we're gonna argue, I need something for my throat." There was a sticky sound as Amber got up, leaving a perfect red butt-print on the chair where the blood had soaked through the newspaper. She stepped over to the fridge, paused, looked at her bloody gloves and then made a sad face at Jolene. "A little help?"

"Go take that shit off, like I said. You can have a beer after you shower. Christ, you're like a child."

"I might as well stay in this thing, I still have to clean up. Just open the fridge for me, please?"

"And then what? How're you going to open the beer?"

"Well, I'd probably need you to do that too."

"And how will you drink it? Without touching it, that is?"

"We have straws around here somewhere. Come on, I'm like dying of thirst here."

"No. Beer can be your reward. Go clean up the workroom, take a shower, and I'll *bring* you a beer afterward – with or without a straw, your choice."

Amber squelched and smacked her way across the kitchen in short, slow shuffles. She halted abruptly in the kitchen doorway and made a red half-circle on the floor as she turned in place to face Jolene.

"What?" Jolene said.

"What're we gonna do about Cornelius?"

"I've been thinking about that. And, well, we either let him fuck one of the corpses, or pay him off with some of what we get from Rhino. I mean, just letting him fuck one of them isn't any worse than us cutting them into tiny little pieces, really."

Amber, face framed by her plastic hood, frowned. "How do you figure?"

"It's still desecration of a corpse. Chopping it up or fucking it is about the same."

"Now, hold on. Heaven forbid what I'm about to say happens, but us getting busted for trafficking in human body parts and Cornelius getting busted for diddling a dead person are two *totally* different cases. A judge would throw the book at him, maybe a whole fucking library for that nasty shit. And us, well, we're just two gals who fell on hard times and decided to utilize unexplored channels of an unorthodox means to get ourselves out of debt. We're broke. He's a pervert. End of discussion."

"But when you start dreaming out loud about what *else* we could do after paying off the mortgage and the bills and everything, talking about moving away from here or just retiring completely…is that not for jollies too? Is that not greed rearing its ugly head? Especially with you looking at living people at the store and wondering how much their parts would go for?"

"Greedy, sure, but it's pretty goddamn different from sticking a wiener in a cold, dead vagina or butthole or whatever Cornelius's predilection is. And I was just saying that I was looking at the world differently now that I have this new, temporary job going for me. If you become a guy who sells used cars who had no idea he'd ever be a used car salesman, don't you think after he's got the job he looks at all cars, his to sell or not, from a slightly different perspective? My world view has opened up is all. There's nothing wrong with that."

"Either way," Jolene said, "we need to be thinking of what we're going to do with him." She took off her glasses to wipe the lenses. "Cornelius hasn't stopped knocking before and now that he thinks he's got something on us he's certainly not gonna now."

"It'll make for good shower-thinking," Amber said, and turned to leave. "I'll report back."

Jolene noticed the strip of flesh was still on the kitchen floor. "God above. Amber! Can you *please* learn to clean up after yourself?"

\* \* \*

An hour later, the workroom sparkling clean and Amber's clothes packed into the incinerator, she stepped back into the kitchen with her hair hanging dark and wet around her shoulders and a clean T-shirt and jean shorts on. Jolene sat at the kitchen table – since it was the only place to sit anymore – painting her toenails. "Where's the beer you promised?"

Jolene showed Amber her wet nails. "Can you get it yourself?"

Amber sat with the beer and took a deep swallow. "So, here's what I came up with in the shower. I say we kill Cornelius."

Jolene continued dabbing the little brush down the length of her middle toe's nail. "I thought you'd say something like that."

"I mean, it's the best course of action, right? I'll show my work. Three things. One, he knows something that could get us in trouble. Two, he is irredeemable already, which nominates him as somebody okay to expel from the population. And three, we have a pretty good way of making a person disappear." Amber paused. "You know I'm just kidding, right?"

"Are you? Or were you just gonna come in here, say all that, see how I react, and *then* decide if you were only kidding?"

"I was kidding," Amber said. "I think we should just let him fuck

a body. Maybe if he gets it out of his system, he'll leave us alone."
Jolene snorted. "Sure he will."

"Yeah, good point."

"Let's say we let him. Which one, though? After Sunday there won't be any bodies for him to fuck. And before you even say it, no, he is not allowed to fuck one of the ones I already got ready. Speaking of which, I still need you to do the makeup – you don't have to do both, just Missus Tamblyn. I did Mister Wicks."

Amber reached across the table for Jolene's cigarettes and lighter. "Then we'll give Cornelius a rain check, take his number, and tell him when somebody's come in."

"And in that time he'll probably have gotten antsy and called the police just for something to do," Jolene said. "Nah. I think we should kill him."

"Okay, well, when we do, we should just jump on him and you can hold a pillow over his face and I'll hold down his arms and—"

"Amber. For fuck's sake, I wasn't serious. What is *wrong* with you?"

Amber put her face in her hands. "I think the heat is getting to me."

"Drink your beer. Stop contemplating murder."

"But it freaks me out to know that he knows, you know? Maybe Rhino knows somebody. Should I text him right now?"

"No. I feel like his trust in us is tenuous enough right now. I mean, with him having to walk us through everything step-by-step like that...."

"He wants things done a certain way. He wasn't a dick about it. It's just steps he probably copied down a long time ago and sends to all the newbies. I still think we should talk to him, see if he has any suggestions about what to do with Cornelius."

"Call me silly, but I don't really think it'd be wise to tell the guy who's buying body parts from us that another guy, who *shouldn't* know what we're up to, does. Just a thought."

"Fair. Back to square one then. Do we let Cornelius fuck a corpse or do we not let Cornelius fuck a corpse?"

"I really don't know," Jolene said and started on her other foot. "What about the other guy, that Frank guy?"

"He isn't dead."

Jolene's eyes went half-staff. "For Christ sakes."

"Sorry, sorry. Kidding." Amber took another sip, then a drag. "What *about* Frank?"

"Should we be worried about him too? He seems kind of shaky."

"You're one to talk."

"I'll admit I was a little…apprehensive to the idea and being faced with what I thought was Frank's murder victim was, yes, a touch nervy for me – but I'm okay with it now. Not *okay*, but, you know, dealing. All in all, I'd say I'm handling things pretty well. Dude was just a gangster who probably pissed somebody off and 'got disappeared' – like they say in the movies. We just happened to be the method by which that disappearing happens."

"But what about Frank, Jo? How much do we pay him?"

"I kind of think we won't have to. He seemed over it when we saw him. Seemed to me he just wanted rid of it. I say we let it ride. You gave him our card. If he wants the money he can call and we'll haggle – once we have the money. When are you due to drop off that stuff with Rhino, anyway?"

"He said to text when I have everything packed." Amber picked up her phone, opened it, closed it, set it back down.

"Did you have any trouble with the dry ice?"

"I spilled some on the floor and it made this weird crackly sound – we might need to replace a couple tiles in there later. But, other than that, no, I used the gloves and all that and everything went in the right container the way it was supposed to. I just feel like I'm forgetting a step."

"Did you wrap everything six times or whatever he said to do?"

"Yep. I wrapped each piece in seven layers of cling-wrap and then in a towel and put each in a cooler, stacking things like he said to, and put a sponge soaked in dry ice on either end and closed the lid, sealing the outside with one strip of packing tape and marking the tape with the code system he sent me yesterday: A for arms and L for legs and E for eyes and H for heart, et cetera and so forth, with the kidneys in a container by themselves because they can't be packed in tight like other shit can."

"So, what are you waiting for? It sounds like you're ready to me." Jolene, done with her toes, screwed the lid back on the nail polish bottle. "The sooner we can get that shit out of here, the happier I'll be. Maybe things can finally go back to normal."

"I'm gonna do it. I'm gonna text him this, 'The cow is packed. When can I drop off?' Does that sound all right?"

Jolene shrugged. "Yeah, sure, sounds fine."

Amber's phone made a *swoosh* sound. "And there it goes. Text sent."

"Can you get me a beer so I can join you in celebrating?" Jolene said.

"Actually…this is the last one. Shit, I'm sorry, honey. Do you want the rest of this? I didn't spit in it."

"It's fine. We can celebrate after – because then we'll have money."

"Fuck yeah we will, girl. High five."

"Nails."

"Air high five."

Jolene laughed – and they almost touched palms.

"We're gonna be okay, babe, you know that, right?" Amber said.

Jolene nodded. "Yeah, I think you're right. Shit was pretty awful there for a minute, but I think, yeah, we're gonna be okay."

"Wow, he's a quick text-backer. He sent an address. Says to be there in two hours for drop-off and immediate payment."

"I'll help you get loaded up."

"Gimme a hug first." They hugged. "This is gonna be good, Jo. Everything is going to be fine."

"I believe you," Jolene said, unable to hug Amber back except by pressing her sides with her wrists, fingers splayed. *I really, really want to believe you.*

★   ★   ★

Frank went into the gas station, paid for his gas, smokes, and a soda, and was walking back to the Lexus when his phone rang. He didn't recognize the number. Ignoring it, he got back in, started his car, and sat there a moment, holding his phone as it continued to ring in his hand, looking at the number he didn't know, wondering if this was the end, the Petroskys somehow found Vasily's body and they were going be nice and give him a running head start. No, they wouldn't do that. Like Ted said, they wouldn't let him know they knew. They'd just find him and kill him.

He answered it. "Hello?"

"Frank, it's Bryce. I'm at my place. Aunt Tasha's taking a little longer than expected getting ready so she asked me to call you to tell you we won't be by until seven."

"Any luck?"

"Finding Vasily? No. Nothing. No hospitals have admitted him, the cops haven't picked him up anywhere. But thank you for your concern, Frank, that really touches me in the bottom of my heart."

"I didn't have anything to do with him running off, Bryce. I was asleep. I woke up and he wasn't on the table, he was just gone, he—"

"You really like telling that story, don't you? We can't prove anything, but I think you had some deal with fucking Robbie Pescatelli. He was probably waiting around the block, waiting for the minute I left. You might not have pulled any trigger, but looking the other way when somebody else does is the same thing."

"Why would I do that after trying so hard to save him?" The golden ticket.

"I don't know, Frank, why would you? Maybe you're fucking nuts. Maybe that was all part of the guise."

"What fucking *guise*, Bryce? It's not like I knew you were going to bring your bleeding-from-the-balls cousin to my fucking house. Why would I have all of that planned? I think maybe you're overthinking this. I'm sure Vasily is somewhere. He may not be well, he may not be alive—"

"So you admit it!"

"No, Bryce, fucking *listen* to me. He was hurt very, very badly. Left unattended without anyone to change his bandages, he would've, without a doubt, gotten an infection – at *least*. That's being optimistic. I really think you should just wait and see if anyone finds him. I hate to be the one to tell you this, but he is probably dead."

"That's fine and good, Frank, but *until* he turns up Aunt Tasha said you're our only lead. So unless you wanna just tell me, right now, where Vasily went, we're still coming over and we're still gonna have that chat with you. You better be home."

Frank could hear people talking in the background. And music – not music, but Muzak. "Where are you really, Bryce?"

"I'm at the mall. I was thinking maybe about swinging over to the food court. I feel like ice cream. Any recommendations?"

Frank felt lightheaded as a black rage swelled up into his throat. "You fucking go near her I swear to fucking God—"

"Listen to yourself. You sound like a fucking movie. But go ahead, finish that sentence. You swear to fucking God you'll – what? You ain't Liam Neeson. You're powerless here, Frank. You have zero control other than what I give you."

"What your aunt gives *you*, I think you mean."

"Not the time to poke the bear, friend," Bryce said in sing-song. "Apparently there's more than one Jessica that works at this Dairy Queen. Their nametags don't have their last names. Does yours have brown eyes and dark hair like her mother?"

Frank took a breath. "What do you want, Bryce? I'm going to be home, like you asked. I've been perfectly cooperative."

"Sure, except you killed Vasily – or had him killed – and now whoever you were working with has left you high and dry. Because that's how I see your situation. I don't know the specific players besides you, and I might be wrong, I don't have all the facts, but I've seen what trapped people look like, people who've been left in a shitty situation and are panicking trying to get back out of it – and they look and act a lot like you. Now, are you gonna tell me which of these Jessicas is yours?"

Frank closed his eyes. "The blonde. The blonde's my daughter."

"See? I *knew* you were a fucking liar. We found her Facebook page, asshole. It's the other one. Were you seriously gonna sell a total stranger out to save your own ass? That tells me so much *more* about you than I already fucking knew."

"I'm sorry, Bryce, I'm sorry – I just don't like the idea of you being near my daughter. I panicked. You're right. I'm panicking. Because you know who else panics? People who are caught in a bad situation who don't deserve to be in one. I had nothing to do with Vasily's disappearance. He left my house while I was asleep and when I woke up—"

"It doesn't matter how many times you say it, Frank. A lie is still a lie. And tonight we're gonna get to the truth, even if it means digging *through you* to find it. Be home. See you real soon."

Someone honked behind him. Frank moved away from the pumps to let the next person fill up, pulled around behind the gas station, and put it in park again. He sat staring at his phone, swiping up and down through his many, many contacts. His parents. His brother out in Seattle. Rachel. Jessica. His lawyer, his ex-wife's lawyer. Several people at the clinic, many of whom he hadn't spoken to in years. Jeremy at Jerry's Organic Grocer – delete. Ted Beaumont. Robbie Pescatelli.

Frank hovered his finger over Robbie's name, ready to press, ready to call, ready to ask for help.

On the dashboard, down where it met the windshield, was the Hawthorne Funeral Home business card. Snatching it up, he dialed the numbers on the card turning it toward the streetlight.

"Hawthorne Funeral Home. This is Jolene."

"Jolene, it's Frank."

"What's wrong?"

"Nothing. I just need to talk to Amber. Is she there?"

"Are you sure nothing's wrong?"

Could anything be labeled as right? He kept this to himself. "Is she there?"

"She's out."

"Where?"

"I don't think I should tell you that."

"Do you have her number?"

A few long moments. "Got a pen?"

Frank dialed the number.

"Hello?"

"Amber. Listen, I—"

"You're kinda breaking up. Have you decided when you might wanna talk about payment?"

"Actually, I was wondering if you might still have him."

A long pause. "I'm actually on my way to drop off right now."

Frank was sweating, pinching the bridge of his nose, feeling sick. "What would it take for you to not go through with it?"

"In full disclosure, right around a million."

"I don't have that."

"Few of us do."

He could hear a rattling hearse engine in the background. "Is there some way we could work out some kind of payment plan? I want him back."

"Why?"

"I changed my mind. I think it'd be better if he was put somewhere where the police can find him, so his family can have closure."

"I hate to be a shit, Frank, but I'm gonna have to decline. They need all of it. I can't have any of him missing."

"Could you leave part of him somewhere for the police to find? Something small, like a finger or a toe or something? Is that something you could possibly do?"

On Amber's end, there was the steady ticking of a turn signal. "Should we really be talking on the phone about this?"

"If you could just leave part of him somewhere, anywhere, then the police can find it and...well, it'd sure make things a lot easier for me. His family's worried."

"Was he a friend of yours or something?"

"No."

"Did *you* shoot him in the balls?"

"No, I didn't."

"Then what's it matter?"

"I can't get into it, but it just does."

"Well, I need all of it," Amber said. "So unless you have the money to buy him back...."

"*Please.* There's a lot riding on this for me."

"For me too, Frank," Amber said. "If it's about the money, after tonight I think I can pay you. Let's say a grand, huh?"

"Listen to me. It's not about the fucking money. It's about him, the body. He can't just disappear. Maybe you could leave a hand somewhere and say you saw some Italian-looking guys throwing it out of their car or something."

Another long pause. "I thought this is what you wanted, why you brought him to us in the first place."

He didn't want to hurt her. He realized he was already telling himself *it's just meat.* "Where are you?"

"Are you serious? I'm not telling you that. But, next time, if there is a next time, maybe you should think real hard whether or not you want to give us somebody before you bring them by. Call me tomorrow and we can talk about getting you that grand."

"Amber. Please. Hello? Hello?"

She'd hung up.

He tried her again, but she didn't answer. "*Fuck.*"

Frank dialed his daughter.

"Jessica, are you at work right now?"

"Dad?"

"Are you at the mall, yes or no?"

"Yeah, yeah, I am. Is something wrong? You sound really freaked out."

"Is there a guy there, young, short hair, probably in a suit? Do you feel like you're being watched?"

"What are you talking about, Dad? Mom said you're not supposed to call me unless she says it's okay."

"This is important. Look around. Anywhere in the food court there, is there a guy watching you? Do you see anybody? Guy, in his twenties, short dark hair, wearing a suit?"

"There's a lot of people around like there always is. Dad, I can't be on the phone right now. My boss wrote me up once already this week when she saw me texting—"

"You need to tell your boss you're not feeling well. You need to go home. Ask mall security to walk you to your car and you go straight home, understand?"

"Dad, are you on something?"

"No, Jessica, I'm not on anything. I just think I may've messed up. I think people who are mad at me might want to harm you and your mother. So I need you to tell your boss you're not feeling well, or just leave, ask mall security to walk you to your car, and—"

"Dad. Dad. Slow down. What's going on?"

"Jessica. You need *to run.* You need to go home, get your mother, and you both need to go to your grandmother's. You can't stay in town, not for a couple of days. Don't blog about this or post anything about this on fucking Facebook or Twitter or anywhere else. You need to stay away for at least a couple of days."

"Okay, okay, I'll leave work. Who's mad at you?"

"Bad people. I'm sorry this has ended up involving you, but it has. Text me when you get home and text me again when you and your mother are at Grandma's, okay? Please remember to do this."

"Okay. I'm gonna go. Are you okay?"

"I'm fine right now. I just want you safe."

"I love you, Dad."

"I love you too, sweetheart. Now go."

Frank pitched his phone into the passenger seat and held his face in his hands. This was how he felt when the cops arrived at the airport and stood him against the wall and put the cuffs on him. It felt like then, but much worse. It was just him going to prison, then. His family wasn't involved, nor would they come to any harm because that, then, had been his crime and his alone. No, this was much, much worse.

Once he'd pulled himself together, he wiped his eyes, and put the Lexus in gear and started for home.

There were no other roads left to take.

# CHAPTER SIX

Whenever she took a corner too sharply, the hearse, which was about as old as Amber, would let out this long, keening shriek of agonized metal. She followed the directions the robot voice on her phone calmly suggested she take, as the part of Minneapolis in front of her headlights was an unfamiliar one. It was mostly factories now, some still functioning but many with their high barbed-wire fences corralling nothing but crumbling, dark structures and smokeless smokestacks. Nondescript office buildings, low, squatty and brick, a lot of them with real estate banners across their fronts reading 'office space available.' Very few cars, other than eighteen-wheelers gurgling past, hauling flatbeds with big pieces of machinery and flashing oversized load signs. She stopped at a red light, waited for no one to go the other way, and pulled through when the light changed, taking a left when her phone said to. *Your destination will be on the right.* She slowed and leaned across the front seat to peer out the passenger side – it was a bowling alley. Lake Calhoun Bowl & Bar.

She double-checked the map app against the address Rhino had texted to her. This was the place, apparently. And as the text had stressed she should park around back, she pulled the hearse through the lot, passing a few pickup trucks with nobody sitting in them, and around to the back of the wide, short building. Behind were a few dumpsters and a trio of refrigerator trucks parked tightly together as if conspiring. She parked and waited, staring out the cracked windshield at the bowling alley's back door. There was a light mounted above it, flickering, haloed by a fog of bugs, but no one was around, no one was waiting for her. She chose to wait in the car, thinking maybe Rhino was running late. There were no further instructions on what was to come next. An address, a time, and where to park. She didn't want to come off more amateurish than she already had. Having to ask him to text her step-by-step instructions on how to package a body was embarrassing enough. This is what she did at the funeral home; she knew this part of things, she worked with people, talking them up into more expensive caskets and headstones. So she sat and waited and smoked, listening to the radio but not really hearing it as her heart hammered in her chest.

She checked herself in the mirror, pulled back her hair, let it back down, and sat drumming her fingers on the wheel, heart still hammering. Maybe she should've dressed nicer, more professional. They'll probably be in tailored suits. Well, too late now. Adjusting the mirror, she saw behind her the three coolers in a row held in place with nylon straps where a casket would normally be. She'd closed the hearse's curtains in the back before leaving, to discourage prying eyes.

Two men stepped outside. Both faces were lit strangely by the light above the door, making their eyes two dark wells. Both black, both in baggy clothing. They lit up smokes and talked – Amber could make out a little of it through the hearse's rolled-up windows. They spotted her and one of them said something about the grim reaper being hot as hell. She waved, smiled neighborly. They flicked their smokes across the lot and went inside. Was that some kind of cue?

She relented and texted Rhino but he didn't respond. She sat clutching her phone, waiting for it to vibrate, and looked around – to her left, at the three refrigerator trucks. California plate on one, New York plate on the second, and Texas on the third.

*Maybe someone inside will know something.* She got out, making sure she locked the hearse twice, and went inside.

It was dark and cool, blaring country music competing with the rumble and crash of the few bowlers on the lanes angling for strikes. A jukebox glowed in the corner. Neon bar signs on every wall, framed photos of people she didn't know but who were evidently individuals of note as far as the bowling alley was concerned. Amber approached the bar, flip-flops sticking to the floor with each step. She could smell that shoe spray they used for the rental shoes, and the appetizing smell of fries, battered fish, and onion rings.

She climbed onto a stool, the bar otherwise unoccupied. Her bladder felt full and her thoughts were screaming through her head too fast to grasp individually. Danger, excitement, the prospect of big money coming soon, and the chance she might get killed – all zooming by at once.

A young woman with a neat bob of black hair and a tube top was at the far end, behind the bar, going through receipts. She had a cross tattooed onto the back of her neck. She noticed Amber in the bar mirror and came down to where she sat, smiling broadly as she approached.

"What can I get you, honey?"

"Vodka tonic please."

"Lemon or lime in it?"

"Lime."

"Preference on the potato juice?"

"Nope."

"You got it." As the bartender, whose nametag read Becky, threw ice in a tumbler, she said without looking up, "Just made happy hour by a couple minutes, lucky girl. And if you want a lane, it's ten bucks a game, five if you're just gonna do some solo practice. You in a league?"

"No." Amber's leg wouldn't stop bouncing.

"Want to be? I'm on a league team, all girls. We're short one since my girlfriend's getting her appendix out. Can you bowl?"

"Not really."

"Not really or no? Because I'll admit I can't but I'm still in the league. We do okay. We've got matching shirts. We're the Pink Ladies. I know, before you say anything, real original, huh? Martine's a big *Grease* nut and refused to even field suggestions on naming the team anything *but* that. It's an excuse to get away from the husbands one night a week, if we're being totally up-front about it, but it's still fun. You should consider stopping by one Wednesday night sometimes. That's when leagues play, on Wednesdays."

Amber didn't know what to say to that. Was she supposed to be paying close attention to that? Was that some kind of code? She just stared at Becky, her knee bouncing under the bar, flip-flop tapping an erratic beat against her heel. "Okay."

"Quiet type, huh? That's cool." Becky tossed down a coaster and then the drink on top of it. "Six twenty-five, honey. Unless you wanna start a tab?"

"No, just the one will be fine, thank you." Amber hoped her credit card had that much room left on it, after shopping this morning.

As Becky swiped the card, she said over her shoulder, "You waiting for somebody, honey?"

"Just in for the drink," Amber said, distant, looking around at the other patrons as nonchalantly as she could. The three guys bowling, each by themselves, seemed pretty invested in what they were doing – not waiting for anybody, but here doing what they came here to do. The two guys she'd seen come outside for a smoke were crowding in close together at an arcade cabinet, pummeling one another with colorfully dressed kung fu fighters. No one sitting at a table by themselves, no one staring at their phone waiting for a call, everyone was busy having fun except Amber.

Becky brought Amber's slip and a pen. Before she could walk away again, Amber said, "Hypothetically speaking, let's say I am here to meet somebody."

"Intrigue," Becky said, smiling a little. "Okay, let's say you are."

"But it's the kind of situation where we're supposed to, you know, keep it on the down low. How would you suggest is the best way to let the person I'm here to meet know I'm here?"

Becky filled a small glass bowl with peanuts and set it in front of Amber. "Are you talking like a blind date or something?"

"In a way."

"You could go around and ask. You know his name, right? Or is this one of those Craigslist anonymous-type hookup things?"

"Not really."

"Or is it more like you're here to *meet* somebody?" Becky brought up her hand to her face, pressing her thumb to her nose and curling her fingers in, all except the pinky – she kept that sharp and high and out. Like a horn. She glanced around, lowered her hand, and smiled at Amber. "Get me?"

Amber nodded. Coolly, she hoped.

"Then do what I just did, so they can see you," Becky said and bobbed her head backward and left, over her shoulder. Amber looked. A security camera was angled behind the bar, up by the mounted TV showing sports highlights, the camera's glass eye staring unblinkingly at her.

Amber brought her hand to her face, thumb to nose, curled in all her fingers except the pinky, and looked into the camera lens – she could see the layers of glass within expand and contract, zeroing in on her.

"Okay," Becky said, "I think they saw you. You can put your hand down now." She leaned across the bar, her breath sweet like peppermints. "Go down that way, past the shoe counter, make a left, go past the bathrooms and at the end of the hall there's a door marked employees only. Knock and wait." With her fingertips, Becky pushed Amber's untouched drink toward her. "You can take that back with you, if you want."

Amber passed the guys at the arcade cabinet, the pinball machines, and turned the corner. She went up the narrow hall, the walls covered in more framed photos of champion bowlers, past the men's room, the ladies' room, and knocked on the door marked employees only. Her glass in her hand, down at her side, rattled its ice.

The door pulled open a gap. A man's heavy face, finely shaped goatee, a flat-bill baseball cap. "*Que?*"

"I'm here for a drop off."

"Name."

"Amber."

The door opened. Two desks facing each other, low drop ceiling, buzzing fluorescent lights, half of them dead. A rack of booze behind padlocked chicken-wire doors. Rust climbing the side of a filing cabinet. Becky sat behind the desk on the far side of the room. For a moment Amber wondered how she'd gotten back here so quick – but then noticed the second door leading in off the kitchen where Spanish hip-hop was blaring along with bleating ovens and hissing deep fryers.

"Sorry for the *Wizard of Oz* routine," Becky said, "but we have to play it safe."

Next to her on the floor, with their backs to the wall, were a couple of young children, a boy and a girl – probably four, maybe five, if Amber had to guess – both holding a tablet together, little faces pressed cheek to cheek, lit by whatever they were looking at, transfixed, their ears blocked up with headphones. They had a handful of toy cars with them, scattered around. A race car, a fire truck, an ambulance with a crooked wheel – far less interesting to them right now than whatever the tablet was showing them.

"Mind pulling that chair over here for her, Fernando?" Becky said as the Mexican guy closed the door behind Amber.

Fernando took the second chair from the other desk and wheeled it over to face Becky. He made a motion toward the seat, several gold bracelets jangling on his wrist. Once Amber had sat, Fernando took his place next to Becky, leaning against the wall with his phone, a cigarette burning between his fingers.

"Are you Rhino?" Amber asked Becky.

Fernando didn't look up from his phone, issued a little laugh. Becky swatted him on the side. "Stop, she's new." Then to Amber: "No, I'm not Rhino, and I'd recommend not throwing that question around much."

"Sorry."

"It's all good, honey. Don't sweat it. So, you brought a load for us?"

"Yeah. It's all out in the car."

"I was gonna give you shit about driving a hearse here," Becky said with a grin, "but I guess that's sort of hiding in plain sight, huh? Kind of like a mask, but one you drive instead of wear." She mimed turning a steering wheel. "Anyway, do you mind giving Fernando your keys so he can go out and get your stuff while we talk?"

"Okay." Amber handed Fernando her keys and he left.

Amber glanced again at the children in the corner as they smiled as one, miles away. Becky must've noticed Amber looking at them.

"They're my friend's kids. I'm watching them while he's at work. You don't mind they're in here while we talk, do you?"

"Not at all," Amber said.

"You can put your drink on the desk here if you want, Amber. You don't have to sit there holding it."

"I didn't bring my coaster."

Becky wouldn't look anywhere else but at Amber. "You're sweet. How is it? Did I make it strong enough?"

"I haven't tried it yet."

"Looks like you could use it right now."

Amber raised the glass, shaking in her hand, and sipped. She'd made it strong. "It's good," she said.

"Good. I gave you the Stoli but wrote it off as the cheap shit. Nobody orders Stoli because it's expensive and then it ends up having to go back to our liquor distributor after a certain date and we end up *losing* money, so…yeah, you got the Stoli."

"Thanks." *Pay me, pay me.*

"So you and your girl run a funeral home, huh? We work with a few in other towns like that. Did your first drop-off at your place go okay? Some back-alley surgeon, I hear. The surgeon being *who* dropped off, not *what* was dropped off, I mean."

"It went fine." *How does she know that?* Amber decided not to ask.

"Rhino walked you through it okay? All of his instructions nice and clear?"

Amber nodded, sipped her drink again. "Uh-huh. Just fine. He was very clear."

"Cool. Well, when Fernando gets back with your drop-off, we're gonna go through it quick and make sure the order's filled. You had the male, twenties, whole, unknown blood type, right? The one missing a nut?"

"Yeah. He was ours." *Cash, bitch.*

"Okay, so once we make sure everything's accounted for – two arms, two legs, one head, heart, lungs, those two glorious little nuggets more commonly known as kidneys, intestines, jugs of blood, and everything – we'll send you out of here with half the pay. Since this is your first time working with us, we'll need to make sure everything checks out with what you brought us. Run it through the X-ray, make sure there's no whoopsies in there like bullets or broken-off knives or needles. This isn't meant to sound like we're doubting you, Amber. Absolutely not, you were great to work with – punctual, professional, easygoing – but it's routine protocol, the same as we do with all our new sourcers. I'm sure you did a great job. Once our tests come back from our guy who does the lab stuff, we'll give you a call and you can come and get the second half of the payment. And here's Fernando now with your load. You can set those down anywhere, honey."

"Okay." Fernando, struggling with his arms full of three coolers and milk jugs of blood in the shopping bag, kicked the door closed behind him and set the load down on the opposite desk. He tossed Amber her keys back. "Thanks. Nice ride. Is that the eighty-three Ford hearse?"

"I think, yeah." She had no idea. It ran. That was the important thing.

Becky got up, patted each of the little kids on the head as she passed – going unnoticed – and walked around to where Fernando had a small penknife out to cut the tape holding each cooler closed. Becky opened the first lid and looked inside, a curl of steam rising out of the blue Coleman cooler.

"Wow, you must be a rock star at wrapping Christmas presents," Becky said. "Fernando, come look at this. It's like a machine did it."

Peering in, Fernando made the not-bad face. "Looks good."

"Rhino will *really* appreciate this." Becky peeled the Mega Deluxo shopping bag from around the three milk jugs of blood. "And this is all his too? Everything's from the same guy?"

"Yeah," Amber said. She took another sip from her drink. "That's his blood."

"You cleaned these jugs out real good before using them again, right?"

"Yeah, with the soap Rhino said to use."

"Awesome. And you kept these under thirty-five degrees, same as everything else, right?"

"Uh-huh. Just like Rhino said to."

"Awesome, very awesome. Okay, Fernando, can you go take this to the walk-in cooler while I get Amber here her money so she can be on her way?"

"Cool." Fernando hugged his arms around the three coolers and the milk jugs and bumped the door to the kitchen open with his back. As the door swung shut, Amber was relieved to have the load out of her hands. Even if it meant no pay, or whatever may come, at least she wasn't in possession of a murder victim anymore. But in the back of her mind, she kept wondering what Frank was talking about needing the body back, wanting her to leave some random part for the police to find so somebody could know, for sure, the nut-shot guy was dead. But it didn't matter now. It wasn't Amber's problem anymore. Out of her hands.

Becky hopped to sit on the corner of the desk, close to Amber. "You were telling Rhino it appeared to you he'd been shot?"

Amber nodded. "Once in the crotch and once in the head. Point blank, the one in his head."

"Did you beachcomb him?"

"I don't think I follow."

"Did you dig out the slugs and/or slug fragments?"

"Didn't have to," Amber said. "He came to us with them already removed."

Becky nodded. "Good. Doesn't matter who did it, long as *somebody* did. What'd you do with the scraps? Meaning, the ribcage and stomach and whatnot, the hot dog stuff."

"We have a cremator at the funeral home," Amber said. "We ran it through that and flushed the ashes down the toilet."

Becky was nodding. "That's what a lot of the funeral home sourcers do. If you hadn't, I would've recommended that method. Clean. Better than tossing it in a dumpster somewhere to let somebody's dog find it, right?" She laughed briefly. "So, before we get down to talking about money, Rhino always wants me to ask if you plan on bringing us anything else. Because the shipment we have going out on Monday – you probably noticed the refrigerator trucks out back – is pretty much full, so you might need to hold off until the fall unless you got something you can bring tomorrow."

"I think this was a one-time deal for us," Amber said. She thought she might want to do this again, until she was here, doing it.

"Well, reason I ask is we're short on A-negative bone marrow with our next delivery going south. If you had anything small A-negative, just a leg maybe, we'd be willing to throw in a little extra more."

"Sorry, we don't have anything available."

"It's all good. Just thought I'd ask. Rhino's breathing down my neck for it but our sourcers can only scrape together what they can, when they can. And don't feel bad making this a one-time thing. You're not indebted to us for anything, Amber. We're actually indebted to you, for all your hard work. And for the amount of money you get per body, well, it can set you up pretty nicely just doing it the once, can't it? Though, if you don't mind, Rhino said he'd like to keep your name handy next time we're up here in Minnesota."

"That'd be fine," Amber said, figuring that was the most diplomatic way of saying no without actually coming out and giving a firm negative to these people.

"Why didn't your partner come with you tonight? If it's okay to ask something that personal."

"It's fine," Amber said. "She didn't want to. She helped me with the load, but didn't want anything more to do with this."

Becky's smile dissolved. "You trust her, right?"

"Oh, absolutely," Amber said. "She won't say anything. She was just nervous about doing it, is all."

"More nervous than you? I can hardly imagine a person more nervous than you are right now." Becky's smile returned. She touched Amber on the knee, two fingers. "It's really okay, Amber. We're not killers. Rhino doesn't want us to go around snatching up homeless people and runaways and hookers. Other groups do that, but we don't. He calls us vultures, we just pick up the scraps. Let the mafia and the gangbangers all kill each other and then we can swoop in and clean up *while* cleaning up." She laughed. "Don't think that was me who came up with that joke, I'm not that clever. That's pure Rhino. Kind of dark, but you gotta have a sense of humor in this line of work. Like cops or EMTs. It's like a pressure valve. Laughter, that's the best medicine. Shit, sorry, listen to me rambling on. You probably wanna get paid so you can get back on the road, huh?" Becky leaned down in front of the children. "Excuse me, babies, but Auntie Beck-beck's gotta get in the safe."

The kids, without breaking focus on the tablet, got up together, walked past Amber, never looking her way, went to the other end of the office, sat down, and continued their tablet-gazing, unbothered.

Amber watched Becky kneel to twist the dial on the safe, left, right, left, and pull it open.

Inside were several stacks of money, each banded and shrink-wrapped in clear plastic. Becky leaned over to her desk to snatch a paper bag, snapped her wrist to open it, and began depositing the money, two stacks at a time, inside, her lips moving as she counted. Amber stared at the money as it came out of the safe and into the bag meant for her. She'd never seen so much cash in one place before. A white-hot thrill rose in her, making her throat clench and her stomach feel warm – she could've squealed with happiness right then, but bit her lip, and watched Becky continue to put the money in the bag, stack after stack after stack.

"It's all gonna be in twenties, I hope you don't mind," Becky said as she put another set of stacks, then another set, into the bag. "Rhino thinks it makes it easier for our sourcers to use right away. Can't find too many places that'll break a hundred."

"That's totally fine," Amber said.

"And, in case you were worried, it's all a mix of old money and new, nothing's in sequence or anything like that."

"I wasn't worried. Not at all." Amber finished the final four swallows of her drink in one gulp and set the glass aside, rubbing the glass's perspiration between her fingers until it was gone. She was practically drooling looking at the money as Becky continued to move stacks over into the bag. *Don't stop. Don't ever stop.*

But when Becky did stop, she had difficulty picking up the bag with one hand – the muscles in her arm rippling from the effort – to set it on the desk.

"First half, four hundred and seventy-five thousand smackaroonies. Do you want Fernando to walk you out to your car?"

Amber stood, knees knocking together with excitement now instead of fear, and picked up the bag, hugging its weight close to her chest, the smell of money washing out and directly into her nose where it splashed over her brain and doubled her excitement. "I think I can manage."

"Well, thank you *so much* for working with us, Amber. We'll give you a call sometime around noon tomorrow so you can pick up the other half. Seriously, though, awesome job on the packaging. You'd be shocked how many people – men, usually, sorry Fernando – just cram the stuff in the coolers like squirrels burying a nut. Anyway, here's to you," Becky said and put out her hand.

Amber uncurled one arm from around the money to shake Becky's hand.

"And we look forward to seeing you tomorrow," Becky said, "when we get our results back from our guy. Oh, and give Wednesday nights some thought; we could really use one more Pink Lady this season."

Amber smiled. "I will. I look forward to your call tomorrow."

"And I look forward to making it. See you, Amber."

"Bye. Nice to meet you, Fernando. Bye, kids."

Only Fernando smiled and said goodbye; the kids never even knew Amber had been in the room at all. It didn't matter. Amber walked down the hall, past the bathrooms, past the two guys playing at the arcade cabinet, the pinball machines, and the bar, her flip-flops smacking against her heels as she moved quickly toward the back door of the bowling alley. She stepped out into the cool night air and went to the hearse, opened up the back, lifted the panel underneath the carpet where the spare tire was, and mashed the money in its bag down deep. She looked around, closed everything up, got inside, and started the engine. As she waited for the car to warm up – and to stop making that awful squealing sound it did every time the engine was first turned over – Amber dialed Jolene.

No hello, just: "How'd it go?"

"Went fine. We got our first half. I'm on my way home now."

"Stop somewhere, get something to celebrate."

"Seriously?" Amber laughed. "Who are you and what'd you do with my friend Jolene?"

"It's me. And yes, I'm serious. I'd say we've earned it. We can have one crazy night before thinking bills and mortgages and getting our furniture back and all that shit."

"Well, what do you want me to pick up?"

"Booze. All the booze you can fit in the car."

Amber laughed. "Anything else, Bukowski?"

"I'll leave that up to you. Just get what you're gonna get and come home so we can finally, *finally* enjoy ourselves."

"On my way," Amber said, pulling out of the bowling alley lot. "We did it, Jo-Jo. We actually pulled it off."

"And we still have another half coming tomorrow?"

"That's what Becky said. And she's super cool, by the way. I think she's Rhino's girlfriend or something. You'd like her."

"I'll like anybody who'll give us a few dollars shy of a million bucks. God, Amber, I'm so sorry I ever doubted you."

"It's really okay. I'm just glad I was able to make this happen. Anyway, I gotta watch the road. I'll see you when I see you."

Given the hour, every liquor store Amber slowed down in front of had its neon sign reading CLOSED in the window. She had thought since it was Fourth of July Eve some might have extended hours, but no. Groaning with frustration, she moved on down the block, slowing at the next she spotted, same deal.

Coming into Dinkytown, taking the Twin Cities in a reducing spiral circling the funeral home in a desperate search, Amber spotted a cozy little tavern with its light still on. Most appealing was the sign that read they offered on/off sale. She parked the hearse, went around back, reached under the cover of the spare tire, and pulled out a stack of twenties. She peeled away half of the stack of one bundle, tossed the rest back in, made sure nothing was showing, closed up the hearse, and double-checked to make sure she'd locked it.

Any port in the storm, so long as that on/off sale sign wasn't lying.

Inside men in cowboy hats in the far corner and the bartender, a middle-aged man with thinning air, who stood looking up at the mounted TV. Amber watched two women pause their game of pool to size her up, cues in hand like sharpened spears. Whatever they were making of her right now, that opinion was about to change. Amber bellied up to the bar. The bartender tossed a coaster down in front of her with a flick of the wrist. "What'll it be?"

"I'll have a vodka tonic, with lime, and everybody else will have more of whatever they're having – the rest of the night," Amber said. And having to shout over the sudden cheers that filled the greasy little tavern, she added, "And if you wouldn't mind, a keg of whatever you recommend loaded up in the back of my car."

"And that is all doable, darling, but I'll need to see the color of your money."

Amber swatted the fistful of twenties down on the bar, and grinned. "How's that shade of green grab you?"

★   ★   ★

Frank turned onto his street and from the corner he could see the three black SUVs sitting parked along the curb in front of his house. He made himself continue to hold the accelerator down, to take him to his driveway, and turn in. He parked in the garage and stepped out, hearing the thump of several car doors. Coming up his driveway was Bryce, his aunt being led by the two burly cousins, and three other men in more casual attire – dress shirts, no coats and ties, pressed slacks. Frank's phone started to go off in his pocket, but he was quick to reach in and turn it to silent. Hopefully it was Jessica saying she'd convinced her mother to go to Rachel's mom's place. He'd check later – if he lived that long.

Bryce led the pack up Frank's driveway, meeting Frank at the side door to the house. Frank had his keys out, but didn't move ahead of Bryce to unlock the door. He held Bryce's gaze, the amused little look on his young face.

"I didn't do nothing to her," Bryce said. "I don't think she even saw me. But Vlad did say he saw her come home from work early and her and your ex take off like the dickens."

"Is he still there, outside their house?"

"No," Bryce said. "I believed you when you said you'd meet us here. We're all here. That's Vlad, if you don't remember."

Vlad, one of the giant cousins, grunted a hello at Frank.

Frank asked Bryce, "Did you not expect me to call them?"

Bryce shrugged. "You did what you had to do." He nodded toward the side door of the house. "You gonna invite us in or what, Frank? It's nippy out here."

Frank glanced past Bryce at Tasha Petrosky, her wet eyes giving nothing, the small grin on her lined face always there, as if smiling that kindly grandmotherly way was its natural state. Frank unlocked the door and let the long line of bodies file into the house. He watched as the cousins eased Tasha onto Frank's couch. Before anyone was settled in, he started for the kitchen.

"Anybody want some coffee?"

Bryce stepped in his way. "Do I need to bother to ask you if you have a gun in the house?"

"I don't own a gun." Frank brushed past him and filled the coffeepot under the tap and poured it into the machine and dumped in two scoops of grounds. "But you can ask if it'll put your mind at ease, Bryce."

"Come on out here while that's brewing, don't be rude to your guests by hiding in the kitchen."

Every seat in his living room was filled. One cousin took Frank's recliner and turned on the TV, flipping impatiently through the channels. Another, seated next to Tasha, poked through their phone. Bryce passed the one kneeling to flick through Frank's meager DVD collection, to sit on the other side of his aunt.

Tasha, nearly buried with a young man on either side of her, stared at Frank — zeroed in on him like she could see everything he'd done, written on his bones, through his thin skin. She cleared her throat, struggling to dislodge something, and said, "We haven't found my son."

"Bryce told me, Missus Petrosky. I'm sorry to hear that."

Bryce went up the hall, stepped into the bathroom, and closed the door. It felt timed, somehow. But Frank doubted, if they were about to kill him, Bryce would be okay missing it. Would how long he had to remain on this planet be determined by how long it took the asshole to go relieve himself?

Tasha's eyes watched her nephew leave the room, then returned to Frank, dragging slowly from one point of focus to the next. Frank's heart thudded in his chest. He folded his arms to keep his shaking hands from showing. It felt like an eternity before she spoke.

"I would like to keep this casual and friendly," she said, her white-white dentures clicking as she spoke, each word seemingly painstakingly selected before being issued. "My husband was unafraid of bloodshed and I think it only worked to make more enemies than friends. Sometimes business does not go as it should. People are fallible. We all make mistakes. We lie when we know, in our heart, the truth is what should be said. I would like it very much if you, Mister Goode, told me what really happened to my son."

Down the hall, the toilet flushed, a faucet hissed.

Frank cleared his throat. "I really wish I knew, Missus Petrosky. Vasily was on my operating table, right in that room right there, when I went to bed. When I woke up, I came out of my bedroom, and he was gone. It looks like he left through the side door because

I found blood on the doorknob. I ran down the street but I saw no sign of him anywhere. I would've called—"

Tasha Petrosky held up a hand. "I asked you to tell me what really happened to Vasily. Not for you to repeat lies you've already told. But I understand sometimes lying, like smoking, can be a hard habit to break – something my husband found out the hard way. I will give you one more chance to explain what happened to Vasily. So, please, the truth this time, Mister Goode."

The relative going through the DVDs paused his fingers. The cousin flipping through the channels landed on an infomercial for knives, and wasn't watching as the demonstrators sawed a brick in half. The other well-dressed young man tucked his phone away. Bryce came back up the hall wiping his hands dry on his pants. "Don't you own any hand towels?"

All eyes were on Frank and it felt like the house had been flung into outer space, with nothing at all going on outside these walls – a total, fathomless vacuum – just them, alone.

Frank licked his lips. "I—"

Bryce, standing very close at Frank's side, drew his gun and pressed its cold barrel to Frank's head, behind his right ear. "The truth, Frank."

He thumbed back the hammer. Frank could feel the mechanism inside the gun shift against his skull. "The *truth*," Bryce said, his lips brushing Frank's ear.

"All I was going to say was…" Frank started, when his phone thrummed in his pocket, the buzz of it vibrating about as loud as a ringtone given the current plunging silence of the house.

With his free hand, Bryce snatched it from Frank's shorts pocket and studied its screen. "You have two text messages and one voicemail. Let's see who you've been talking to. First text message from Jessica, received two minutes ago: Dad, I'm home. Second text message, received one minute ago: We're going to grandma's. Well, nothing we didn't already expect. Now, on to the voicemail. Let's listen to it on speaker, shall we?"

"*Frankie, it's Louie Pescatelli. Big Robbie told me to tell you he got a call from some guy calling himself Giraffe or Hippo or some shit, saying you was in hot water. Robbie and his boys should be there in a few minutes, just hold tight, buddy, cavalry's on its way.*"

Frank had his eyes closed, ready for the sudden crack and pounding heat on his temple and the Great Whatever that waited for all of us – but it didn't come. He opened his eyes, still alive, and saw everyone in his living room before him was getting to their feet. Bryce said, "Did you hear that?"

Then Frank heard it too, struggling to pick up whatever it was through the pulse chugging hard in his ears. Car doors whacking shut. Hushed talking, getting closer. And footsteps coming up his front walk – several sets of feet.

The doorbell rang.

No one moved to answer it.

The gun barrel, pressing hard against Frank's head, began to shake. Bryce whispered, "What the fuck do we do?"

From outside, Robbie Pescatelli boomed, "You fucking Slavs can keep as quiet as you like but we seen your cars out at the curb. You might as well open up so we can talk this over. And Frank had *better* be breathing."

Frank stood, heart pounding, hands up, gun to his temple. The doorbell rang a second time. Robbie's fists shook the house, thunder, thunder, thunder, rattling the windowpanes.

Tasha motioned at the giant galoot cousins nearest the door. "Answer it."

The door came open and Robbie stepped into the house, silk Hawaiian shirt clinging to his girth with sweat, a curl of dark hair drooping down into his face. He walked in scowling, empty hands at his sides, leading in four of his own men.

Bryce's cousin closed the door and the heat in the house swelled immediately. Frank couldn't remember the last time he'd had this much company over. The house was threatening to split at the seams. Robbie and his men remained near the front door, one Russian cousin standing behind them. Robbie looked through the wall of bodies between him and Frank, and locked on the ex-doctor – and shifted his dark eyes to Bryce, next to him, holding the gun on Frank.

"Ain't no need for that, kid."

"You think so?" Bryce said. "He fucking killed my cousin. Or you did. Somebody fucking did. And we're gonna figure it out tonight, eye for an eye."

Tasha Petrosky released her nephew's arm and shuffled on small shoes across Frank's stained carpet toward Big Robbie, having to crane her head all the way back to meet his eyes high above her. "Did you kill my son, Robert?"

"No. I didn't," Robbie said. "But that don't mean I ain't glad his ass is dead. Same as your husband – though I wish it coulda been a bullet that did him."

Tasha's face didn't change. That small smile, that slight tremor that accompanied her every movement and slightest gesture. She just stared up at Robbie after what he'd said, saying nothing in return.

Robbie sighed. "That was a little harsh. I apologize, that was your old man and your kid I was talking about. I take it back. But, for the record, your old man? You *can't* look me in the eye, Tasha, and tell me he wasn't a dyed-in-the-wool son of a bitch."

Tasha still said nothing. Shivered, stared, smiled.

Robbie glanced around at Bryce's men. "I think she's broke, fellas. You wanna plug her in for a while and we'll try this again?"

Robbie's men laughed. Tasha's men did not.

"I'm waiting for you to tell me the truth," Tasha said up to him, at eye level with his massive gut expanding and contracting as Robbie's powerful breaths filtered the air. She poked a skeletal finger into his silk-draped paunch, sinking it to the second knuckle. "You still haven't said whether or not you were involved."

The young man with the pompadour, who was standing closest to Robbie, slowly opened his motorcycle jacket. From it he produced a submachine gun, letting it hang at his side, finger curled into the trigger guard.

Through the gun pressed to Frank's head, he could feel Bryce's hand begin to shake at a quicker tempo now.

One of the other Russians produced a snub-nosed revolver, and like Robbie's man, drew his weapon but didn't aim or raise it – just let it be seen in his hand, ready.

Frank wasn't sure if his legs were going numb from fear or if he'd actually just pissed himself.

"Look here, you dumb old fuck," Robbie said down to Tasha, "I ain't no fucking squealer. I know who done your son, yeah. I got the name right here on the tip of my fucking tongue. But I ain't gonna give it to you. Now, we're here to see after our sawbones. Which means escorting' you cabbage-chewing assholes out of his fucking home – because by the look on his face, I don't get the impression none of you were invited. So, if all of you wanna put your fucking shooters back in your pants and fuck the fuck off, that'd be just peachy. Otherwise, we're gonna have some real big fucking problems in a minute."

Tasha withdrew her finger from Robbie's belly – the indentation of it remaining in the soft material of his shirt. "So my Vasily is dead? You know this, for sure?"

"That I do," Robbie said, proud. "But I ain't telling you by who."

Frank watched Tasha's long frail arm lower to her side, then curl around to the elastic band of her tracksuit, wrapping her bony fingers around the pearl handle of a knife. Robbie remained glaring down at her, looking at her like he could swallow her whole.

Nobody breathed.

Frank slowly took a step backward. Bryce remained with his arm out, holding the gun on the empty space where Frank had been standing – staring at the scene ahead. Frank moved backward into the kitchen, near the trickling coffee maker.

"Then if you know, you were involved, and that makes you accountable," Tasha said. And with a flash of steel winking into Frank's eyes from the living room, her arm moved shockingly quick, her tremors allowing her this one unmarred moment of grace, and brought the knife up and out – sinking it to its handle in Robbie's gut.

Gasping hugely, Robbie tried stepping back, to pull himself off the knife. Tasha shuffled forward, little steps, with him – twisting the blade like trying a sticky doorknob, then wrenched, hard, to the left. A gout of blood erupted onto the floor.

In one smooth motion Robbie's hand scrambled into his pants pocket, took out his gun, mashed it into the wrinkles of Tasha's cheek, and fired.

Tasha Petrosky, seventy-two, crumpled to the floor, most of her jaw taken away, broken dentures leering out of her dead face where she lay – the carpet accepting the deluge of dark blood and brain spilling from her head, mopping it up.

All the remaining men looked at each other. Robbie's men, Tasha's men.

Bryce turned his gun from the ghost of where Frank had been standing, and took aim at Robbie. "You're fucking dead."

Robbie raised his gun and aimed at Bryce. "Not as dead as your fucking aunt."

The guy in the motorcycle jacket and pompadour hoisted his submachine gun in both hands.

Robbie pressed a hand over his torn shirt and torn belly, aiming at Bryce, sweat dribbling into his eyes. "What're you gonna do, kid? Eyeball me to death?"

Bryce fired – and set in immediate motion Frank's living room tearing itself apart with noise. Frank leaped back further into the kitchen, threw himself to the floor, hoping his cabinets would shield him. Plaster dust and dishes in the cupboards rained down on him as the bullets tore through the house. Large caliber, small caliber. The next room, one thin wall away, for three cacophonous seconds, was a cube of condensed noise.

As quickly as it had begun, just as quickly was it over. One last small pop, a grunt, and a thump Frank felt in the floor as the last man collapsed.

Keeping low, Frank touched his shoulder, feeling something wet and hot running down his back. He glanced up and saw his coffee maker had been blown to pieces on the counter, dark coffee dribbling over the edge and onto him.

He stood, moving through the thick fog of dust and gun smoke, and peeked out into the living room. Nothing moved.

With the wall-to-wall aftermath, the still bodies and spilled blood and smoking bullet casings, no square inch of the carpet was visible. His TV spat sparks from its shattered screen. Every wall had holes peppered in lines across it. The front windows lay in shards, blood-spattered curtains curling out of the jagged holes from the wind.

His ears rang. He carefully found gaps between the bodies to step, the wet carpet squishing under his sneakers. Bryce stared empty-eyed at the ceiling, his neck blown open to the point Frank could see his spine. He lay near his aunt, now splattered with blood that wasn't hers. Dentures, bright white against all that red, winked out at Frank as he stepped over her.

The giant cousins were each hit several times across their chests, their injuries almost perfectly mirroring each other's. The well-dressed kid who'd taken an interest in Frank's DVD collection was missing the front part of his head, now bearing a flat red wreck for a face. The young guy with the leather jacket and pompadour lay against the wall, the submachine gun smoking next to him on the floor, its hot barrel melting the carpet into a dark gooey crater. He'd been shot in the cheek, ripping it from the corner of his mouth to his left ear. His teeth were showing on the one side in a lopsided rictus. They clicked as he muttered, low, "Simone... Simone, I'm sorry...."

Simone's baby daddy, Frank surmised, and stepped past him as Joey, presumably, faded away and slumped over, clicking exposed teeth falling still as his chin dipped to his chest and his eyes evacuated any sign of life.

Big Robbie, lying in a mound, his belly's underside looking like it was uncoiling a long pink tongue. Robbie's bloody hand felt around at the dangling bit of gut and tried stuffing it back inside, tucking in some of his shirt with it, feeling around blindly.

Frank knelt, his knees touching warm, blood-soaked carpet. He helped Robbie push his intestines back in. "Jesus Christ," Frank heard himself say, through ringing ears. "Jesus fucking Christ."

Robbie lay in a heap by the blood-soaked couch. His shirt was darkening in three different spots across his chest. One of them was blowing bubbles when he inhaled, a struggling deep wheeze. His sweat-slicked face raised a little, landing dark eyes on Frank with the ex-doctor's hand mashed deep in his belly, trying to find the source of the bleeding. There were far too many.

"I didn't expect shit to go that way," Robbie managed to say, some blood slopping out of his mouth and down his double chins. "I...didn't think there'd be so goddamn many of them here. But you're our boy, Frankie. We look after our own."

Frank found the worst of the bleeding, the rent in Robbie's guts gushing hard and hot against his searching fingers. He pinched at the artery, slippery as it was, and held it closed, feeling the pressure immediately build and balloon behind it. He'd need a clamp.

"Why's it smell like shit?" Robbie gurgled.

"She cut open your large intestine," Frank said.

Robbie dropped his head back. "That probably ain't good, is it?"

"No. But I can help you."

"You should run, Frankie. The cops will be coming." His eyes, slowly blinking and unfocused, moved around the room, seeing all the bodies that lay around them, arms and legs draped every which way, smoking guns in many hands held with loose, uncurled fingers. "The war's over, but some of these boys, they got boys of their own. And they'll grow up and hear about this shit and...and they'll do something about it. They'll see it gets straightened out...you gotta tell them, Frank. Tell them what they did to Big Robbie, okay?"

Frank held on to Robbie's artery, pinching hard until he thought he might break his own fingers, the lips of the tear in the man's gut gumming at his wrist softly, swallowing him. "I gave Simone an abortion yesterday morning," he said. "Bryce brought Vasily here. She killed him."

Robbie's lips pressed together. When they parted with a pop, a red bubble swelled between the edges of his teeth as he said, "You what?"

"She asked me to do it. She paid me to do it. I didn't want to, but I did it."

"Was she raped?"

"I don't think so."

Robbie tried looking over at the pompadour kid. "Did Joey know...?"

"No. She said she wanted to fit into her maid-of-honor dress. She—" Frank felt a warm barrel of a gun touch his temple.

"And you fucking *kill it* just because she asked you to?" Robbie said.

"Yes," Frank said.

"You fucking piece of shit. They got so many of us here."

"I know."

"Was it a boy?"

"I'm sorry, Robbie, I—"

"Was it a fucking *boy*, Frank?"

"Yes. But, Robbie, listen to me, this is all her fault. If she hadn't killed Vasily—"

*Click.* Frank flinched. He'd let go of the artery. Reaching in, he couldn't find it again. Blood came out in a gush, dampening Frank's legs and chest.

Robbie glared up at Frank all the while, pulled the trigger again. Again. Again. Nothing but dead clicks. "You fuck. You little *fuck*."

Frank withdrew his hand, the wound slapping shut but continuing to drool a wide pool of blood onto the carpet. He stood as Robbie tracked him with the gun, still squeezing the trigger, still not firing.

Robbie paled. His arm slapped wide, the gun spilling out of his clutch. And his eyes, as Frank stared into them, made himself stare and watch and witness, lost their light without a sound.

With a wet, slippery hand, Frank picked up the empty gun. He'd never held a real one before – a rubber one in drama class in high school had been his only experience. The real deal was much heavier.

Frank stood, blood slathered on his clothes up to his elbows, ears ringing, dust settling in his hair and across his shoulders. All of these bodies, knee-high in his living room, all of them beyond saving. He had to do something. He couldn't stay here. Someone would have certainly called the cops. He had to run. Like he should've, like Ted said he should've. Fuck.

He looked around his house. Bare walls now full of holes. Broken TV. He had no photos to take with him. No treasures from his childhood. No heirlooms. No one and nothing to lift, rescued, to his chest to come along on his escape. Just him. They would find the bodies. They'd find his operating room too and the illegally obtained equipment and tools and drugs. He didn't have any money to take. Nothing but himself. But he might be able to contact some help, he thought, and struggling to wedge his hand in, Frank fished out Robbie's phone from his slacks pocket. He tucked it into his own pocket, stepped over Robbie, shoes squishing in the carpet as he tried to avoid stepping on any dead men's hands or necks. He picked his way over to the side door of the house. Stepping out slowly, listening for any stragglers that might be running up on him, the cool night air lapping on all the wet parts of him – blood, sweat. He glanced across the street before running to his garage.

One of the pickup trucks across the street was hissing down on one side, its front right tire punctured. A house alarm was going off kitty-corner from Frank's place, the house's front window lying smashed in the yard and a perfect circle piercing the curtains. Then, drawing him around, he heard an old man howling in pain. Facing the Shulmans' house, there in the window stood Mister Shulman, whom Frank seldom saw outside their home, clutching the sides of his head and screaming down at something Frank couldn't see, on the floor. "Cynthia. Oh, God, my Cynthia."

And when the wind turned, Frank could hear the sirens. Several going at once, their peals mingling and overlapping, sometimes syncing – but all of them, together, were growing louder.

Frank, only hearing his footsteps and not feeling any part of his body as he ran, moved up the driveway and into the garage. He got behind the wheel of the Lexus, tossed Robbie's gun onto the passenger seat, and smeared the door handle and the wheel and his keys with blood as he got the engine started and backed out of the driveway. He took off, in the opposite direction from the sirens, turning the first corner that came up so he could no longer see the flashing red and blue in his mirror behind him.

He had to stop a few blocks away to be sick. He didn't get the door open in time. He got back on the road, flew through a red light, turned onto the highway, and filled his car with screams and curses, forgetting all language but the animalistic noise of precise agony, bottomless regret, and self-aimed anger, as he tore off into the night at ninety-five miles per hour.

★　　★　　★

The world felt soft and unsure under Amber's flip-flops as she stumbled out the front door of the tavern, an arm draped over the shoulders of her new friends. Everybody laughing, she knew so many new names. In a loud pack of red faces, they stepped together out to the lot. No traffic on the nearby street. The few streetlights in this part of town flickered, those that worked. The bartender followed them out, stood at the door and watched everybody navigate the parking lot, weaving like flies banging against a windowpane, toward their cars.

"And there's my buddy," Amber said as her new friends approached the hearse with her. The keg sat in the front seat, as if waiting for her. "Think I could use the carpool lane now?" She remembered walking the bartender out to the hearse to load up the keg but couldn't say, for sure, how many hours ago that'd been.

Amber, released by her friends, receiving many thanks and loving claps on the back, was set free to try poking her key to one side of the car handle, then the other, as everyone else filed off and left, some of whom probably couldn't afford another DUI on their record but were going to chance it anyway.

The bartender called from across the lot, "Maybe you should consider calling a cab, darling. Be kind of ironic to die in a ride such as yours."

"I'm fine," Amber said. "I got a funeral tomorrow, I need to get home."

"Might be *your* funeral if you don't take a cab. They might even let you put the keg in the trunk if you ask real nice."

"What, are you my mom or something? Said I'm fucking fine, okay? Jeez."

"Eight vodka tonics would make even an elephant drive kinda screwy, girl. And you ain't no bigger than a whip. I can't tell you what to do, but this is just me, a concerned citizen."

"Then shut up, butthead."

"Say the word and I can call a cab *for* you—"

"Fuck you." Amber got behind the wheel, pulled the door closed, sat in the sudden silence of the hearse. She gave the finger to the bartender until he shook his head and went back inside.

The lights along the front of the tavern went dark. Amber murmured a curse; she'd been using them to try and get the key in the ignition. She stamped the gas in time with twisting the key, unable to find the right synchronization of movements to get the finicky engine to relent and turn over. She paused, counted to three, breathed deep, tried to get her hand on the key and foot on the pedal to cooperate and work together, and tried again. Twist, stamp, twist, stamp.

The car rumbled to life. She put it in gear and, meaning to go backward, instead shot forward. She heard the underside of the hearse bark sharply as she ran over the cement parking strip. But since she was already in motion, she decided to just keep going, went over the sidewalk, slammed onto the street, took a really wide turn to get aligned with the lane, and drove leaning forward over the wheel, squinting in the dark to get the watery world beyond her eyes to focus, fighting to line up the front left corner of the hearse's long hood with the double yellow line.

Soon, the line was on the right, somehow, and she tweaked the wheel with one hand, fumbling to light a smoke with the other, and got back on her side of the road.

The light ahead changed, yellow, red. She braked a little early and had to creep up to the intersection with small shoves of the accelerator. Once stopped she noticed a crimson comet flaring across her blurry vision. Next to the red light was a little white light hung on the same line. It usually indicated an ambulance was going to come through the intersection soon, or a cop car on a chase after somebody. Shit. Killing the radio's distraction with a swat on the knob, Amber straightened up in the seat, made sure she'd actually buckled up, and watched out the rearview mirror for flashing lights.

She glanced to her right. In the passenger seat sat the keg. Well, maybe this was a poor choice after all. But when she finally heard the sirens and saw flashing red and blue blasting near out of the darkness, they weren't coming from behind her, but going past her, ahead of her car. Six police cars tore past, followed quickly by an ambulance struggling to keep pace. Amber sat watching them, mesmerized by the flashing lights as, soon, only the lights, not the vehicles they were attached to, were all she could make out, several blocks down. She watched them, *flash-flash, flash-flash*, as she leaned over the steering wheel to see.

Despite her condition, she almost wanted to follow them just to see what the big ruckus was about. Maybe somebody got shot. Maybe she could load them up and take them to Becky. Those lights were amazing to watch, either way, flashing off into the night like coked-out lightning bugs on a mad run....

The hearse was drifting out into the intersection.

Amber, realizing she was moving, cursed, and tried slamming the brakes but hammered the gas instead. The hearse's engine screamed and tires squealed, lurching her further out into the intersection. A car coming the other way flared the inside of the hearse with its headlights. Squealing tires, it swerved, blared her with its horn, and narrowly avoided T-boning her.

The hearse was still going – her feet couldn't remember which pedal did what – and the chain-link fence, dead ahead, jumped forward to snag her like a catcher's mitt.

There was a rattling clatter of metal as the fence flew up and over the hood and draped across the windshield. Amber screamed when the pavement ended and it was just dirt and trash as the path ahead angled sharply downward – and the car, nosing down, even once she found the brakes, would not slow.

The hearse banged and jumped and lurched side to side as it picked up speed, tumbling down the ravine under the highway overpass. She heard something crack, saw a bright flash of light in one eye, and felt something warm drawing a line down her neck, safety glass embedded in her cheek. The pain came on a delay.

The headlights caught something gray and unmoving ahead. Through the blood in her eyes, Amber watched, helpless as the hearse ran straight at the cement pylon keeping the highway above her standing. Fighting the wheel did nothing. The hearse was determined to kill itself.

With a deafening slam of metal on cement, the hearse's slope-made inertia was violently ended – equal and opposite forces and that.

Her head, and the keg, both lashed forward upon impact. But whereas her head was stopped from flying out through the windshield by still being attached to her neck, and bouncing off the steering wheel as well, the keg wasn't likewise restricted – it leaped through the windshield with a splash of breaking glass, and struck the support structure of the overpass ahead with a resounding *clang*. Hitting the trash-strewn ground outside the hearse, hissing, bleeding beer, it spun and hopped around, foaming the ground as it depressurized, finally coming to rest in a bubbling puddle a hundred feet away.

Amber lost consciousness, tasting blood.

# CHAPTER SEVEN

Jolene, for a lack of anywhere else soft, lay in one of the caskets in the display room. The one with the pearlescent finish and platinum hardware, which they always called their 'hip-hop special' but never in front of clients.

The satin interior was comfortable, the pad good and pillow soft under her head. She lay watching a movie on her phone, one earbud in to listen for when Amber returned. But that was half a movie ago when she started thinking she'd be back any minute. She sat up, lifted the casket lid from over her lower half, swung her legs out and hopped to the floor. She stepped out into the reception area. The vaulted ceilings – meant, probably, to evoke the feeling of a church – repeated the sounds of her steps. She went around the counter and studied the CCTV screens. No hearse pulling into the driveway, nor parked out at the curb at the edge of the yard. She sat and watched the grainy feeds, watching the time stamp click one minute by, another.

She was still thinking about Cornelius telling on them, and Frank's questionable behavior. Now, with it being nearly three in the morning, and having not heard back from Amber, despite Jolene having left ten messages, she was beginning to wonder if maybe this Becky chick Amber mentioned had changed her mind – if Rhino changed his/her mind. A whirlwind of possibilities, all bad, circled Jolene.

Deciding sleep wasn't going to be likely tonight, she went into the kitchen to get the coffee started. Her eyes burned, her nerves were shot, and she tried, yet again, to call Amber. Still nothing. She sat at the kitchen table, taking her coffee with sugar unlike usual just for the spike of energy she hoped to get from it, and waited. Nothing more could be done. But people were due to show up in five hours expecting their loved one to be taken to their final resting spot, and that would require a hearse.

"You better have a *damn* good excuse, Amber," Jolene said to herself, and lit the last cigarette left in her pack.

★    ★    ★

When the news started to repeat Frank's life story – beloved local surgeon turned criminal turned back-alley surgeon turned supposed mass-murdering mafia-killer – Frank turned off the radio. His whereabouts were still unknown, they said. Well, he could confirm that better than anybody. He knew where he was. They didn't. How much longer it'd stay that way remained a mystery.

In Frank's glove box, he had a pack of Wet-Naps from the last time he went to a barbecue joint. He turned on the dome light of his car, and dabbed at his arms and face and neck, scraping hard at the blood to try to get it off.

The Wet-Naps only did so much. Mostly they just pushed the blood around. But he got his hands clean, at least.

He checked himself in the rearview mirror. Yep, he still looked like somebody who just walked away the sole survivor of a shootout.

He sat in his car behind a closed Pizza Hut in West St. Paul, headlights off, doors locked because West St. Paul wasn't exactly a great part of town, and brought his cigarette up to his lips. His hands were still shaking and his ears still ringing two hours on. Ahead of his car, over the dead Kmart's parking lot, the sun was due to start coming up soon. He couldn't remember the last time he watched the sun come up.

It took him a few tries to figure out how to get the magazine to eject from Robbie's gun. He sat looking into the empty handgun – which he thought maybe was called a Glock – and slid the magazine back inside. Even empty, it might be useful. Worse comes to worst, he could always go out via suicide-by-cop.

But he wasn't at that point yet. He still had people he could call, but was afraid to, thinking the cops would ping his cell phone signal. So he kept his phone on airplane mode, sitting at half-charge on the passenger seat. Another twenty minutes slid by without a police helicopter hovering over his car or a SWAT team wrenching him out through the window. A silent summer morning, dew on his windshield, a rainbow in each little perfect hemisphere of water.

He thought about his daughter and his ex-wife mostly. He thought about happier days. And some of the not-so-great ones, in the later, grayer stages of his marriage. Even those, weeks on end sleeping on the couch, paled in comparison to what his life was now. All he had was his car. His car, the clothes on his back, and the mountain of awfulness his life had become, swelling up over the horizon to blot out the sun. Currently, in reality, the sun was peeking up in the distance, burning away purple and gray clouds, the kind of orange that always made him think of sherbet.

He couldn't sit here forever watching the sun. Soon it'd come up all the way and people would start driving by. Eventually he'd be seen. He needed an escape.

Reluctantly, Frank took his phone off airplane mode and dialed Ted. One ring, two, three. It never went to voicemail, just kept twittering in his ear, no connection of any kind possible. He had mentioned he was going off the grid, maybe he already had. Frank ended the call and flipped through his text chain with his daughter, those last two desperate messages roaring out at him.

*Dad, I'm home.*

*We're going to Grandma's.*

And then that voicemail. Frank listened to it again. Rhino, whoever the fuck they were, had tipped Robbie off about the Petroskys. Why did Rhino want to intervene? What did Frank mean to them, to anybody, besides the cops right now? And on top of that, how did they know *to* send Robbie over in the first place? Frank had told no one about the Petroskys planning to come by except for Ted.

Okay. So he followed that possibility a second. Maybe – maybe – Ted had sent it up the food-chain; maybe someone in the red market saw value in what Frank did for a living. Maybe Frank, since giving those funeral-home girls Vasily, was being unwittingly recruited as a source for bodies in the future. Maybe they wanted to help him so, if caught, he wouldn't squeal about what he knew about Rhino and what Rhino did. Or maybe Rhino wanted to keep Frank from harm's way so Rhino, himself, could kill Frank to make sure all loose ends were tied up. But if he wanted Frank dead, why not just let the Petroskys kill him?

Maybe those funeral-home girls were Rhino, together, and just put on a good show to *seem* like they had no idea what they were doing. Maybe Ted was Rhino. Maybe that dumbass Slug was Rhino. Fuck, maybe Frank's ex-wife or the mailman or the goddamn Pope or the Loch Ness Monster was Rhino.

It didn't matter. They had saved his life, whoever they were. And for the moment, he just savored that small nugget of luck he'd been tossed.

Frank set his own phone aside and took out Robbie's and sat for a while edging off the hard little dots of dried blood from the screen with his thumbnail, considering what he should do. He was lying low right now, afraid to get on the highway. He had to get rid of his car, he knew that much. He had to have someone hide him. But who owed him anything? It wasn't like he could call Rhino for another favor – it seemed he deigned to intervene when he wanted. Plus, would that be putting himself deeper in his pocket than he apparently already was?

Robbie's phone's wallpaper was of an overweight woman smiling, sitting in a gondola with what could only be Venice in the background.

If Robbie had been married, no mention of a wife had ever come up in the brief conversations Frank had had with him when Robbie dragged in some underling of his with a bullet or knife in him. Just small talk. Sports scores, the weather, where's good to eat, shit like that. Frank sat looking at the picture of Robbie's fat wife, wondering if she'd heard the news yet. And, for that matter, if it'd circled back to Robbie's niece, Simone. Simone, who without her putting a bullet in Vasily, none of this bullshit would've ever happened.

Maybe it was laying blame. Maybe it was like it was at the clinic, when a fuck-up happens, your mind, wanting to save your career and social standing, rushes to fill in holes, packing whoever was available into the hole you'd made, sacrificed. But Frank didn't think, though he'd done such things in the past, that this case was like that. Replaying it all over in his head, these past two shitty days, he decided, no, this *was* really all her fault.

If she'd just gone, like he had asked, and *not* shot Vasily in the head for no real concrete reason, none of this would've happened.

Frank remembered trying to tell Robbie it was all her fault, back at his house, but felt like he was trying to find a scapegoat. He hadn't been. No. He'd been telling the truth. It was her fault. All her fault.

Frank found her name in Robbie's phone — the little profile picture was of her, with longer hair, fuller in the face, sitting at a kitchen counter in somebody's house, chin on her palm, elbow on the counter, smiling that absent-eyed smile. He could hear her voice as he stared at her picture. That fucking accent that felt half-pretend. That loose hold on the English language she had, the little slips of racism, the ignorant fucking girl who was born with a silver spoon in her mouth from her fucking mobster family and didn't give a shit about anyone but herself. She was a murderer and it was a shame she hadn't been in that room when the bullets had started to fly.

He called her. She was going to be Frank's square peg for this hole and he'd make sure she fit it.

"Who is this? Who's got Robbie's phone?" Simone said, voice wracked. Many female voices were howling and crying in the background. Simone sniffled. "Who the fuck is this, huh? You gonna tell me I'm next or some shit? Well, speak up, you fucking asshole — because when I find you these will be your last fucking words."

"It's Frank, Simone."

"Frank? You're all over the news. What happened? Where are you?"

"Do you really think I'm just going to tell you that?"

"Were you there? Did you see it happen? They killed my uncle and my cousins, Frank. My Joey was there. He's dead. They fucking *killed* him, Frank. Every man in my family's dead."

"I know they are. I was there."

"How did you get away?"

"I need you to help me."

"Why should I help you? You just left them all to die. Half my fucking family died in that house, you piece of shit, and you're gonna ask me for a goddamn favor?"

"There was nothing I could do. And I think you owe me."

"I *owe* you? I don't *owe* you shit. Fucking nerve of you to say such a thing to me, my family's been torn apart, we're all over crying our guts out and you're gonna—"

"But you do owe me. You have no one to blame, Simone. No one. If you hadn't shot Vasily none of this would've happened. Bryce would've picked him up and everybody could've gone their separate ways but you just *had* to shoot him, didn't you?"

"Why are you saying all this to me? Don't you know I'm in fucking pieces right now; I lost half my fucking family tonight, Frank. Don't you have no *heart*?"

"I need you to come pick me up. I need a room. I can't stay here."

"So go rent one."

"I can't. I'm covered in blood and I'm sure they're watching my bank account. After that, we need to figure out some kind of way to get me out of the country. I'm not going down for this. I didn't do a goddamn thing, but they're saying on the radio I masterminded the entire massacre."

"Well, didn't you?"

"No, Simone, I didn't. I tried to keep your uncle *away* from my house. Somebody tipped him off. I was prepared to deal with the Petroskys myself, take whatever was coming – that *you fucking caused* – and then everything blew up. So, now, you're going to help me get out of this."

"My mom and my aunts are here. I can't just leave."

"You're going out to get breakfast for everybody. That's the story. I'm in West St. Paul. Call me once you're on the road and I'll tell you where exactly."

"Tell me now."

"So you can give an anonymous tip to the cops? I don't think so. Call me when you're on your way."

"Why should I help you?"

"Because if you don't I'll call the cops and tell them *you* set the entire thing up – that you wanted to usurp your uncle or something."

"I'd never do that."

"Then prove it. Get moving. It's six thirty-four right now, you have until eight to get here."

Frank hung up and watched the sunrise, thinking, remembering. It all came back so clear. The flop sweat. The dry throat. He'd tried running before, four years ago. That crime he'd actually committed. Then, he'd tried crossing up into Canada, a straight shot north from the Twin Cities. At the time, he thought the shortest route meant the best, but it turned out to be the most obvious, thus his apprehension. He'd tried going by plane, second stupid mistake, especially since his passport got scanned at the terminal, undoubtedly setting off all kinds of alarms. Idiot. Rich idiot. Rich, spoiled, sheltered, selfish idiot. No, those were two things he wouldn't try again. They might have the record of the arrest, know what he'd attempted before and expect him to pull a repeat, betting he hadn't learned. But he had learned. He'd play this smart. He would not make the same mistakes twice.

He noticed something white on the floorboard. Grunting to bend himself in half to reach it, he lifted the tramped, bloody Hawthorne Funeral Home business card off the floor – and put it in his pocket.

★   ★   ★

Amber shot awake. The first thing she noticed was she had tubes up her nose. The second thing she noticed she was in a hospital bed. The third thing she noticed was her left wrist was in a handcuff, the other end fixed to the bedrail. She tried sitting up and a thousand little hurts all over her body started yelling at her. She couldn't see out of her left eye. She reached up with her free hand, which was wrapped in a thick cast, and dabbed at her face, hoping she hadn't lost the eye – but it was just swollen, a giant goose egg above her eyebrow. She remembered leaving the tavern with her new friends, a few fractured blurry seconds of driving, cop cars screaming by, flashing lights, then a busted keg hissing and hopping around on the ground, the smell of smoking car, blood, and Michelob filling her nose.

She was alone in the hospital room. The door was closed. She could hear people just outside, nurses and doctors, phones ringing, phones being answered. The TV in the corner of the room was currently displaying the local morning news. The word *shootout* grabbed her attention and with her one good eye, she watched.

"—is thought to be the home of Frank Goode, a former surgeon at the Hennepin County Medical Center, who authorities believe, following release after drug-trafficking charges, was running an illegal medical practice out of his Minneapolis home."

A picture of Frank, a mugshot clearly taken some years ago, appeared on screen. He didn't look pleased with himself. A little less gray then, a little rounder in the cheek, but definitely the Frank Goode that Amber knew.

"We take you live now to Northeast Minneapolis, where Ella Knudsen is live on the scene. Ella?"

Cut to a brunette woman in a smart business suit holding a microphone, overly lit, standing in front of a squatty little green house with yellow tape running every which way.

"Thanks, Tom. Behind me is the home of Frank Goode, former surgeon who was released from the Stillwater Correctional Facility two years ago. Late last night, 911 calls were placed complaining about loud noises coming from the home. Authorities, arriving on the scene, found the body of Robert Pescatelli, head of the Pescatelli crime family, and several of its members inside. Also found dead in the home were several members of the Pescatellis' enemies: Natasha Petrosky, head of the Petrosky crime family, and several key members of the Russian mafia. Among the casualties, Frank Goode's eighty-four-year-old neighbor Cynthia Shulman, who sustained a gunshot wound to the shoulder. Goode is thought to have coordinated the two rival gangs against one another where the deadly shootout occurred, at his home. Police are unable to find Goode at this time and believe he may still be in Twin Cities."

Cut back to Tom. "Do the police know what Frank Goode's plan was, Ella? Perhaps he was trying to help establish some kind of truce between the two gangs maybe?"

Back to Ella. "Right now the police are unable to discern the reason for the meeting at Goode's home. It's theorized Goode may have deliberately arranged to have the two families meet so as to provoke a shootout, but they are unsure. Back to you, Tom."

Tom in the studio. "Thanks, Ella. Well, folks, any second now we'll have a number on screen for you to call if you see Frank Goode during your morning commute. We recommend you do not attempt to approach him or apprehend him, but call 911 or the number we'll have – yep, there it is. This is the Minneapolis-St. Paul Police

Department tip line. Stay safe out there this morning. We'll be back in a moment with what we can expect the weather to be this Fourth of July weekend. Keep it here, folks."

Amber said, "Holy shit." And for a moment, she'd forgotten about all of the aches and pains dotting her body. She tried sitting up again but something in her hip sent an electric bolt through her. She slumped back, feeling drugged and hungover and beat to hell. And blasting her to sitting upright again was the thought – *the money.* Where the fuck was the money? She yanked on the handcuffs, only managing to hurt herself more. She mashed the button on the side of the bed, hearing a bell ringing in time outside the door, at the nurse's station.

A doctor came in, red eyed and rumpled. "Miss Hawthorne, good morning," he said flatly, as he shuffled into the room with his clipboard open, never looking her way.

"Why am I handcuffed?" *Please don't say for the trafficking of human body parts.*

"I should probably leave that up to the officer to tell you. He's down in the cafeteria now getting coffee. But I'm pretty sure it might have something to do with driving around St. Paul with a BAC of point thirty-one percent."

"BAC?"

"Blood alcohol content." The doctor, having heard some snippet of the news apparently, turned to look up at the TV. He stared at the face of Frank Goode, sighed, turned the TV off, and faced Amber again. "Which is a near-lethal level, if you didn't know."

"That's fine, whatever. Do you happen to know where my car ended up? It's a hearse."

The doctor flipped some pieces of paper around on his clipboard, running his tongue around the inside of his cheek like he'd recently eaten something sticky.

"Did you hear me?"

"I heard you, Miss Hawthorne, but I believe that's another topic for the officer. He should be up to read you your rights in a moment. I'm here to talk to you about your injuries and lifestyle choices."

"I drove drunk, crashed my car, bumped my head, yeah, yeah, yeah. Can I get you to call the bail bonds place so I can get this ball rolling? I need to get outta here. Do you think they'd take the car to the impound or straight to the dump? I don't know how bad it was messed up."

"They had to use the jaws of life, so I'm going to assume it's 'messed up,' yeah."

"Look, man, don't be an asshole. Write me a script for pain pills or something and bring the release form – I need to *go*."

The doctor stared at her a moment, two, sighed again, lifted the clipboard and began reading. "Severe contusion to left forehead, no internal bleeding, no fractures, minor concussion. Fractured cheekbone, clean break, will remodel on its own in time. Spiral fracture in left radius. Two fractures to left ulna, near the wrist and at the elbow. Hairline fracture to left collarbone. Dislocated left shoulder. Muscle tearing and lacerations across right shin and ankle—"

"I get it, you're a miracle worker," Amber said. "I'm the Bionic goddamn Woman now. Go outside and flip God the finger or whatever doctors do after a big win, but just bring the release form, okay, Doctor Dickhead?"

The doctor grumbled something about goddamn alcoholics, slammed her chart into the wall-holder, swatted open the door, and left.

Amber sat up as much as her pains – and the handcuffs – would permit, looking around the room for her clothes or her phone. There, on the window sill, was a plastic Ziploc bag with a familiar shape in it. The screen was lighting up and the phone in the bag was slowly scooting across the window sill as it vibrated. She couldn't reach it, not attached to the bed with all the tubes, handcuffs, IV drips, and the catheter in her. She needed to call Jolene. Somebody had to go track down the hearse. The money, if nobody found it, was still in the back under the spare.

The door swung open and a middle-aged man with a hard scowl on his fry-tanned face entered, pushing an empty wheelchair.

He was in light blue scrubs that didn't fit him very well. No soft-soled nurse's sneakers on his feet. Big heavy black boots. He closed the door behind him, parked the wheelchair to one side, and stood staring at Amber lying in the bed. Then, slowly, he took a scan about the room with his deep-set green eyes. Studying Amber again, he looked her over – not like he was checking her out, but like she was a piece of unwieldy furniture that needed to go up a steep flight of stairs.

"If you're here to change my bedpan," Amber said to him, still trying to fling an arm to the window sill to reach her phone, "I haven't had my morning coffee yet so you're gonna have to wait."

The hard-faced man took the chart down from the wall, opened it, read it, tossed it onto the seat of the waiting wheelchair. "You're Amber Hawthorne?"

"That's me. Say, if it's not against the rules, could you bring my phone over there?"

The man, with heavy steps, moved around to that side of the bed. He looked at the phone, then at Amber's reaching, cast-swallowed arm, then back at the door. "Will you make a fuss?"

"If you do the thing I asked you to do? No, I'll say thank you. I just need to call my friend. It's an emergency."

The man reached for the phone and Amber prematurely gushed her thanks at him – until he stuffed the phone, bag and all, into his scrubs pocket. It was then that Amber noticed he wasn't wearing an ID badge and his clothes weren't fitting too snugly on him because the scrubs were the wrong size, but he appeared puffy strictly around the middle – like he was wearing something thick under there, like a bulletproof vest. When he turned to the side, she could see the thick straps peeking out of the V-neck.

She had to swallow before she could speak. "Who are you?"

He was looking at the door, listening. "I'm nobody. I'll ask you again. Will you make a fuss?"

"Make a fuss about what?"

"I'm going to take you out of here," he said, "and we're gonna go see your friends. They want to talk to you. Which will mean me moving you through the hospital, down to the parking garage. I don't want to knock you out because they want to speak to you as soon as I get you there."

"What friends? What're you talking about?"

He reached into his pocket and snapped open what Amber thought, at first glance, was a knife, but was a long, narrow screwdriver. He stepped to the side of the bed and began clicking around inside the handcuff's keyhole.

"Answer me," she shouted up at him. When he continued to say nothing, she jerked on the handcuffs to make them snap tight against the rail, causing him to drop the lockpick. He bent to pick it up, patiently, and stood holding it in front of her face – the precise little tip close to the eye that wasn't swollen shut and could see, easily, as it hovered near. Her eyelashes flicked against it.

"Do that again and I'll pop your goddamn eye."

"Okay, okay, okay. I'm sorry, I'm sorry," Amber said, thankful for the catheter suddenly.

He watched her pee trickle through the clear tube into the bag hanging on the side of the bed. He seemed pleased by having something to do with that happening. He took the lockpick away and went back to work on the cuff.

She watched him, smelling his aftershave. "Tell me what's going on," Amber begged. "Please."

"Please be quiet."

"Who are you? Who are these 'friends' you're talking about? Did I do something wrong?"

"Be quiet please," he said, still clicking around inside the handcuff. "I'm trying to concentrate."

Once the lock relented, he left the one metal hoop around her wrist on, the second dangling open on its chain. He dropped the bedrail, pulled up her hospital gown.

"Hey!"

He stared down at her as she scrambled to cover herself. "Then you do it. Remove all the tubes and IVs and the catheter." He steered the wheelchair over to the bed. "And get in."

With shaking hands, fingers restricted by the cast, she pulled the IV from her arm and the tubes out of her nose. She reached down between her legs, found the catheter tube – and tugged.

"Get in the wheelchair."

She scooted to the side of the bed, sitting up fully now that the drugs in her system were bouncing around her head, making everything feel about the way it did last night as she was leaving the tavern. The man helped her, plunked her down in the wheelchair and dropped her chart into her lap. "Hold on to that."

He wheeled her out into the hallway. She begged with her eyes as they passed nurses and doctors and patients similarly being carted around. No one gave her a second glance. She felt something sharp on the back of her neck, that little screwdriver. He leaned down over her shoulder, his breath rich with coffee and tobacco. "If you ever want to walk again, do not say a fucking word."

They waited for the elevator to arrive. The cop that supposedly was going to read Amber her rights came strolling up the hallway with a steaming cup of coffee in hand, radio barking on his hip. The man in the heavy boots turned her away to face the wall until the cop had passed. The elevator doors parted and he pushed her in. They had the car to themselves. He hit the button labeled P. The smell of exhaust, summer heat, and city stink rolled in as the doors parted. He pushed her along the parking garage ramp, passing car after car until coming to a plain suburban minivan. Bumper sticker: *Proud Parent of an Honor Student*.

"Can you stand?" he asked her.

"I think so."

He gave her a tap on the neck with the screwdriver. "Don't try to run."

"Okay, okay. I won't."

She got up on legs that felt far away. Trying to memorize the license plate, the digits and letters failed to connect with Amber's drug-altered understanding of them – her one open eye blinking slowly. Every sound felt like it was hitting her brain after a long delay. The hot wind curling through the parking garage hurt her skin as it brushed over her many bruises and scrapes.

He lifted the minivan's hatchback. In the back weren't soccer balls or groceries as she expected, but the back row of seats had been folded down to allow room for four full body bags.

She tried issuing a scream but it came out as a hoarse wheeze. Trying to run, she twisted in place, tripped on her own numb feet. The hard cement floor of the parking garage caught her, hard.

He scooped her up without a sign of struggle, like she weighed nothing, and carried her to the side of the van. She kicked her feet and swung her arms, the handcuff jangling around on her wrist. She struck him on the side of the head with her cast – probably hurting her more than him. He made an angry growl, suffered the blow, and pulled open the side door of the van. As he threw her in, he leaned partly inside to wind back and punch her in the face. She couldn't get her body to cooperate in time to avoid the fist and her head snapped back. Blood ran down into her face – she touched at her forehead, her goose egg had burst.

The man in the heavy boots wiped his bloody hand off on his scrubs pants, grunted a swear, and rolled shut the door.

As he came around to get in on the driver's side, Amber tumbled onto the floor and reached for the door handle, trying to lock him out. He yanked the door open before she could hit the lock switch.

Beyond the dark-tinted windows, she saw an older couple approaching the Buick parked right next to the van. She screamed for help. The man in the heavy boots started the van and cranked the radio to a deafening volume. Amber still screamed and knocked her cast on the window but the old man helping his wife into the car never even looked up.

Before backing out of the spot, the man in the heavy boots turned around, having to shout over the radio to be heard. "Be quiet. They don't need you alive. They told me that. If you gave me too much trouble, they said I could dump you anywhere I want. Remember that."

"*Who*, though?" Amber said. "Who said that? What's happening?" Her elbow brushed the black vinyl wrapping a dead body behind her seat – the body bags familiar sights to her, she having unzipped close to a thousand or more during her lifetime at the funeral home. "Who are these people?"

The man in the heavy boots said nothing more. He kept the radio blaring, exited the parking garage – the sunlight burning into Amber's eye – and out onto the street. They were in Minneapolis, she recognized the area immediately. She passed old haunts and stores she loved, feeling like this would likely be the last time she'd see any of them.

The man in the heavy boots lowered the volume on the radio once they were on the interstate – Amber assumed out here it wouldn't matter how much noise she made. She considered pulling open the side door of the van and jumping out, but they were moving at nearly eighty. She'd be dead instantly. She had to wait for the right opportunity. Maybe once they stopped the drugs would be out of her system enough she could run. She had to call Jolene. She had to tell her to run.

"I can give the money back," Amber said. Her eyes welled with tears. "I just have to find it. It was in the car when I crashed it, in the back. If there was something wrong with the body.... I'm really sorry, I didn't know. Would you please talk to me? Please say something."

The hard eyes in the rearview mirror wouldn't look back at her.

"I don't know what I did wrong," she said. "If you could just tell me what I did wrong, maybe I can do something to fix it. Are you going to kill me? Please say something. Please."

"Be quiet. You can talk it over with them when we get there."

"Talk it over with who? I don't know where we're going."

"We're almost there," is all he'd say.

★   ★   ★

Jolene tried one last time to get a hold of Amber and gave up. She saw she'd made forty-eight calls to her phone since last night. She showered, checked her phone, blow-dried her hair, checked her phone, brushed her teeth, checked her phone. She got dressed in her work blacks, checked her phone. She went into the workroom, got today's burial in her casket, touched up her makeup, got her wheeled into the viewing room, checked her phone, and started setting up folding chairs for the people who'd be there any minute.

Jolene felt fine with running a funeral on her own as its sole director. She'd done it before when Amber went on vacation with some of her other old sorority friends – none of whom Jolene ever established such a deep connection with as Amber – but the problem, this morning, was that there was no hearse to take the body to the cemetery once the viewing was over. Which, naturally, would cause some complaints. But Jolene went to the front of the funeral home, unlocked the front doors, stood in the reception area, wishing they had flowers or at least something to bring some color into the place, and went back into the living quarters half of the house and started the sixth pot of coffee she'd made since midnight. She stood smoking, flicking ashes into the kitchen sink, staring at her phone's screen, trying to send a telepathic smack upside Amber's head over the phone lines, wherever she was.

The priest arrived first, as usual. He was one Jolene and Amber had met before and as soon as he walked in, announcing his arrival with a friendly, "Knock, knock!" Jolene tossed her smoke in the ashtray and clopped out in high heels to meet him. He was looking at the clean spots on the carpet where the rented furniture used to be, last time he'd been here. He made no mention of it, but smiled that big broad priestly smile Jolene's way.

"Good morning, Miss Morris."

"Hey."

"Is something the matter?"

"Well, my partner is currently AWOL – with the hearse."

"You don't have a second?"

"No. Just the one."

"Hmm. That may be a problem."

"Yeah."

"Do you suppose you could rent one? Is that such a thing, a rental hearse?"

"I don't know. I didn't think of that."

"Maybe we should google it and begin making arrangements, if such a thing is possible, soon. The loved one's family will be arriving shortly and we'll need some mode of transport for the deceased."

"Unless you've got a wheelbarrow handy."

"A wheelbarrow, Miss Morris? I hardly think that'd be appropriate for—"

"I'm kidding. Anyway, could you maybe do crowd control if anyone arrives? I'm gonna go look into finding a hearse I can rent for the day. Good suggestion, by the way."

"Thank you. And certainly, Miss Morris, I will welcome those who arrive as if this were my own home. And Miss Morris? I hope everything works out in your favor this blessed day."

"Yeah. You and me both."

★   ★   ★

The minivan turned into the Lake Calhoun Bowl & Bar. The man in the heavy boots drove around back and parked and sat with his hands on the wheel, watching the back door. Amber said nothing, waiting for her chance to run. The minute the doors unlocked, she'd bolt − or try her best to, in bare feet. She noticed two of the three refrigerator trucks parked behind the bowling alley were gone. Only the one bound for Texas remained. Exhaust trickled from its back end, running, keeping things inside cool.

The back door of the bowling alley swung open and three men emerged. A tall, clean-shaven black man in an orange polo shirt and jeans, Fernando whom Amber had met last night, and the third − upon seeing him − filled her with a red spike of anger. It was Slug, in his low-slung jeans and tank top, cornrows now studded with colorful plastic beads.

The tall black guy waved the van forward. The man in the heavy boots eased them into motion, drawing the side of the van even with the back door of the bowling alley. The doors unlocked and Amber rushed to pull open the sliding door. The three waiting outside the van formed a net of outstretched arms. She went for the smallest, Slug, grabbing at his face and hair, screaming at him. "You piece of shit!"

"Whoa, bitch, cool down, you're among friends here."

"What the fuck, Shawn? You're working with these people?"

"I fucking made the hookup, didn't I? They liked my style, I guess, and made me full-time. Damn, girl, you ripped my shirt − this is new."

She spat at him. "We went to kindergarten together, you *fuck*. We've known each other our entire lives."

Slug lifted his eyes from his torn tank top to meet her gaze. He made a pathetic little shrug. "I got bills like anybody else. People kept shorting me, yo. Ten bucks here, ten bucks there, 'I'll pay you next week.' I had to stop being a friendly dope slinger and do what was best for me."

"I'll fucking *kill you*."

The tall black guy said, "Bring her inside. Luke, help Fernando if you would. Slug, grab the chair out of the back."

Amber tried wrenching away when Fernando came up behind

her. The man in the heavy black boots, Luke apparently, bent to grab her by the ankles. They got her inside the bowling alley. Most of the lights were off and every lane was empty, the pins at the end of each standing waiting. Amber twisted and thrashed as much as she could. Fernando had her around the middle, Luke her ankles. She watched Slug come in last, pushing the wheelchair in ahead of him, drawing the door shut behind, and snapping the deadbolt. He flipped around the OPEN sign to CLOSED, and followed. Amber continued to scream things at him, calling him every name she could think of, but Slug, head down, walked along behind with the wheelchair, unable to meet her eye. Her hospital chart rode in the seat of the chair.

Together, they went down along the head of the lanes, to the far wall, and to the maintenance door. Fernando walked with her backward, lifting his chin each time Amber tried to throw a head butt at his face. They carried her down a steep flight of metal stairs. It smelled like grease and disinfectant, like a mix of an auto body and a hospital.

The basement was walled-in cinderblock. High steel beams above, the underside of the lanes. The machinery keeping each pin-setter at the far end was paused – it looked like they were inside a massive piano with so many mechanical jointed arms and cables running the length of the room in neat rows. Along the far wall were four buzzing freezer chests and four exam tables, tools scattered about on trays, adjustable lights angling down at the blood-spattered slabs. Amber recognized the three blue Coleman coolers sitting on the one table immediately. Becky stood with rubber gloves that reached up beyond her elbows and a filtration mask dangling around her neck. She noticed the men dragging Amber into the room and stepped out from behind the coolers, her easygoing demeanor from last night gone. Straight-faced, hair back tight, her voice even, she said to the tall black man, "We got a problem."

Slug, coming down the steps last, snapped the wheelchair locked, and continued rolling behind after everyone else. He still wouldn't look Amber in the eye. Luke and Fernando dropped Amber into the wheelchair. Luke snapped the dangling handcuff around the armrest of the chair and knelt next to her with the tiny screwdriver in his hand again. "Behave. One word and this goes in your eye. Understand?"

Amber nodded and nodded. Though she still wanted to fight, find a way to run, when she heard Fernando, returning upstairs, throw the basement door's bolt, another fraction of hope died in her. This didn't look good. But once given the opportunity to explain, she would definitely try.

Standing, Luke snatched the medical chart from Slug and approached Becky and the tall black man with it.

They hushed their whispered conversation. Becky took the chart from Luke and glared over at Amber, then briefly at Slug, standing beside her, then down at what she held in her hands, riffling through the sheets. With the droning freezer chests and the buzzing lights above her, Amber couldn't make out what they were saying – but they weren't pleased about something.

Becky handed the chart off to the tall black guy and came walking over toward Amber, peeling off her long rubber gloves. "Your drop was a fucking disease bomb. It may've been packaged nice, but whoever that was had hepatitis C. And as for the blood, that was from three different people, all mixed together. There was even some O-negative in there. Care to explain?"

"It came to us like that. The guy who dropped it off, he—"

The tall black guy said, "Frank Goode."

Becky nodded, understanding, and glanced over at Luke and the tall black guy, then back at Amber in the chair. "This puts us behind. Like everybody, we answer to somebody too. And you fucked us, bringing in this filth-riddled shit. That could've killed somebody. Imagine if one of those kidneys got put in somebody who was already on their deathbed. That'd be the same as a fucking bullet in the head, you dumb little bitch. Didn't you ask Frank the background on this guy? Any info at all on him, where he came from, what killed him, any of that?"

"No, I didn't get the chance. He just dropped him in my driveway and drove off. Please, I'm really sorry, I can give you the money back. I only spent about a grand of it."

"We don't care if you spent every penny of that first half,"

Becky said. She put her hands on the armrests of the wheelchair to lean in close to Amber's face. "That doesn't mean jack shit to us. What we do give a shit about is clean product and yours, barring AIDS, couldn't have been any dirtier."

"I'll do whatever it takes to make it up to you," Amber said. "I didn't know he was sick."

Becky stood back up from the chair and angled her eyes over to Slug. "Go upstairs, Shawn, and help Fernando bring those other bodies down." She turned back toward Luke. "Who all did you get?"

"Bryce Petrosky, his aunt, Robbie Pescatelli, and Joey Stefano."

"Wish I'd known beforehand, otherwise I would've told you not to bother bringing Bryce," Becky said.

"Why?"

"He was the one, apparently, who gave Vasily the hep."

Luke glanced over at the three blue coolers sitting open and steaming on the nearby table. "So we know that was Vasily Petrosky for sure?"

"Simone and I pieced it together. It's him and Bryce got him sick." Becky looked over at Amber. "Tough luck, girlie. Your load got the hep C the same night he died. It all would've been fine if Bryce had decided not to play the hero and give his cousin his blood." She sighed, folded her arms, and looked at Luke and the tall black guy again. "So we won't need to bring Bryce down here. Have someplace you can dump him?"

Luke nodded.

Becky had started to turn away. "Wait, Joey's in the van? Joey Stefano?"

"Yeah," the tall black guy said.

"Why did he go to Frank's?"

Luke shrugged. "Dunno. But he did. Now he's in the van. And I hate to be the bearer of bad news, but I got their charts all right here." Sneaking a hand under his scrubs and beneath his bulletproof vest, Luke drew out four manila folders, a few pages spilling out. "Bryce and his aunt were both A-positive. Robbie Pescatelli's B-negative. And Joey Stefano is a good ol' A-negative."

"Well," Becky said, "at least we got our little ace up our sleeve sitting pretty right here."

Amber stuttered, trying to say: "What...what do you mean? What are you gonna do to me?"

"You're AB-positive, Amber," Becky said. "Which is exactly the blood type of the bone marrow we need."

Screaming again, Amber tried to overturn the wheelchair. Becky slammed her hands down on the arms to keep it in place and jammed a firm finger against Amber's burst goose egg. "Stop wasting your breath. Nobody can hear you."

"Please don't kill me. Please. *Please.* Let me call my partner, maybe we have something."

"For your sake, you'd better fucking hope to hell you do. Otherwise...Ted?"

The tall black guy stepped from the next room with something in his hands Amber couldn't quite make out in the poor light – but he was dragging behind him a length of extension cord. One quick rev of the electric engine and Amber recognized the sound of the BranchBuster.

Amber turned and shouted at Slug, who by now had gone to the far wall and was standing with his arms folded, back turned to everyone else. "Stop them, Shawn. *Do* something. You're going to let them do this to me?"

"I'm sorry, Amber," Slug said.

"I didn't know he was sick! Please!"

With quick angry strides, Becky went to one of the tables, snatched Amber's phone up, ripped the Ziploc bag from around it and shoved the cracked screen toward Amber's face. "Tell me who to dial," she shouted. "We have until the end of the day and that shipment needs to be on the fucking road – whether it goes to Texas with your leg is *entirely* up to you."

★ ★ ★

Jolene sat in front of the office computer with the door closed, typing 'rent a hearse' into Google over and over again, getting nowhere. There were plenty of hearses to *buy*, but none to rent. Her phone went off in her pocket and she scrambled to tear it free of her suit coat's small pocket.

"Amber? What the fuck happened last night? Where are you?"

"Jo, listen to me. I'm in a lot of trouble. They have me."

"Who has you?" Jolene's blood iced. "What's going on?"

"There was something wrong with the stuff. The guy was sick and they can't use it. They need bone marrow, AB-positive. Do we have anything at the house? It has to be AB-positive."

"No, no, everyone's embalmed." Jolene lowered her voice. She could hear just outside the door as the priest was welcoming people into the funeral home, shadows moving past the bottom of the office door. She cupped her hand around the phone. "Where are you?"

"They said I can't tell you that. We need to figure something out. They're gonna cut off my leg. Jo, please do something, I—"

Another voice came on the line, female. "Is this Jolene Morris?"

"Yes. Let her go, please, don't hurt her."

"Shut up. You have until three this afternoon. Lake Calhoun Bowl & Bar. Don't call the police. We'll just leave her here to bleed to death. Or, if you really piss us off, your gal pal here can learn there are things worse in life than death – I can only imagine winding up a quadruple amputee is right up there. Do you want that for your friend, Jolene?"

"No."

"Neither do I. AB-positive. Leg. Fresh. By three."

# CHAPTER EIGHT

In his mirror, Frank saw the sky-blue Honda come around the corner of the closed Pizza Hut a few minutes shy of ten o'clock. He watched Simone, alone, pull up behind his Lexus and sit staring out through the windshield, eyes narrowed. He gathered his things – his phone, Big Robbie's phone, and Robbie's handgun, which he tucked into the back of his cargo shorts. Frank stepped out, used the keychain to lock his car, but paused.

There was no point in thinking he'd ever be back for it.

Tossing the keys on the ground, he got into Simone's car on the passenger side.

The car was full of trash, up to his ankles in the floorboard. She sat behind the wheel, glaring over at him. "Where to, Miss Daisy?" Gum crack.

"Cut the shit."

"Still need to know where you wanna go."

"We can't stay in the city. Take the highway, we'll find something on the outskirts."

Simone put the car in gear. Frank watched out his window as they passed his Lexus, leaving it abandoned behind a closed restaurant. He considered what Ted had told him just the day before yesterday – which now felt like a lifetime ago. He had to let go of that old Frank, because he was no more. And though the separation was proving to be painful, Frank knew his friend was right. He watched the Lexus fall from sight behind them, and faced forward. He reached behind him and took out Simone's uncle's handgun and held it low, in his lap, the barrel – with nothing in its chamber at all – aimed at her.

She glanced as she drove, and snickered. "Seriously?" Gum crack.

"Where's yours? In your purse here?"

"Don't you go through my fucking purse."

"Just drive the car, Simone. Watch the road."

Simone got them on the highway. Frank found her small chrome handgun, stuffed Robbie's gun in his shorts' cargo pocket, and held Simone's gun on her. "I'm sorry about your uncle and your boyfriend."

Simone drew in a sharp breath, perhaps ready to scream at him, but only sighed. "An entire generation of Pescatelli men wiped out in one fucking night. That's gotta be a record, even for us. Wait, why'd you switch guns? Ah, fuck, that other one wasn't even loaded, was it?"

"No. But this one is."

"Far as you know." Grin. Gum crack. "Maybe I took the bullets out."

Frank leaned over to press the barrel to Simone's ribs, easily found through her thin spaghetti-strap tank top.

"Okay, all right, stop, stop," Simone said. Gum crack. "I'm just fucking around. Gawd."

"Spit out that fucking gum."

"It's a fresh piece. Keeps me from smoking."

"I don't care."

"Fine, Jesus." Simone rolled down her window and spat her gum out. "Happy, sourpuss?"

In the cupholder between them, Simone's phone rang. Frank watched Simone glance from the highway ahead to the phone, to him, and back at the road. "Can I answer that? It's my girl Becky. She might need something."

"No. Where'd you tell your mom and aunts you were going?"

"I did what you said, I said I was going to Denny's to get breakfast."

"How long before they'll suspect something's up?"

The phone in the cupholder stopped ringing.

Simone shrugged. "Couple hours. They'll call me to see what's up before calling the police. We don't like the cops."

"And you spoke to no one about coming to get me?"

"No, nobody."

"Not even this Becky person who just tried calling you?"

"No. She's my friend. She probably heard what happened last night and she's worried, wants to be a good friend and be there for me. But you probably don't know nothing about having friends, do you?"

"Stay in this lane," Frank said. "And keep it under sixty-five."

"Wait a minute. Why're you asking about my family being worried about me being gone? You planning something I should know about, Frank?"

"I don't want them to know I'm with you."

"Is that all?"

"All *you* need to know."

"Killing me won't unfuck anything, Frank."

"Who said anything about killing you?"

"Well, according to the radio that's what you do. You kill people. Russians, Italians, don't matter. You're the Twin Cities' own Doctor Hannibal Lecter and the Punisher rolled into one."

"I didn't kill anybody. They killed each other. Because of what *you* did."

"Okay, I fucked up. I shouldn't have killed Vasily. I should've let Joey and his crew or Uncle Robbie do that, at a better time when innocent bystanders, like you, wouldn't get pulled into the mix. There. I'll admit I screwed the pooch on that one."

"I'd say it was a bit more than that. Eleven people died in my house after, yet another, you murdered. And you basically murdered me, too. I'm lucky to fucking be alive. I can never go home, I'll probably never see my daughter again, and as far as ever setting up a practice – illegal or otherwise – it's never going to happen. I'll have to get a fake name and do factory work in Mexico just to keep a roof over my head. You ruined my life, Simone. I don't think you understand that."

"Understanding and giving a shit about something are two different things."

"So you don't even care? I had no part in any of this."

"I mean, sure, it sucks Uncle Robbie's dead, but me and Joey were kinda on the rocks anyhow. From what I could tell the only reason he was even with me was so he could secure his place in the family by fuckin' his way into it."

"Just drive the car."

They went a few miles in silence. Becky tried calling two more times. Frank saw it flash on Simone's phone that she had nine voicemails waiting.

"So you want a motel, huh?" Simone said.

"Yeah."

"And after that?"

"A ticket for a bus heading south."

"Mexico?"

Frank said nothing.

"Why not Canada? Closer."

"That didn't work out so well for me last time."

"Right, *right*, I learned your whole life story on the way over here. Why was you even selling pills on the side anyhow? Didn't they pay you enough playing doctor?"

"Slow down. I think I remember there being a motel along here."

They were coming into the outside fringe of South St. Paul where it was mostly auto dealers with the dancing inflatable noodle men beckoning potential buyers and RV lots and miles of motorboats sitting beached in the sun. Frank told her to turn into the Land o' Ten Thousand Lakes Motel. The place was like any you'd see on long road trips: a few short buildings ringing a a diseased-looking swimming pool. Desperate-looking people sat by the ice machine in moldy lawn chairs, smoking, one arm tanner than the other, road-worn.

Simone pulled them up alongside the office. Frank slunk low in the seat. "Go inside and get a room. Don't tell them anything."

Simone went inside. Frank watched from the car as she talked to the cashier. She came out a moment later, got back in, and drove them around the back of the building where the rooms, evidently, didn't have many people staying in them. Few cars were parked before the rows of doors on this side.

Frank waited until Simone opened the door and went inside the room before he got out, scrambling inside with his cargo pockets full of phones and weaponry. He slammed the door behind them. Simone turned on the AC and sat on the corner of the bed, waiting for the old CRT TV to warm up enough so there'd be a picture to match the sound.

Frank tossed Simone's phone onto the stained bedspread next to her. "Get on the internet and use your credit card to get me a bus ticket. Laredo, Texas. Today. Earlier in the day the better."

Simone fished her credit card out of her purse and held it alongside her phone as she keyed in the numbers. "You really think they won't have somebody with your picture sitting at the border?"

"I'll take my chances." Frank sat at the small table by the window after drawing shut the curtains – leaving them open just enough to see if anyone came around the corner to the back side of the motel. He set Simone's chrome pistol on the table, then Robbie's next to it, Robbie's phone, and his own phone, and sat staring at the collection of gadgets and guns.

"There. Done. You'll leave tonight at eleven-thirty."

"Eleven-thirty p.m.? There was nothing earlier than that? That's twelve hours from now."

"What, do you want me to eat some metal and shit you a bus that'll leave whenever you want? It was either at eleven-thirty tonight or noon tomorrow."

"Fine. Whatever. We can wait." He noticed she wasn't on the internet anymore, but clicking through her text messages. He snatched her phone from her and tossed it on the table with the other two. "Don't think I'm not paying attention."

"I wasn't doing nothing. I was fucking checking my messages."

"You don't need to talk to anybody right now."

Simone stood, kicked off her high heels, and padded over to the bathroom. She left the door open. Frank watched as she leaned into the mirror, poking at the corner of her eye with a pinky finger, clearing some wayward mascara. Finished, she scooped a hand down the front of her shirt, lifted a boob back into place and adjusted her shirt's straps, giving herself puffy-lipped looks.

"Lost some of the baby weight already, I see," Frank said.

"I did a cleanse."

Frank stared at the TV. Midday talk show. Jabbering heads talking about nothing. A scroll along the bottom of the screen kept repeating his name and the police tip line. He glanced out the window again, saw nothing, and tried to convince his heart to slow down – but it wouldn't. He still had a question he had to ask, one that would decide how things would go for Simone. He didn't want to ask it, but decided to leave it up to fate. He could learn for himself, without her even saying anything, by looking in her purse where she'd left it, right there on the bed. But he wanted to ask her, to have it be a decision that, in some way, they made together.

Simone sat down on the edge of the bed again and turned the TV back on. "I was watching that."

Frank asked his question. "How much cash do you have?"

"Huh?"

"Cash. How much do you have on you right now?" He felt sick.

"I don't carry cash. I got a check card and a credit card. Look, I just paid for your stupid room and your stupid bus ride, what more are you gonna want from me? And, out of curiosity, am I your fucking hostage right now? Is that what's happening? Because I got shit to do today."

"Shut up," Frank said. "Just shut *the fuck* up."

"I'm gonna go. I think we're square now."

Frank snatched up the gun and snapped back the hammer. "Sit down on the bed."

She remained standing, only a small shine of fear in her eyes. "I could go out to the ATM, but—"

"Sit down." He stood. "I said *sit down*."

"Fine, all right, okay, I'm sitting."

Frank sat again too, after dragging the chair over in front of the door. He leaned forward, elbows on knees, gun heavy in his hand. "Turn the TV off."

Simone turned the TV off. "Okay, Frank, it's off."

He could see she was scared. He couldn't look at her as he said, "When I was still at the clinic, I saved four hundred and forty-two people's lives during my time there. I breathed life back into children who'd been hit by cars running into traffic after balls. I gave elderly people a few more years with their loved ones, lasering out tumors on their brains. And I helped bad people too, because that's part of the job. A woman with ten kids sitting out in the waiting room, each one with cigarette burns running up and down their arms and legs. A meth head who came in with third-degree burns after he blew himself up in his garage. I gave mouth to mouth to a man who, I later found out, had a little girl in his basement lying dead inside a dog crate. It wasn't my job to decide who lived and who died because I'd taken the Hippocratic oath. I was beholden to saving people, regardless of who they were and what they'd done to themselves to wind up in my O.R. needing my help. I wanted to let a few of them die. I knew the world would be better without them. But I never hesitated, because hesitating even half-seconds can decide everything. And I want to think that if there is a God maybe saving those four hundred and forty-two people permits me, now that I'm not under any oath, to end one life I know doesn't deserve to continue."

Simone turned on the bed to face him fully. After pushing a strand of hair from her eyes, she rested her hands in the lap of her denim miniskirt, movements even. Her dark-ringed eyes were calm. "So all that blah-blah-blah boils down to you're gonna throw the whole do-no-harm thing out the window because I messed up your day? Okay, let's talk hypotheticals. You kill me and do *what* with me exactly? Call your funeral home girls to come pick me up? Get some cash for trading me so you'll be nice and comfy once you're in Mexico? Was that the plan?"

"How do you know about them?"

"That doesn't matter. What matters, Frankie, is you just threatened me. I don't like being threatened."

"How do you know about what they do?"

"Because you do like everybody does. Like everyone in my family did. You wrote me off thinking I'm just some stupid tart that spends all day taking selfies and going to the tanning salon. But I ain't. I'm smart. I got connections. Yeah, pick your jaw up off the floor. Shoe Store Simone's got connections she made all on her own. Like ones in the red market."

"You're part of it? You...you're Rhino?"

"Nobody's Rhino. That's just some scary-sounding bullshit they tell us to use because one man, in control of all the shit's far scarier than thinking, in each town, there's a group of people who meet in cars behind the mall to decide on strategies – who to trust, who to off, and all that. So maybe we're Rhino together, I dunno. I never put too much thought into it."

Frank's hand tightened around the grip of the pistol. He sat up in the chair. The air conditioner kicked back on, its sudden whining making him flinch. "You knew that would happen at my house. You knew your uncle was going there – you made that call, you knew you were sending him to his death."

"I didn't make the call. They'd know my voice. But it was my idea to chum the water like that."

"They were your family."

"True, but they were all pieces of shit. Drugs and shitty apartment buildings, that's all they dealt with. They were a disgrace to the Pescatelli name. I was gonna bring it back and make it something worth fearing again. The Russians wouldn't have ever fucking set foot in either of the Twin Cities if we still had the hold we used to, like back in the day. But Uncle Robbie was scared. Shit, even my Joey was scared. Scared of change, like all men are. I asked him not to go last night, knowing what would happen if he did – but he said he had to prove himself to Uncle Robbie if he ever wanted to get made. Well, he got made all right – into a fucking corpse, the tiny-pricked peacock. Surprised he even managed to knock me up."

Frank raised the gun, aiming between her breasts. She didn't react.

"I came to your house for two reasons," she said. "One was to get rid of that parasite in me and two, I was giving you a trial run, to feel you out. And with Vasily coming up to your doorstep, I saw no better way to see you in action, see what you'd do. And what do you know, we called your good buddy Ted – who was also on a probationary period, like you and the funeral home girls, though he's doing better than all of you is by a *long* fucking long shot."

"I thought Ted just had contacts with…the people doing this."

"He did, and that's all he was for a long time. In the network, but just on the edge of it. They brought him in, wanting him to lead up the Midwest sourcers with my girl Becky. He's fitting in real good. Anyway, back to my point. With the new girls coming on like they were, well, it all worked out with you taking them Vasily. All of a sudden we had us a burgeoning network in Minnesota finally. For, like, one fucking day."

"Did something happen?" The gun rattled in Frank's hand. "Are those girls all right?"

"Don't pretend you give a shit, Frank. But, the issue was, I don't know if Vasily already had it or if it was you or Bryce who gave it to him giving him you two's blood, but when they checked him, turns out he was full of hepatitis. Of the C variety, no less. Unfortunately, when the funeral home girls chopped him, the ick went along with the parts – you can't just wash that out when you drain a body." She paused, eyes moving down to his left arm.

Frank, too, was looking down at the small square of tape on the inside of his elbow, the red dot in the middle having gone brown a long time ago.

Simone grinned. "Did you two share a needle, Frankie? You might, once you're down in Taco Land, get some hombre to test you. Anyhoo, now the girls are in a heap of shit because their stuff ain't clean. We got an order to fill, real specific blood types and items they need down south. And because we're short everything we were counting on Vasily having 'cause he was sick, we need to fill those gaps back in." She started to stand.

"Stay on the bed," Frank said and took the gun in two hands. "Sit back down."

Simone lowered herself, slowly, back onto the bed, crossed her legs at the knee. She peeled a stick of gum from its wrapper and folded it into her mouth. "What blood type are you, Frankie? Were you the O-negative they found in Vasily or one of the two A-positives?"

"That's not happening to me."

"O-negative is a universal donor. We like your stuff *a lot*. Think how many more lives you could add to that four hundred and some. Think about all the people who can't get on any list. People who can't afford to get a new heart or a new set of lungs or a fresh kidney that works because they ain't rich – like you used to be. You could help from beyond the grave, Frank. What doctor can say that?"

"Where are they?"

Simone furrowed her brows slightly. "Who?" Gum crack.

"Amber and Jolene."

"I ain't telling you shit more about shit, Frank. You seen what's behind the curtain enough. Listen, I'm gonna stand up and get myself a glass of water – please don't shoot me in the back. You can see I ain't got no other gun." She flashed up her skirt. "*Anywhere*, heh. Wait, did I leave a pair of panties at your place?"

"Yes."

"You still got them? Ah, shit, they're probably in an evidence bag somewhere now, huh? That sucks."

"I threw them away with all those fucking feathers that were all over my house." He flicked his hand in the direction of the sink. "Go get your glass of water."

She stood watching him in the mirror as she filled a plastic cup, drained it, and set it aside. She came back over to the bed, sitting on the side closer to him, their knees nearly touching. Her jaw worked slowly, meditatively. She blew a bubble, sucked it back in, and said, "Your life is over."

He shoved the gun barrel at her, thumping it hard against her jutting collar bone. "Be quiet. I need to think."

"Go ahead and shoot. Death don't mean nothing to me, Frankie. You can kill me and I know it don't matter. Nothing matters, not in this country anyway. Just money. I wanna walk outta here, sure, go make some money, do whatever, kick back with my girls, go clubbing and shit, but I know it don't matter. We're just all running down the clock and with money, well, that time can be a little more easy going. Spend more time at home instead of at the office. And really that time don't mean much to anybody anymore anyhow, being home around family. Do you know the average person spends more time staring into their computer or phone or tablet or TV or whatever than looking into the eyes of their loved ones by nearly nine hundred percent? We're fucked, as a species. Distracted. Just going through the motions. Yeah, ask me, the only thing this species has done that's worthy of comment is we invented the word cruelty then expanded on that definition in every way we could possibly dream up. Everything else? Shit to fill time.

"You've seen some of the worst of what people can do to each other," she said. "You don't wanna be a part of this any more than I do. So why do you wanna keep running? Do you think you'll ever have a good life, after all this? Anything remotely close to what you had back when you was a surgeon? The house, the wife, the kid, the Lexus? No. That shit's over. And you don't wanna live like *this*, do you? Running all the time. Sleeping with one eye open."

"I didn't do anything wrong." He lowered the gun from her chest – her tan skin showing a perfect O that quickly filled back in with color. "I shouldn't go back to prison for this, for what *you* did."

"We ain't talking about prison."

"*That's* not going to happen to me either."

"Let's calm it down a second. Here's what I think you should do, Frankie, okay?" Gum crack. "I think you should go over there, lay down on the bed, and I'll put a pillow over your face. You did a lot of good in the world. You never killed nobody. And if you're clean, then you can help people. Don't fuck up that record of those four hundred lives you saved." She edged closer, her hand gently taking his wrist. "Give me the gun, Frank, and let's see you off, nice and gentle, into the next—"

A flash of white between them. Abrupt silence.

What Simone said, wide eyed, with a hand over her chest, was lost to him – just a low whine to his ears overlaying everything. Blood ran down the front of her shirt and onto the floor. She slipped off the bed, fell heavily to carpet.

Frank stood, watching Simone pulling herself along the floor on her newly flat stomach, leaving a trail of blood behind her. She got to the door of the bathroom, tried pulling herself inside, tried closing the door behind her, leaving red handprints on everything she touched.

Stepping over to her, Frank pushed the door wide. He pointed the gun down at her and she raised her hands and maybe screamed or just made her face into a scream and tried turning away as the dark bathroom flashed shadowless.

More of Frank's hearing was permanently ruined with a second, then third, shot down into her.

Simone slumped over, twitched once, and didn't move again. He stared at what he'd done, the result he'd made of her. Long tan leg hooked over the other, arm draped across her face. Mouth open, lipstick smeared, white teeth, hair a wreck clotted through with pink bits of ruptured brain. The wad of chewing gum dropped, *plop*, from her open mouth.

It's just meat.

He felt numb. But guessed, probably, once the shock of it wore off, he'd be suicidal. He'd think about how she, like anybody, wasn't beyond saving. That she probably wasn't a complete piece of shit, that everybody has some good in them somewhere. Maybe. Until then, Frank was fine being numb and decided to use it while it lasted, savor the temporary barrier between himself and his conscience.

He glanced up to look at himself in the mirror holding the gun. The spatter of blood on him, fresher than what was already all over his face and clothes, which had dried dark since last night. He could hear voices through the wall, people shouting excitedly, having undoubtedly heard the shots, running for their vehicles. Yet again, the cops would be on their way.

*Or,* Frank considered, *if this place was the kind that it seemed, maybe those who'd heard would just run – also wanted by the law themselves. Why draw the cops here? Just go.*

Right now, ears ringing and hands feeling waxy and hollow from the shock of vibration from the gun, Frank didn't care much either way. He went over to the window unit and cranked the AC as cold as it would go. He tossed the gun onto the bed, sat down next to it, and turned on the TV. He didn't know why. It felt right. Noise, any other noise than the ringing his ears. He should go. Take her keys and go, just run like Ted had advised, but he felt empty and sick and all he wanted was to sit down in front of the TV. The screen gained clarity. His own old mugshot stared back at him. He raised the volume until his ruined ears could make out what was being said.

They were calling him Doctor Bad. And the police, it seemed, no longer thought he was some vigilante who, on a quest for redemption, tricked the two gangs to face off in his living room – but that he'd orchestrated the whole thing in some kind of twisted body-harvest scheme that went south. The reason they believed this was because the bodies of Big Robbie, Joey Stefano, Bryce Petrosky, and Tasha Petrosky were now all missing from the morgue. The thief, best to the cops' estimation of things, being Frank Goode, who was still at large.

He hooked a finger into his pocket, taking out the business card with the red fingerprint, his fingerprint, sitting in the corner of the card like a watermark. They had the girls. Wrapped up in this shit, desperate for money, just like Frank, and lo and behold into the grinder they went too.

He crushed the business card and tossed it over his shoulder. He was still waiting for someone to kick in the door, but it'd only been a couple minutes – it may take a while.

He glanced over toward the bathroom and saw Simone's bare feet sticking out, not moving. Maybe they wouldn't be picky about who they got, if they were, as she said, rushing to fill an order. Maybe they'd take one of their own. Maybe he could get something out of this, some small win of some kind.

Problem was finding them. Frank opened Simone's phone. Her wallpaper was blank, just a black rectangle with a handful of apps. He brought up her contacts and scrolled through. A lot of women's names he didn't recognize, likely her friends. Uncle Robbie. Aunt Judy. Joey. Becky's name appeared on screen, the phone trilling and vibrating in his hand.

He answered, but said nothing.

"Jesus Christ, Simone, where *are* you?" Becky, presumably, said. He let her rant. "We're at the bowling alley fucking waiting on your ass and you haven't been answering your fucking phone, girl. Get with it! Ted's about to shit his pants outta anger and we need you here, now, to help handle this. The Amber chick ain't cooperating. Simone? Hello?"

Frank hung up. He thought about asking which bowling alley exactly, but didn't want to tip them off, and doubted she'd just blurt where they were at the strange voice answering her friend's phone. The phone began ringing again almost immediately. He didn't answer this time.

They were at a bowling alley. That's all he could safely glean from Becky's call without alerting them. He could work with that. How many bowling alleys could the Twin Cities have? He looked it up on Simone's phone.

A lot, apparently. "Shit."

He saw she had some emails. Expecting to maybe find an address for this bowling alley, he saw, instead, at the very top, the confirmation email from Greyhound. His one-way ticket would be waiting for him at the bus depot, eleven-thirty. His plan only took him that far. Get out of Minnesota, get out of range of the cops and where they expected him to be. Keep clear of the house, the airport, anywhere crowded since his face was plastered all over the TV. But once down in Laredo, without a passport, there was going to be no border crossing without haggling with somebody who might be willing to hide him in their trunk – or show him, in the middle of the night, some weak part in the wall. Nearly as dangerous as staying in the Twin Cities, maybe more so. But there was that bus. It could take him away from where it was most dangerous for him currently. Out of the frying pan, and maybe into a bucket of ice, if he could get a new social security card, maybe a little job somewhere. Start over. Come back to his home state a few decades later, maybe reconnect with his daughter. Maybe.

He thumbed through Simone's phone some more. He opened her internet browsing app and saw Facebook was one of her most frequently visited sites. She was still logged in. He read her dreadfully spelled posts about how much she disliked Mexican people and video clips she'd shared of Channing Tatum dancing without a shirt on. Scroll, scroll. Further down her feed, a few weeks ago, she'd 'checked in' at a few restaurants. Reducing the posts to just recent check-ins, Frank scrolled through all of the clubs and bars and seafood places Simone had gone to, stopping when he saw she'd visited a place called Lake Calhoun Bowl & Bar.

He loaded Simone into the back seat of her Honda and threw in the motel room's bedspread to cover her. He got in, fought to get the engine to turn over, and pulled out of the spot. He kept it under the speed limit along the frontage road, the highway to his right. Six lanes, three going north, three going south. He got up to where he could go left or right, north or south. He knew where Lake Calhoun area was. He also knew where the Greyhound station was. North or south.

He used his turn signal.

★   ★   ★

"What do you mean you don't have a hearse?" the old woman screamed into Jolene's face. "How are we supposed to bury my sister without a hearse? Carry her ourselves?"

"I'm really sorry, ma'am, but my partner got into an accident last night. Now, if you want to come back tomorrow, I'll keep your sister comfortable while we figure something out. You had the viewing, we'll just take her to the cemetery tomorrow bright and early if it's all the same to you."

"It's *not* all the same to me. I'll sue you. That's what I'll do. I'll sue the pants off you, young lady!"

"Look here, bitch. I got a lot more to worry about right now than your dead fucking sister. *My* sister needs me right now so I suggest you leave and come back tomorrow when I have a hearse or you can take her casket with you right now."

"I never!"

"Yes, yes, you never, you never, get the fuck out."

Once the last funeral attendee was out the door, Jolene slammed it shut and locked it. She didn't have time to wheel Missus Tamblyn in her casket back downstairs. She charged into the workroom and pulled open the drawer of the only person they had left to bury. He was embalmed already. That and his blood type was A-negative. They needed AB-positive. Fuck. Jolene tore off the suit coat she was sweating through the entire funeral, flung it aside, and ran back upstairs. She paused passing through the reception area, thinking she heard footsteps just outside the door. She went to the CCTV monitors. It was only the mailman. The old lady she'd shouted out of the house still hadn't gotten down the front walk. A dark thought slipped through Jolene's mind. *No. Don't even* think *that.*

Her mind clicked onto a different candidate, a more worthy one, someone she wouldn't feel so bad about hurting.

He was supposed to be by today, after all, to discuss keeping one another's secrets. Jolene was half-surprised Cornelius hadn't been by already. He typically showed up in the a.m. hours to unfurl the latest draft of his proposition on her. In the office, she looked up on her phone the number for the local Mega Deluxo and dialed it.

"Mega Deluxo. How may I direct your call?"

"Hi, I need to know if Cornelius is on the schedule to work today."

"We can't give out employee personal information."

"In that case, can you connect me with the register he's working on today?"

"He's…on his break?"

"Learn to lie. Bye."

She couldn't look him up in the White Pages because he'd never given his last name. He only ever introduced himself as Cornelius – and she'd thought that was a fake, all the way up until seeing it on his name badge at the store. She went outside, crossed the lawn, stood on the sidewalk hot under her feet, looked up the street and looked down the other way, and did not see any sign of that butter-yellow suit on approach anywhere. She could hardly believe she was considering this. Nor did she ever imagine a day when she'd *want* Cornelius to ring her doorbell.

But who was to even say he was AB-positive? And to ask him before clonking him out, who was to say *he'd* even know? Jolene didn't even know her own blood type and figured most people didn't. She remembered she'd learned it once, when she gave blood in college for some fundraiser the sorority had hosted, but that'd been years ago. A-positive? A-negative? B-positive? B-negative? AB-positive? AB-negative? O-positive? O-negative? It was anybody's goddamn guess what Cornelius had rolling around in his twisted little heart. One in eight. Not great odds.

That, and of course there was also the small matter of: could she really do that to another living person, even a serious creep like him?

She returned inside, slamming the door behind her. In the kitchen, she took a sip of coffee from her cup that'd since gone cold, staring at the digital numbers on the microwave – it was two minutes until one. She had two hours. Two goddamn hours to make a human leg magically materialize. She stood in the reception area with a cup of coffee in one hand and one of the rubber mallets they bought the other day, waiting for the doorbell to ring.

The grandfather clock in the other room tolled two-thirty.

Jolene tossed the rubber mallet onto the floor and dropped her head, staring at the floor for some answer, some solution, to rise up out of it – it never came. But she saw two feet in her patent leather shoes. What she stood upon. A possible means to saving her friend's life, a friend who'd saved her life.

In the basement, Jolene tore through all her old boxes of college stuff. Various textbooks and old reports she'd decided to keep that she'd aced. She hadn't seen a lot of it in years. Some framed photographs of the sorority house, captured moments of the bake sales and car washes they'd held – Amber and Jolene in bikinis, car sponges in hand, smiling, young, stupid. Jolene dug through more papers and files and stuff she didn't even remember why she'd kept. She paused only when she caught a piece of letterhead that featured a red teardrop. She pulled out the form and saw it was a little print-out certificate thanking her for her blood donation. There was her name, and her blood type.

AB-positive.

From the garage Jolene dragged in the camping cooler and tossed it onto the floor of the workroom at the foot of the stainless steel table. Pulling on the thick gloves, she poured enough dry ice into the cooler to cover the bottom and dropped the lid to keep it cool. She set out the plastic wrap, some gloves, and extension cord.

Heart pounding, questioning herself and this possibly fatal decision, she moved into the house's living-quarter side and unzipped her suitcase that still lay on her barren bedroom floor, rooting through until she found her leather belt with the double-tongued buckle. Draping it over her shoulder, she moved into the bathroom, filling her arms with the half-bottle's worth of hydrogen peroxide they had and several bath towels. Dropping those onto the table in the workroom, she went back out into the reception area and approached the front door, using the peephole to make sure, last chance, Cornelius hadn't arrived. Their front steps stood empty, no necrophile in sight. She unlocked the front door and on the walk back to the workroom, dialed the cab company.

"Yes, could I order a taxi for two-forty-five please?" she said and gave the address. She hoped the driver would take her where she wanted, even in the state they'd be picking her up in. She pocketed her phone and returned to the workroom and surveyed what she'd laid out, running down a mental checklist. In one of the lower cabinets she kept a bottle of bourbon hidden for emergencies. Not even in the worst of times did she allow herself a drink from it, only when it seemed that burning the funeral home to the ground would be the best option. Today warranted a deep swallow of it. Once she felt the warmth in her stomach begin to spread and make her hands feel light, from the bleach bath, she lifted the BranchBuster 9000, shook the water out of its chain, and set it on the table.

When she started going through Amber's dad's old cassette tapes, trying to decide on something that might help the process, she realized she was stalling. She didn't have the time to mess around with this. She slapped in *Motown Greatest Hits*, hit play, hopped up next to the saw on the table, kicked off her shoes, drew off her pantyhose, and paused when she noticed she'd forgotten to shave her legs this morning.

Would they still take a hairy leg? The shit you think sometimes in weird situations.

She sat with her unshaven legs, the same two legs she'd had her entire life and had gotten quite attached to, hanging off the edge of the table.

Her left had a tiny scar on the knee from when she crashed her bike in a gravel parking lot on her way to class her senior year of school. She should've gotten stitches, but hadn't. On her right leg, down by the ankle, in the trickiest spot to shave, she had a tiny scar that looked like the Nike swoosh. It almost matched the set of scars on the inside of both her wrists, faint from the years, which refused to tan no matter how long she laid out in the yard.

Both leg scars were a story, same as those on her wrists, all of which she'd miss seeing every day for the reminders of things they could cultivate so quickly in her mind. But one had to go.

She decided. She'd crashed her bike in that gravel parking lot because she'd been really hung over, she remembered, and her equilibrium was all screwy. That was a memory she could stand to let go; one less reminder hanging around. She'd keep the Nike swoosh.

Jolene lifted her thigh and fed the belt under, wound it tight, and pulled until the leather band was pressing deep into her skin. She clicked the tongues into the holes – she couldn't squeeze a finger underneath. Almost immediately her toes started to feel cold.

The next song on the tape was 'I Can't Help Myself (Sugar Pie Honey Bunch)' by the Four Tops. She always liked this song. She doubted she would after today.

One last cheek-swelling swallow of bourbon and she picked up the chainsaw and clicked on its electric motor.

It shook in her hands, the chain hungry, all those tiny teeth.

It would lurch on its own, the chain always slowly turning even without putting any pressure on the trigger.

Her leg was starting to ache from blood deprivation, her pulse hammering hard against the belt, desperate to push the red stuff where it needed to go. Her toes were blue, almost matching the shade of her chipping nail polish. Pins and needles now, and in a few seconds a waxy numbness. That's what she was waiting for.

When it came, Jolene took one deep breath, held it, let it go. Held another, let it go. *Amber saved your life. You owe her. She saved your life. You owe her. This is for her. She would do the same for you.*

Jolene told herself the same thing she did when she cut her wrists.

"Fucking do it."

Squeezing the trigger all the way down, the electric engine screaming and the blade throwing off a faint breeze as it spun, Jolene lowered the blade, inching it close to just below her knee.

The first bite. She screamed and pulled the blade away, letting the trigger go. The blade slowed, the engine quieted.

She stared at what she'd done to herself.

Blood ran down her leg, dribbling off her toes onto the floor. Just a divot. She could see pink inside her skin — and though she'd taken care of hundreds of dead people, seen their blood a million times, gallons washing down this very same table's drains, this time, it was different. She breathed deep until the wooziness cleared, and squeezed the trigger again and brought the blade down, pushing down behind it.

The screaming motor guttered, struggling. The blade screeched hitting the bone. Jolene screamed, the pain filling her. It felt like lava that was shooting out of her from every pore, detonating in her brain, tearing her apart, not just her leg — it was like all else in the world had gone away and only the pain existed, this burning-hot tearing.

She squeezed the trigger harder, though it could go no faster. The bone snapped, cut through.

"Fibia," she said.

As the blade continued down through the thick part of her calf, the entire blade buried in her leg, she screamed and screamed and pushed and pulled the trigger, working the saw forward and back, rocking it through the meat of her leg.

More screaming of blade on bone.

"Tibia."

She gunned the motor and pressed in hard.

Her glasses were dotted with blood. She cleared it with a finger swipe and continued, sweat dribbling off her chin. She may've pissed herself. She may've shat. She may've thrown up in her mouth and swallowed it.

She let up on the trigger, squeezed again hard, and pushed.

Only a couple more inches.

Only a couple more goddamn fucking inches.

When the saw met the table with a scream of metal on metal, she lifted the blade back out and bits of herself were flung from the free-spinning chain.

She tossed the saw aside, clattering to the bloody floor, and sat, for just a moment, staring at what she'd done to herself.

There it lay, her pale leg no longer attached to herself. She could not remember seeing a stranger sight in her life. Something so familiar, so very, very familiar and hers, totally hers, no longer warm and attached and part of her.

"Oh, my God."

The open end of it, red, pink, the yellow layer of fat. The brown cores of her fibia and tibia staring at her like wide, surprised eyes, mirroring her shock.

A half-second where the world blinked out. Fuck. She'd nearly gone unconscious. Maybe it was shock. Maybe it was the pain mashing her brain's go-to-sleep button, too much, too much. "Stay awake. Stay fucking awake."

She turned herself around and watched the ragged stump leak blood in a few different streams of varying power onto the floor, dribbling fast. Shit. The belt could only restrict so much but right now it was the only thing keeping her alive.

Her stomach felt hollow, her ears rang from the trilling noise of the saw and her own screaming. Remaining on the table, she snagged the box of cling-wrap and with heavy hands, and fighting her eyes trying to close, she wrapped her leg in plastic, over and over in enough layers until the details of it – the nail polish on her five toes, the stubble of dark hair running down its length – were buried. Once it was swaddled to satisfaction and wrapped in a couple towels, she tossed it off the side of the table, into the cooler, and it made the same *whack* sound as dropping a fish onto a hard, cold surface – soft, but firm too.

Now to get it out into the reception area and wait for the cab.

Turning herself around on the table, she let herself drop onto the floor. One bump against the raw stump and she screamed out in pain – she clawed with her fingers, reaching for a leg that was no longer there.

She rolled onto her back, screaming, crying, laughing a little at how fucking insane this all was, and looked up at the ceiling…as her vision started to darken around the edges.

"No." She cracked herself across the cheek. "Do not pass out."

She sat up and pulled some towels off the table onto the floor with her and, as gently as possible, began tying some around her stump. The towels filled immediately, growing heavy. She replaced one for another and filled that one too. Tightening the belt meant having to loosen it first. *No. The cab will be here any minute. You just have to hold on that long.* Maybe if she died they'd agree to take the cooler where it needed to go. Maybe she should've just called a very morally lax courier company.

Slow blinks. Hands cold. Breathing shallow.

She pressed a towel, hard as she could stand to have any pressure on the stump, and hissed through her teeth, "Keep it together, girl. Keep it together." She felt immediate dampness on her hands through the towel.

One small nod off. She started awake, the towel having slipped off onto the floor.

Another small flash where all sound around her stopped. She slapped herself. "No. *No.*"

Each time she snapped awake again the pool of blood around her was wider.

Grabbing the bottle of peroxide, she unscrewed the cap, lifted her thigh to bring up the raw end – and upended the bottle. She *roared* – the sound inhuman even to her ears, the one who'd made it.

The stump hissed and, as if growing rabid, a frothy pink foam dribbled off onto the floor. But it'd be clean.

And something, deep inside her, clicked. It had had enough, whatever determined consciousness, and triggered.

She'd later remember smelling blood and overworked electric motor as she watched the room tilt – wall, wall, ceiling. And the sound it made when the back of her head cracked against the tile floor. The double slap of the backs of her hands as her arms fell wide, releasing the towel from her leg and the soft trickle like a creek of her body slowly, slowly emptying itself.

And somewhere, in the fog, maybe dreamed or maybe heard – a doorbell was ringing.

The cab. She tried opening her mouth to shout for them to come in, but like a nightmare, she was mute. Her words wouldn't come out. Oblivion took her.

⋆   ⋆   ⋆

Amber sat shivering in the thin hospital gown, the drugs wearing off now, and she began to feel, fully, every bit of her that was broken. She listened as the proceedings continued around her. Becky spoke in Spanish to someone on the phone – she sounded like she was begging for someone's patience. Fernando, Luke, and Ted had left to dispose of whoever Bryce Petrosky was, since he was apparently the cause of her drop being dirty and they wouldn't need him. On three of the slabs across the room, three body bags lay – one much more round and full than the others. A large man was inside, Robert Pescatelli. She knew none of these people. She had never felt further from home than now. She wanted to call her parents. She wanted to run away. She wanted to start over. She wanted to go back in a time machine and make so many decisions differently. She noticed Becky, who stood facing away on the phone, had a gun peeking out of the back of her cut-off jeans.

Slug stepped away from the corner he'd been standing in for the last hour, wiped his eyes, glanced at Becky, and moved over next to Amber.

"Do something," Amber begged, whispering. "Let me go. Please. Don't let them do this to me."

"Here's the plan," Slug said. "I'm gonna go over there and hit her. And I'm gonna get you out of here."

"Be careful. She has a gun."

Slug knelt next to Amber's wheelchair. "I got this, boo. Don't worry. We'll—"

A shot rang out and Amber felt a hot spatter on her face as Slug's body was flung to the floor. Becky stood across the room, smoking gun in hand, still pressing the phone to her ear. She said something in Spanish into the phone, ignoring Amber's screams and curses, and continued on with her conversation not missing a beat.

Amber looked over the arm of the wheelchair as Slug's dead eyes stared up at her – an expanding pool of blood circling his corn-rowed head. "Oh, God. Oh, God. What the fuck. What the *fuck*." She screamed across the room at Becky, "Why did you do that?"

Becky tucked her phone into her back pocket and approached Slug's body. "Because I was just on the phone with my contact in Juarez. And Shawn Klegg didn't check out. His brother works for the ATF."

"He wasn't doing anything, you crazy bitch. We were just *talking*."

"I know you were just talking, I know," Becky said with faux sympathy. "But it's better that we weeded him out now than have it become a problem later when he might've gotten scared and decided to place a call." She paused. "Christ, why am I bothering to tell you any of this? I'm talking to ground chuck. You're product in an hour."

Becky unzipped one body bag. A man in a silk Hawaiian shirt lay inside, pale, eyes open, covered in blood. The next was an elderly woman missing half of her face, dressed in a red tracksuit. The third was a young man in a motorcycle jacket and tight black jeans. Becky stared at the three bodies, shook her head, and began unbuttoning the one corpse's Hawaiian shirt. She sat him up, peeled it off, tossed it aside, and let his weight drop him back to lying down – his head clanging loudly off the metal slab under him.

Becky noticed Amber watching. As she uncoiled a long garden hose and began spraying the first corpse, she said, "In Japan the blood type means a lot more than just compatibility for transfusions and organ transplants like it does here. Unlike everyone else in the West, they know, right away, what type they have. They look at it like it's their horoscope, determining everything from personality to tendency to go into certain lines of work, to how well they'll get along with other people. They call it *ketsueki-gata*. Like horoscopes, it's all bullshit, really, but they've been believing *ketsueki-gata* affects so much of their lives since blood types were even discovered to be a thing. They say people with A-type are more logical and B-types are more inclined to be artistic, that they think outside the box. O-types are the most level-headed and clear thinkers, adaptable. But then we get into the discussion of AB-types and things get kind of confused. Because they're often unpredictable, tend to have poor impulse control and are the most likely to end up homeless or die by suicide. They're the most likely to develop drugs or alcohol problems. They spend their lives confused, torn between their A-side and B-side. Gutter blood. But, again that's all superstition. Hokum. B.S." She sprayed off the dead man for a while, not saying anything. "Of course, then I look at you and see what kind of a pretty little mess you've made of your life, Amber, and I think, maybe there's something to that. The A-type half of you did a really good job packaging up your load. You were professional when we were texting, you always said thank you after each time I sent you some tips on what to do next, and you were on time for your drop. Then the B-type rears its ugly head and you fail to ask whether or not the body you received had any history with drug use or had any background whatsoever. So, I guess maybe *ketsueki-gata* might not be total crap. It sure got you pegged."

"Are you really going to cut off my leg?"

Becky tossed the hose aside and stepped through the pink water on the cement floor. "Yes, I will. Because I made a promise to my bosses that I could fill the order, completely, without any gaps. I'm responsible and professional and I do not allow myself any fuck-ups. I'm A-negative. So, again, maybe the Japs are onto something." Becky took out her phone, flashing a glance at its screen. "Your friend has forty-five minutes to get here or your gutter-blood leg is going on the truck. Think she'll pull through for you? Or do you think she's on her way to the airport to leave your sorry AB-positive ass to suffer for your own mistakes?"

The basement door at the top of the metal stairs banged open. Ted, Fernando, and Luke clomped down into the room, Ted in the lead. All three paused when they saw Slug dead on the floor.

"Fuck happened?" Ted said.

"Had to," Becky said. "Home-base ran his name and he has a brother in the ATF."

"Shit," Fernando said. "Should we be worried?"

"Only if he'd made a phone call," Becky said, "but that doesn't seem very likely anymore."

"Any word from Simone?" Ted asked.

"Not a peep. She answered a while ago but I think she butt-dialed, or, you know, butt-*answered*. She'll be here."

"She better be," Ted said.

"Oh, chill the fuck out, Ted. I vouch for her. She'll be here if I say she'll be here. She has more of a cover story to maintain than any of us. You think dealing with a house full of crying relatives is an easy thing to get away from? Can't just slip out when someone's fetching a fresh box of Kleenex."

Ted was shaking his head. "She flakes out on us too much. She needs to learn, regardless of personal shit, punctuality means something. What, does she think her time is more valuable than ours?"

"We're not waiting on Simone, Ted. We're waiting on Amber's friend. Don't try to blame Simone for shit just because you don't like her." She continued spraying. "Talk about not being professional."

Luke bent down to take Slug under the arms and drag him over to the last open slab. He stopped, Slug dangling, head lolling. "Wait. What blood type was this one?" He raised Slug a little to indicate to whom he was referring, making the corpse issue a lazy shrug.

"His blood's practically orange from all the OxyContin he was using. Just process him, Luke. Leave the ideas for those properly equipped to be making them."

"Cripes, all right. Just thinking out loud." As he began undressing him, starting by removing all of Slug's cheap jewelry and fake diamonds, he said, "We dumped Bryce off in the river. Figure he'll be found after we're on the road."

"You could've dropped him on the front steps of the courthouse for all I care."

Ted was standing next to Amber, towering over her, arms crossed. "Think we should start getting her cleaned up, then?" He checked his watch. "We're running up on time and I figure it'll probably take around twenty minutes altogether, with packaging and everything."

"Please don't do this," Amber said. "Please. Fuck, I'll do anything. Just don't cut off my goddamn leg." She started to cry again.

All four looked at her – each set of eyes giving her nothing.

Becky, as she hosed off Robbie Pescatelli, chewed her lip in concentration, eyeing Amber from across the room. Luke was pulling off Slug's pants, after checking his pockets. Ted, closest to Amber, stood looking at her dangling legs like he was trying to guesstimate their dimensions and thickness. Fernando used a push-squeegee to move the bloody water dribbling off Big Robbie's corpse toward the drain in the floor, whistling while he worked.

"I say we start," Ted said finally. "But that's just me. Objections?"

Becky shrugged, spraying around Robbie's dead face, under his double chins. "Your call. Her friend *might* still come through. You never know."

"Please don't," Amber continued, still going ignored. "Please. Please. *Please* don't."

"Yeah," Ted said to Becky, "but if she was gonna come through with something, she would've been here by now I'd figure. I mean, right? We're a quarter to three now. And I still need to get gas in the truck before we get on the road."

"Again," Becky said, "that's your call, Ted. My work's finished. You and Fernando are driving the truck, not me."

Ted cleared his throat. "Okay. Luke, leave Shawn for now. Go get the kit. We need to get Amber ready for surgery."

When Luke came over biting the cap off a syringe, Amber, though abundantly aware it was over for her, refused to go down without a fight. She sprang out of the wheelchair, turned, and tried to run for the stairs – but with the chair still fastened to her wrist by the handcuffs, all it took was for Ted to sit down in the seat. On the wet floor, her bare feet swung out from under her. Ted remained sitting in the chair, setting the brakes, anchoring her. Fernando set aside the push-squeegee. Luke tapped on the needle's tip, stepping over to where Ted had her pinned. Fernando came up behind her and hugged her arms down flat to her sides. Amber screamed and kicked and bit, but feeling the pinch in her bicep – and the slowness everything took on around her suddenly – she could only make gooey sounds with her mouth. The last thing she saw was the floor under her as she was carried above it – and the gradation of the lights brightening on the wet cement, shining, as she was taken over to the slab they'd cleared just for her.

★   ★   ★

Jolene remembered another time she had made a widening pool of blood around herself. That lonely co-ed bathroom stall, listening to the muted bass of someone's music through the wall, nobody knowing someone was killing themselves mere feet from their dorm room. And the sound of a door opening, someone calling her name, and Amber was there, standing in the open stall door looking in at Jolene, going saucer-eyed at the horror she'd made of herself. But Jolene had been relieved, then. Happy to see her, happy to see someone had come. She didn't really want to die, but only knew that when it seemed it was too late.

And now, years later, a door was opening. Someone was coming in to save her. Someone was standing over her, looking at her with a shocked expression. But it wasn't Amber. Jolene's eyes couldn't focus; she'd lost her glasses at some point. Maybe they weren't looking down at her with shock. No, it wasn't Amber. And they weren't sad and scared for her, but smiling. Cornelius stood over her, hands working his belt, smiling at the discovery he'd made on the funeral home floor.

"I'm not dead," Jolene said. "Stop, I'm not dead."

Cornelius's hands paused, his fly halfway down. "Miss Morris?"

"Help me," Jolene said, only able to manage a hoarse whisper. "I need to go get Amber."

Cornelius looked around the room – as if seeing its state for the first time. Like he'd come in, seen Jolene lying there pale and still and had seen nothing else. "What did you do?"

"We need to go to the bowling alley."

"I don't think you're in any state to go bowling, Miss Morris. We should get you to a hospital." He sounded disappointed as he buckled his belt up again.

"No. Not the hospital. Help me up. Where's your car?"

"Outside." He wouldn't take her reaching hands. "What do I get?"

"What?"

"If I help you will you reconsider my proposition?"

"Yes. Just help me. Amber needs me."

"You'll really reconsider?" Cornelius said, smile widening. Those awful tiny teeth.

"*Yes*, Cornelius, just get me to your car." Her jaw felt heavy, tongue fattened and numb. "Lake Calhoun Bowl & Bar. We need to go now. What time is it?"

"Just a little after three."

"Shit. Where's my phone? Help me up."

The next half hour hit Jolene in flashes. One arm draped over Cornelius's shoulder, she could smell his cologne. Hopping on one foot as he helped her through the garage. The rumble of plastic wheels as he dragged behind the cooler with her leg in it, leaving a thin trail of dry ice smoke in its wake. Then she was screaming in pain but didn't know why – until, returning to herself, she saw the round red stamp she'd made on the car door as Cornelius tried putting her in the passenger seat. Then the wind coming in through the open window. Traffic. Other cars. People staring at her, concerned and sickened and worried. Cornelius's awful taste in music – Air Supply or some other soft rock group. More traffic. The smell of asphalt heated up by the summer sun. Car exhaust. The grinding car engine as Cornelius sped them across town. The slow trickle, though, was constant. The smell of blood and Cornelius's cologne, mixing, turning her stomach. She caught flashes of him talking to her, at her, about something. Asking if she was okay, maybe. She answered that question, whether he truly asked it or not she didn't know. "I'll be okay," she said. Same as she told Amber when they closed the ambulance doors between them that night of her senior year.

Cornelius held the phone for her as he drove with his other

hand. Jolene didn't remember asking him to call anyone. She heard Amber's outgoing message: "—calling Hawthorne Funeral Home. We're not in right now, but leave me a message and I'll get back to you as soon as I can."

*Beep.*

"Amber. Tell them I'm on my way. I've got a leg. I got one. I got one. I got one...."

# CHAPTER NINE

Frank kept the pedal pressed to the floor, batting at the wheel to keep the Honda on the road as he took the final turn – the Lake Calhoun Bowl & Bar stood straight ahead at the end of the street, lined on either side by closed factories and empty office plazas up for sale. He spotted the refrigerator truck waiting parked in the side lot and drew the Honda up ahead of it, parking sideways in front of its tall grille. Texas plates, he noticed. He sat in the car a moment, looking ahead at the bowling alley's back door, glancing down at the chrome pistol in his lap. He struggled to get the magazine to release. Ten bullets. He had no idea how many people were inside, how large the network was, how many Rhinos were within. If this was even the right place at all. Maybe Simone just liked bowling alleys and he'd picked to go to the first one he saw she'd 'checked in.' It didn't matter. If this wasn't the one, he'd try the next.

He didn't feel responsible for Amber and Jolene getting wrapped up in all this, that wasn't his doing, but they didn't deserve to die for messing up an order. Ted, this Becky person, and whoever else was potentially inside the bowling alley could just let them go. No one had to get hurt. He would do something. He'd try to save their lives, albeit by a method he wasn't accustomed to, no scrubs or scalpels here, but he'd still try.

Frank swallowed down the bile burning the back of his throat, took a couple deep breaths, and stepped out of the car, closing the door on Simone lying in the back – his potential bargaining chip, a means to start a trade maybe.

He could feel the heat of the baking asphalt washing up his bare legs and under his chin as he approached the bowling alley's back door – marked 'closed' currently – the gun warm from his own body in his pocket, beating against his leg with each step. He approached the glass door and cupped his hands to see inside past his own reflection.

A few neon bar lights, a couple arcade cabinets shining out in the dark, nothing else.

He tugged on the door. Locked.

Turning, he noticed a pale blue minivan. That was Ted's car. This was the place.

Lifting the lid on the dumpster, Frank spotted an old printer inside and struggled to lift the slop-drenched thing out. He swung it in his arms and released it, sending it crashing through the glass door. Drawing Simone's gun – nearly forgetting to pull back on the slide to chamber a round – Frank crunched through the shards, into the air-conditioned bowling alley, seeing no one behind the bar, no sounds other than the whoosh of air from the vents above him, the hum of the ball return, the electronic chirps of the various idle arcade games and pinball machines.

A door marked employees only. Sweat coursed down the sides of his neck. He paused to wipe his palms on his shorts so he wouldn't drop the gun, should he need to use it. He hoped he didn't. He hoped the threat of it would be enough.

Bumping open the employees-only door, he found two desks, both standing empty. The next room, through the swinging kitchen door, he found nothing but recently mopped floors and glistening shiny appliances. Maybe he was late. Maybe they'd already gone. Maybe that refrigerator truck sitting outside was a decoy. Maybe—

"Who are you?" someone asked, behind him.

Frank started to turn.

"Whoa, man," they said. "Don't fucking turn around. Stay looking that way." A shotgun loudly racked, a cold barrel pressing on Frank's spine. "Who are you?"

Frank kept Simone's pistol close to his belly. They didn't see he was armed yet. "I'm looking for the manager," he said.

"Well, she ain't here right now. You're trespassing, buddy. I suggest you go back out the way you came in."

Frank turned his head to look over his shoulder. In his peripheral vision he could make out little detail of the young man. He was olive skinned, dark hair, wearing a baseball cap cocked sideways on his head.

"Don't look at me, dude," he said. "Keep facing forward."

"Are you going to shoot me? Because I'm type O-negative. I'm here for a trade. Amber for me. Or Simone, if you prefer. She's out in the car."

The guy lowered the shotgun barrel slightly. "Who the fuck are you and how do you know about all this shit you're saying, man? And *where's* Simone? What?"

"Simone is outside. I'm here to trade. Me and her for Amber."

"Simone was fucking *playing* us?"

"No. She didn't turn on you. I should clarify. Her being part of this deal I'm suggesting isn't exactly her say, but given her current condition—"

"Whoa, what you mean she ain't got no say? What'd you do to her? You got a gun on you, man? Turn around."

If he saw the chrome pistol, he'd shoot. This was Frank's only chance.

Frank planted his sneakers, hoping their tread wouldn't fail him on this freshly mopped kitchen floor. He twisted around, fast, snatching the shotgun barrel with one hand and lifting up and away as he thrust the pistol toward the guy's chest, the barrel clinking against the guy's golden crucifix necklace.

"Okay, man, okay," the guy said, one hand raised open with the other still clutching the shotgun's wooden stock.

"Let go of the shotgun," Frank said.

"Just let me take it and I'll go. Got my prints on it. I'll just go, man."

"No, let go of it or I'll shoot you," Frank said. He felt like he might have a heart attack any moment. "I'm here for Amber. I'm willing to trade as long as you don't hurt her."

The guy blinked at him. Frank could see it. It was the same look he used to see as he went to tell a patient's family in the waiting room bad news – often, before he'd even opened his mouth, somehow, they knew. Something had happened. But now it was Frank getting the bad news, no need for words, just a look.

"I'm not supposed to shoot you," the guy said. "You have type-O. That's gold to us. But I'll do it, man, if you don't let me go." When he tried wrenching the shotgun down – the kitchen exploding with the sudden flat noise as it discharged inches from

Frank's head – Frank, entirely involuntarily, squeezed the trigger of the pistol at the same time.

Shot point-blank, the guy made a guttural, low grunt, stumbled back through the kitchen door, and fell across one of the desks. He lay with a smoking hole in his shirt over his heart next to his nametag that read Fernando.

*It's just meat. It's just meat.*

Frank held his head, his skull vibrating. The heat of the shotgun going off in his face tingled painfully. Though his ears had been ringing for days, the left wasn't picking up even that much anymore. He touched at his face. One eyebrow was crispy, same as the hair on his left temple. He was only bleeding from his left ear, but none of the bullets had punctured his skin.

Gun still hot in his hand, Frank stared at what he'd done to the young man lying draped across the desk, bleeding a thin line out of his shirt.

Nearly a decade of school, all those hours at the clinic, days and nights one to the next saving people, double shifts, triples, sleeping in his car, pulling people back from the brink even as their bodies begged to be let go, to just die, again and again – and in one day Frank had personally shoved two souls spiraling into the Great Whatever. He stood, stared, and breathed, concentrating only on slowing down his heart for a while. He told himself he was under no oath, like he'd told Simone; maybe someday he'd believe this was justified, that this was okay. But right now it felt sickening, as necessary to saving Amber as it may've been.

Woozy, he bent to collect the shotgun from the floor. He pocketed the pistol and used the shotgun barrel to poke open the kitchen door, stepping back out into the bowling alley behind the bar.

Immediate gunfire chewed the floor at his feet to splinters. Frank dropped, only seeing a flash out over the lanes before shattered booze bottles rained liquor and glass down around him. Staying low, he racked the shotgun, letting them know he was armed.

"Might want to identify yourself," a male voice shouted. Not Ted. Someone else.

"I'm here for Amber."

"I didn't ask what you're here for, asshole," the voice said. Frank could hear heavy boots on the polished wood of the lanes as a man stepped out. Sitting up a little, Frank used what remained of the mirror behind the bar to see. Though the cracks made the reflection unreliable, he could see a bald man in blue scrubs, several of him it seemed, all moving together as one, crossing the lanes, each with a compact machine gun in their many, many hands. "Name."

"My name is Frank. I'm here for Amber. I want to trade."

The heavy boots stopped. Frank watched in the mirror as the multiple blue-scrubbed bald guys lowered their machine guns together in unison, all of them screwing up their heavy-browed faces. "Frank as in Frank Goode?"

"Doctor Bad himself," Frank said, and shook his head at himself. *Idiot.* "So are we going to talk or are we just going to shoot each other?"

"Did you kill Fernando?"

"Unfortunately, yes. I didn't want to, but I did."

"You have anything to do with the fact Simone hasn't answered her phone since this morning?"

There was no point in lying. "She's dead."

The man in the scrubs and heavy boots brought the machine gun up to his shoulder again, taking aim at the bar. Frank, behind it, slid along the floor on his knees through the broken glass to put the reach-in freezer between him and the potential bullets, thinking maybe, like at home, he could make himself a shield. He waited for the hail of bullets, but none came.

"Did you kill her?" the man shouted.

Frank couldn't see him in the mirror. He tried angling his head around to use his right ear, the one that still functioned. "I did."

"Why?" He didn't sound mad, but slightly irked.

"Because I had to."

A muffled gunshot rang out somewhere in the building. Neither man standing at opposite ends of the bowling alley said anything for a couple heartbeats.

When the guy in the scrubs called out, fear was strangling his voice. "Ted? Becky? You guys all right down there? Fuck." He called out to Frank, "So you're the universal donor, right? You were some of the blood in the jugs, the shit that came out of Vasily?"

"Yes. That was mine."

"So you *did* try to save him. What do you know? Looks like I owe Ted twenty bucks."

"I tried," Frank said, "right before your friend Simone shot him."

"I see. And you're here because you're after Amber? She family to you?"

"No."

"But you still wanna save her?"

Frank sighed. "Look. Why don't we just cut to the chase? I already know what you're going to say. And I'll agree to it, without you even needing to ask. I'll give you me if you let Amber go. Bring Ted out here, I'll talk to him."

"No. And I call bullshit. There ain't nobody who *wants* to get chopped. I'll come back there and shoot you and *then* chop you – but I don't believe it for a fucking second you'd give yourself up *knowing* what's in store for you."

"I will. Because, at the risk of sounding melodramatic, man, I don't have jack shit to live for," Frank said. "The cops are after me, as you probably heard on the news. They think I wiped out both the Pescatellis and the Petroskys. And if either family has relatives around, in other states, I'm sure they've heard what happened and they're on their way here to find me right now. Long story short, I'm fucked. And since all this stuff you take across the border or wherever you take it, helps people, I'd rather do that than rot in prison the rest of my life or end up buried in a cornfield somewhere, not helping anyone. I might have hepatitis C from sharing an IV with Bryce, but I'll sit still if you want to test me before making your decision. Just let her go, please."

"That's real kind-hearted of you to say and all, Frank, but I still don't buy it. So let's do it my way, huh? Put Fernando's shotgun on the floor, come out from behind there real slow, and we'll—"

Frank jumped at the loud, sudden pop. He stood up from behind the bar, and saw the man in the blue scrubs lying facedown on the floor, his blood running into the ball gutter, as Ted, one hand full of a gun, another holding a plastic-wrapped leg by the ankle, went running for the door.

"Ted! Stop!" Frank charged out from behind the bar, stopped to take aim, and fired. He hadn't braced for the shotgun's kick enough – something in his shoulder snapped, pain flaring hot.

Ted hopped through the glassless doorframe and out into the parking lot, the shot only stirring the broken glass on the floor. Frank, reaching the broken door, shirked back when a bullet sparked off the ground at the doorway. "Don't follow me, Frank. You don't wanna go where I'm going."

Standing to one side of the doorway, Frank pumped the shotgun. He was pretty sure he'd broken his collar bone. "You piece of shit, Ted. What the fuck are you *doing*, man?"

The throaty rumble of a diesel engine started. Frank stepped out, raising the shotgun. Ted was behind the wheel of the refrigerator truck, window down. Ted looked out at Frank. Simone's Honda blocked his path. Frank approached, barrel out, aiming up at the window as Ted glared down at him.

"If you came here to save her, man," Ted said, "you'd best get down there. I undid her tourniquet. She's bleeding out. So you can either shoot me or you can go save her."

"Or I can shoot you, then go save her," Frank said.

"But you ain't got it in you. You're a healer. You can deal with killing these folks you don't know. Or Simone, I see you brought her with you, but you know *me*. You've known me since school, man. We came up together. And when you think about it, I didn't do *shit* to you. Nothing directly, anyway. But go ahead, Doctor Goode, shoot me."

Frank lowered the shotgun. "I hope this was all worth it, Ted. I really fucking do."

"I'll see you, Frank." One parting look – maybe a tinge of regret there – and Ted rolled up the window.

Frank took a step back from the truck as Ted put it in reverse, the engine rumbling as he started to nose the front end around the narrow gap Frank had left parking Simone's Honda in the way. He was about to turn and run back inside the bowling alley for Amber when Frank noticed Ted pause, hands still on the wheel, to watch something coming up the road. An electric-yellow sedan was screaming toward the bowling alley, the shape of two people within. Frank, wanting to believe it was someone after Ted, who might finish the job, left them to it and ran back inside, slipping on the broken glass in the doorway a second time.

He ran across the ten lanes, hopping over the gutters, until he reached the maintenance door on the far side. Inside, the stink of machinery and blood hit him. Over the railing he could see from the top of the stairs four exam tables. Three were empty, with a fourth, covered with blood, holding Amber sitting halfway up, her hospital gown soaked with red up to the waist. From under the gown's hem only one leg was sticking out.

On the floor lay two other bodies. A woman, shot through the head, with a large cross tattooed on the back of her neck. The second Frank recognized immediately – the kid, Slug, Snail, whatever – lying on his side, also shot, also not moving. Fellow vultures Ted didn't want to share the score with, Frank guessed.

Frank started down the basement steps, undoing his belt. Hopefully Amber hadn't lost too much blood. He felt under her jaw. She had a pulse. Very slow, very faint. He wrapped the belt around her leg, above the knee, and growled with the effort as he pulled as tight as he could. Amber sat up, her lips parting as she issued a soft gasp of pain.

"Where's Jolene?"

He'd said it countless times. "You're going to be okay."

\*    \*    \*

More time traveling for Jolene. Stoplights, then suddenly in motion again, the edit between choppy, loud, and jarring.

Cars around them, then not.

She was lying one way, then the other, flopping side to side when unconscious in motion with Cornelius taking sharp turns.

She woke one time to find her chin resting on his bony shoulder. Cornelius smiled down at her. Despite her injuries, she could summon the energy to slump herself the other way; anything to not be touching him.

She sat up and glanced down, hoping she'd only cut off her own leg in a dream. But the car seat under her, soaked through with blood slowly going cold, told the whole story. "Shit."

She watched, vision blurry, the wind sharp in her face, as they took the next turn. Dead ahead lay the bowling alley, neon squiggle of its sign shining bright, flaring at the edges to Jolene's eyes. She saw a small blue car parked in front of a refrigerator truck. One man, in a bloody shirt and shorts, running back toward the bowling alley as the driver of the refrigerator truck hopped out and took aim. Cornelius screamed and started flinging the wheel left and right. Loud snaps of gunfire sounded as the windshield fell into the car, in shards. Jolene reacted to everything on a delay, screaming too late as more bullets zipped into the car. Cornelius fought the wheel, the tires lost traction, and spinning a full circle in the road, they came to a stop.

Jolene, dizzy, eyes trying to roll themselves back into her head, only heard the sharp *click* of something metallic near her ear – then fought to lift her chin to look at the man leaning into the car with the gun in his hand. Cornelius was slumped over in the driver's seat, face pressing the horn – it droned, echoing about the dead factories, unheard by anyone but them.

The man in the orange polo shirt aiming the gun at Jolene twisted up his face. He'd probably seen all the blood. Jolene didn't have the strength to push the gun barrel out from under her chin where he held it, smashing her teeth together.

He leaned into the car, past Jolene, peering into the back seat. He laughed, loud, in her ear, as he withdrew. "Two for one, huh? I'll take it."

The gun came out from under her chin. She heard a car door open, its rusty hinges squeal, and then heard it boom shut. Jolene blinked slowly, watching the man in the orange polo shirt and black shorts lug her camping cooler away from Cornelius's crashed car, heading back over to the truck he'd gotten out of.

The refrigerator truck, belching two puffs of black exhaust from its high pipes, nudged its grille into the side of the tiny blue blocking its path – it skidded sideways, the side window breaking. Jolene tried tracking the truck as it passed but her head refused to turn that quick. She caught Texas plates. That was about all – before she fell unconscious again.

Somebody was talking. She heard footsteps on rough concrete. She raised her head, not realizing she'd passed out again. The driver's seat was empty. Cornelius was gone. Out ahead of the hood she saw

Frank carrying a limp, bloody shape. He was looking where the little blue car had been, which, like Cornelius, was now also gone.

"Over here...." Jolene raised her hand, waving for Frank as much as she could. Frank spotted her through the broken frame of Cornelius's car where it stood half on the sidewalk and shuffled over, carrying...somebody. Once in range of Jolene's vision, she saw it was Amber and her heart exploded with relief.

Mashing down an elbow on the seat, Jolene pushed herself up to sitting – the damp seat made her keep sliding down into the floorboard. "Is that her? Is she okay?"

Frank said nothing. He pulled open the back door and struggled to lay her across the back seat. It was only once he stepped back from her and her blood-soaked hospital gown peeled from his belly and fell draped over Amber again that Jolene saw...she only had one leg.

"No. *No.*" Jolene's heart couldn't summon a faster pulse than the dim occasional thump it was giving her now.

"She'll be okay," Frank said. "She's going to be fine."

"They cut off her leg." Jolene's eyes welled with tears as she reached into the back seat, fingers cold and numb. "They cut off her fucking leg." She touched Amber's cheek and she stirred, sitting up, her face as ashen as Jolene's reaching fingers. Amber coiled her fingers with Jolene's. She could hardly squeeze at all.

"I'm okay," Amber murmured. "I'm okay."

Frank got behind the wheel, looked over at Jolene sitting in the sodden seat, and his mouth fell open seeing she too was in the same state as Amber.

"Fuck," he said. "They got *both* of you?"

"No. I did this," she said. "I did it to myself."

Frank swallowed. "Jesus Christ. Okay, well, I'm taking you two to the hospital. This goes beyond my expertise. Just hold on, okay?"

Frank struggled to get the car to turn over, stomping the gas in time with twisting the ignition.

"Start! Come on! *Come on!*"

With one last stomp on the gas, the car spurted to life, smoke rolling out from under the hood. He backed the front wheels off the sidewalk and hammered the gas. Jolene felt mashed into the seat with the sudden movement. She couldn't keep anything squared up in front of her eyes – but she had Amber's hand, and she would never, ever let go.

⋆   ⋆   ⋆

Frank broke the speed limit when he felt it would be safe. Other times, he dodged the bright yellow four-door around other cars, picking up speed toward yellow lights. Without a windshield, his eyes watered whenever they picked up speed. Amber and Jolene would nod off in turns, one slumping over in their seat while the other would wake with a start, a gasp, and a low scream of agony. Frank told them to keep pressure on their wounds; he was driving them to the clinic, taking his old route to work, the fastest way he knew. "We're almost there, we're almost there."

They crossed over the bridge between St. Paul and Minneapolis, and hit traffic on the far side. There was no way around and a few cops, ahead, were directing traffic. Frank heard the initial *pop*. And then, out over the summit of the Cathedral of St. Paul, he saw the first flash. Blue, then red. Then another arcing, sizzling trail and a set of flashes, pink and orange. Jolene, in the passenger seat, let her head fall toward the window. Frank watched her slow blinks, the shine on her face, lighting blue then red then green, as the fireworks continued. She reached into the back seat, shaking Amber's shoulder. "Look. Happy Fourth of July, Amber."

And while they waited for traffic to resume, they watched fireworks from their stolen car full of blood. Maybe the distraction helped to make the pain, just for that couple of minutes, tolerable. When it came time for them to take the turn, the lights finally working at the intersection ahead and the cops pulling off – thankfully – before they rounded the curve, Amber and Jolene continued to moan and hiss and curse and groan, pain rushing back in, fully felt.

Frank pulled the car under the drop-off awning, a space clearing at the curb as they arrived. He left it running. Pulling open the passenger door, he reached in, trying to pick Jolene up in a way that wouldn't hurt her too much. He screamed for help while she screamed in his ruined left ear. The orderlies came running with a wheelchair. Frank told them to grab a second, he had another in the same condition in the back seat. The orderly rushed off with Jolene, Amber screaming from the back seat. Frank helped her out next, turning her around, holding her under the arms, feeling the blood soaking through her hospital gown. They set her in the chair, his belt around her thigh – she left a trail across the sidewalk, people gawking, as they rolled her in through the doors, not far behind Jolene. Frank watched doctors, nurses, and patients alike spring back as the two women were carted, wailing, into the hospital. All stopped for them. Frank followed, blood on his hands, blood dried on his clothes, exhaustion catching up to him now. He slowed as he watched two doctors toss down what they were doing – one was wrist deep in a bag of chips – to get Amber on a gurney, then Jolene. They rushed them off through a set of doors. Frank watched them being run, side by side, the two women never letting go of one another's hands. He waited there, watching them go. They took a corner, and were gone.

And then all eyes in the ER turned toward him. The TVs about the room were all showing his face, his old mugshot, and people were putting it together. *He did this to those women*, he could see them all thinking. A few, slow on the uptake, noticed what the others were looking at. One woman stood, and pointed. "That's him! That's Doctor Bad!"

Frank turned and sprinted back out of the ER, to the little yellow car sitting on the curb. He hopped in as he heard, behind him, squawking police radios and heavy boots and authoritative shouting for him to stop. He got the car in gear and tore out of the clinic parking lot, merging with traffic, the shouting and blaring horns of the people he just ran off the road behind him.

He didn't want to spend a lot of time on the highway. He kept to side streets and quiet neighborhoods, moving toward his house in a zig-zag pattern, pulling over and cutting off the engine every time he heard a siren anywhere nearby. Resuming after all was quiet again, he passed a few public parks where further fireworks displays were going off. With no windshield, the smell of people grilling was easy to pick up on the air. He listened to the dull thump of the colorful explosions in the sky going off all around him, and the faraway cheers of people enjoying themselves. The flashes found their way into the car, painting his bloody hands on the wheel different colors as he drove. He heard sirens, figuring it was somebody who fired a Roman candle into their own bedroom window by accident. That it wasn't for him, they didn't know where he was. He would go to the last place they'd think to look. They were at the airports and bus depots showing cabbies his picture. They wouldn't think he'd go home.

He parked a few blocks from his house, left Simone's and Robbie's phones, but took his own and Simone's handgun – fearing some kid might find it. He walked up the sidewalk, the wind tossing his hair, even the burnt parts of it on his temple. He cut through backyards. Most people weren't home, they were likely at the stadiums and parks to watch the fireworks displays. He avoided houses where the fog of grilling swelled over the hedges. He had a few dogs bark at him, had one motion-sensor light come on, but no one shot at him, no one told him to freeze. He hopped the last fence, finding himself in his own overgrown yard. There was no smell of grilling here, no laughter of friends, no beers or hot dogs or tiny firecrackers for the kids. His house was dark, the back windows each black with his thick curtains all closed. He stepped around the side of the house, peeking toward his front yard and the street.

The Pescatellis' cars, as well as the Petroskys', were all gone, hauled off, impounded. At the sidewalk, small wooden stakes had been driven into the ground, yellow police tape keeping no one back. No one was here to gawk anymore, no more reporters, no rubbernecking neighbors elbowing for their chance to tell the camera, "But he was such a nice, quiet man." He'd be forgotten in a handful of weeks, maybe even days. Something else would come along. Doctor Bad would become yesterday's news.

He climbed onto the back deck and found his back door laced across with three strips of yellow police tape. He tore it away and stepped inside, the rank smell of congealed blood hitting him like a wall. They'd turned his AC off and the house smelled like a slaughterhouse in peak summer – which, really, wasn't too far from the truth. He closed the door behind him and stood in the dark and stink of his place, listening. He was alone. He clicked on the kitchen light. And from the doorway he could see his living room's carpet. All the bodies were gone but they'd left their stains. More red than beige, some outlines were faintly visible, the source of each one where both families had lain dying. The house felt haunted, but at the fresh point before the ghosts knew they could be seen and heard and were just waiting for someone to notice things out of place. Frank felt like a ghost himself. He stepped onto the stained carpet, hearing it crunch instead of squish now – each fiber was rigid with dried blood.

He moved to his front windows and peeked out. No one. Nobody. The side window. Mister and Missus Shulman, he could see, were in their living room. She'd lived, but she had a massive cast taking up her entire left arm from shoulder to wrist. Her husband was waiting on her, bringing her dinner on a TV tray. She motioned for a kiss and he clutched his back, but smiled, to bend down and give her one. They watched something together on TV, Mister Shulman glancing over as his wife ate, and laughed at whatever they were watching, Mister Shulman's eyes lingering on his laughing wife a little longer before returning his focus to the screen. Frank let the curtain fall shut before they noticed the cause of her agony was watching and smiling along with them, trying to steal their happiness and relief after nearly causing her death.

He couldn't stay in the house forever. The police would be back. Someone would see the lights on and call. The house would be watched, if not currently, *somebody* would be by before long. Frank went into the kitchen and pulled open his fridge. A half carton of milk and the Tupperware of leftovers he couldn't remember saving. He closed the fridge and went into the bathroom, figuring he'd at least get cleaned up if not fed. He didn't feel that hungry anyway, not after all of this. He sometimes stored excess supplies for his practice in the bathroom, packing the linen closet with coils of tubing and hypodermic needles and pills and whatnot. Pulling the closet door open, looking for a towel, he noticed the ten STD test kits he'd gotten from Ted with his most recent restock.

The plan had been assembling itself on the drive home, since dropping off Amber and Jolene. Perhaps in the background of his mind, perhaps just thought and considered on the fringes, but now, seeing the test kits, waiting to give him the status of his blood – tainted or not tainted – he had his answer. It would determine what he did next. He took a sample of his own blood, smeared it on the first stick, the second stick, then the third stick. He cranked an egg timer to one hour, set it on the bathroom counter, and undressed. He showered, listening to the soothing ticking beyond the faucet spray, giving the fates their time to determine things for him.

He faced the shower wall, letting the spray run down his battered body. Even warm water hurt. He had a bus ticket waiting for him at the Greyhound station. He could get across town in an hour, and still have time. He could still run.

He watched the final seconds of the egg timer tick by. When it rang, it sounded faraway to his ruined ears.

The bus bound for Laredo would have an empty seat on it.

He dressed in a clean T-shirt and his last pair of cargo shorts. He wanted to be barefoot, but because of the carpet, slipped his shoes back on. Returning to the bathroom, he looked at himself in the mirror. One eyebrow was gone, burn marks around his left eye. The hair that'd been fried by the shotgun blast had rubbed off in the shower. He looked more like his mugshot now. Taken that night they dragged him from the airport bathroom, slicked with stress sweat, malnourished and afraid. He forced his eyes down to the counter before him, where the three strips sat in their small plastic trays with his blood smeared onto each. Three negatives, on all three tests. He had nothing. Nothing but the clean O-negative in his veins.

It may not go to the right people. It might all end up keeping the affluent, self-serving – like he used to be – above ground, staving off the inevitable for a few more years of golfing and not leaving a tip. But no one would get hurt.

Frank crunched over his blood-hardened carpet and sat in his recliner again in the dark. His phone had three percent of a charge left, just enough for two quick calls. He keyed in three numbers.

"911. What's your emergency?"

"Ambulance," Frank said and gave his address, slow and clear, and hung up.

In his contacts, he pressed his daughter's name on the screen. She answered on the first ring.

"Dad? Are you okay? We're still at Grandma's. Mom's worried. We saw the news. What's going on? Why are they saying that about you? Dad, I—"

"Jessica," Frank said. "You and your mom can go home now."

"Where are you? Are you in jail?"

"No, I'm at my house." He nearly said home. This wasn't home, never had been. "Listen, Jessica, I have to go soon but I just wanted to call to say I love you very much."

"Dad, you're kinda scaring me. Do bad people have you or something?"

"No. I'm okay. But, just let me get this out. I'm sorry I missed so much time with you, Jessica, between work and my time away." He paused. "No excuses, I was a bad dad. I should've been better to you, been there more. You deserved so much more than what you got with me."

Jessica said nothing for a moment, but Frank could hear her quickening breathing. "Dad...."

"Take care of your mother for me. I love you."

"I love you too, Dad."

"Bye, Jessica."

"Dad—"

He hung up and turned off his phone so he wouldn't hear it when she tried calling him back, if she tried calling him back. He sat in his recliner in the dark with the pistol on the armrest. He waited until his curtains lit up again. They did, but not as he was expecting. The grand finale fireworks, the color of each blast fading quickly from the far wall of his living room. It ended, and he could hear people cheering a few blocks over, his room staying dark around him. Then, soon after, swelling bright and never fading but instead flashing, harder and brighter and faster. Sirens screamed, a sound he always thought sounded like *hold on, hold on, hold on*. He heard tires screech outside his home and feet stamping up his front walk.

Frank Goode took one last deep breath, held it, closed his eyes, and gave himself up.

★　★　★

Amber woke up in a hospital bed for the second day in a row. She sat bolt upright expecting the man wearing the bulletproof vest under his scrubs to be there with the tiny screwdriver near her eye. But it wasn't the same room, the view out the window was different. And she had a roommate. It hurt her neck to turn to look. Jolene lay next to her, multiple tubes running in and out of her, her IV stand loaded with bags of blood and clear liquids. Her heart-rate monitor bleeped, each peak strong and steady. The shape of Jolene's blankets over her lower half was odd, like she was lying with her legs crossed at the ankle – but that wasn't quite it. Just one hill at the end of the bed, one foot.

Yesterday – or however long it'd been – came back to Amber in a cold flood. She looked down at her own hills and valleys under her blanket, her body that lay hidden by the scratchy hospital blankets. She only had one foot mound and she could feel that she didn't have her legs crossed under there, but she felt like, maybe, she had both legs. She forced herself to pick up the corners of her blanket, lift, and look.

She didn't need to press the button to summon the nurse. Her scream did that.

It was enough to rouse Jolene from whatever drugs they had in her. She woke, blinked, looked over at Amber crying, and started crying too. The nurses didn't want her to, but Amber insisted they help her over into Jolene's bed. The nurses scrambled to keep their IV lines and oxygen mask tubes from getting tangled. Amber pulled Jolene close, who could barely do more than sob and wheeze apologetic-sounding noises. Neither cared about their loss. It was a shock, certainly, for Amber – but the prospect of losing Jolene was so much more scary. She would've given both legs. Both arms. Her goddamn head. All of it, if it meant keeping her Jo-Jo alive. And though she'd never asked her to, Amber saw Jolene would do the same – and had done the same. But they were alive. They were alive, and they had each other.

\*　　\*　　\*

Middle Texas was about as flat as flat could get. And quiet. Ted Beaumont couldn't pick up a radio station no matter how slowly he turned the dial. Just fuzz.

He'd been driving for nearly eighteen hours, only stopping for gas and pissing in an old soda bottle sloshing side to side around the floorboards. But he was making good time. He glanced over at the rumpled paper bag in the passenger seat he'd put the seat belt across to hold it in place. He counted it leaving the Minneapolis impound lot, quickly – roughly half a million. It was a serious pain in the ass prying open the back of the hearse, but he did it, he got the money. And nobody, *nobody*, had to know he'd taken it. The story he had prepared was that Slug was, as suspected, a mole for the ATF. After cutting off Amber Hawthorne's leg, Slug shot Becky, Luke, and Fernando. It was by Ted's quick thinking alone that he managed to kill Slug and make it out of town with the load before the cops were drawn to the bowling alley by the gunfire. He would get the load to Juarez. He would get his payday – on top of what he retrieved from the two troublesome bitches' hearse – and he would be set for life. It was all beaches and playing with his kids in the sand and fucking his wife under the stars listening to the ocean from here on. Fuck, he might even dump the wife and kids and hook up with some young thing. He had the money to do it now. And he always had a thing for Latin women. Hot-blooded, he heard. Just as likely to crack you across the head when they come as bring you breakfast in bed the next morning.

It would be a good life, once he got there. Just a few hundred more miles.

Dead, flat landscape and the highway ahead of him and the numbing vibration of the truck's wheel in his hands. It felt like he'd traveled the same stretch about a million times, like the planet wasn't a sphere but shaped like a rolling pin and he was just going down and around and up and over, down and around and up and over....

Glancing in the side mirror to see if anyone was following him – a habit he'd developed as soon as he'd left Minnesota – he didn't see any cop cars or Frank chasing in that ugly little yellow car, but a flock of black birds. Dozens of them, all flying low, all keeping time with the truck, some even trying to sink their talons into the sheet metal, it seemed, in an attempt to get Ted to brake.

Then the alarm started yelling at him. One dial next to the gas said the refrigerator unit was dying and the temperature back there was rapidly spiking to degrees unfriendly to delicate human tissue.

Ted pulled over to the side of the road. The truck was making weird noises, both the engine up front and the second one behind the cab that was supposed to – as he'd been told – be pretty reliable.

But no. Of course fucking not.

It'd failed and now he was in the middle of nowhere with an entire load warming up in the back. He dropped down out of the truck, immediately getting pummeled by the heat. It turned his stomach, made his brain feel loose in his skull. He couldn't even hear the truck idling because his ears were being filled with the noise of the cloud of crows that, now that he'd stopped, swarmed the truck. They swooped low, beaks angling for Ted's neck and cheek and forehead. One pecked him on the crown of his shaved head, and it hurt.

"Piss off!" he shouted, waggling his arms around. He went to the back of the truck, stepped up on the bumper, and tugged on the lock release. One breath and he was vomiting, violently, on hands and knees on the red-dirt roadside. The open truck door released a shallow stream of viscous brown-red fluid that dribbled off the bumper, thick as cheap syrup, each drip clinging before letting go.

The birds dove past him, diving into the truck. Ted watched in horror as they tore at the melting load inside, pecking through the cling-wrap over arms and legs sitting piled on the shelves within. They had finally caught up to him and were now, after a long chase, set about devouring everything.

Staring, seeing but not believing, Ted got out his phone to call his wife. He barely had one bar out here and the connection showed for it.

"Hey, baby," she said, "you just missed it, the twins just had their first dip in the Gulf. I got pictures. You should really see them, they love it down here. When are you going to—"

"We have a problem. A big one."

"What's wrong, baby? Everything go all right leaving Minneapolis?"

"No. Nothing went right. And I got another problem staring me in the face right now." Ted paused to swallow down the urge to gag. He picked up a rock to throw at the truck to chase off the birds – maybe something was salvageable down in there, buried deep where it was still cold. But the birds ignored the rock, and continued to peck, tear, and devour. "The truck broke down and everything's melting. We're fucked."

"Can't you call somebody?"

"Call who? They're all dead. Get your head out of your ass."

"Don't you talk to your wife like that, Theodore, I'm just trying to help. Nobody told you to get wrapped up in this shit. I wanted to stay in Minnesota but *no,* your greedy ass just had to 'step yourself up into the next business bracket' didn't you?"

Ted sighed. "I know, baby, I know. I'm sorry. It's just...they're expecting me down there with a load tonight. They were willing to let go what was going to New York. Load going to Cali they let slide, but only if I could get them this one. This isn't going to be good."

Maybe, just maybe, if somebody came along *right this minute,* someone who wasn't going to ask questions about that smell coming from the back, somebody who knew how to fix the cooling system of a truck like this, Ted might be able to squeak by un-murdered. Maybe.

A sound turned him. An approaching dust cloud, made wiggly by the heat waves. He hung up on his wife, stepped up onto the bumper to slam the truck's back doors closed – the fucking birds can *stay* in there if they like their free meal so much – and took off his shirt. Ted stood waving it over his head in the middle of the road, squinting to try and make out details of the approaching vehicle just over the distant hill. "Please don't be a cop. Please don't be a motherfucking cop."

The little blue car solidified as it emerged from the heat waves rising up off the blacktop – snapping to sudden sharpness in Ted's squinting eyes. A familiar car, familiar color. But they showed no signs of slowing down and he stepped aside, waving the fistful of money from his pocket at them. And as they ripped past him, he had only one second to look inside at the driver, and his passenger. The man driving tipped a trilby hat, smiling a friendly hello. The passenger, pale-skinned and asleep, lay with her head on the driver's shoulder.

Ted turned with the car, watching it go screaming on down the highway without ever showing any signs of slowing to help him out. The car, the woman in the passenger seat.

"Simone?" Ted said, coughing away the road dust and the pervasive stink radiating from his own stranded vehicle. He watched the blue Honda reduce to a pinprick on the horizon. And he was about to call his wife back when, again, from behind, noise drew him around. A second dust cloud was on approach out there in the far-flung, sun-blasted distance. This cloud was bigger, almost like a building sandstorm. And from it, not thunder came ringing out but many sirens layering over each other – it had to be a hundred police cars. And they too started to develop sharpness to their shapes as they emerged from the heat waves, in dogged pursuit.

Ted lowered the shirt he was waving overhead and the crumpled cash in his hand going soggy from palm sweat. He glanced back at his vehicle, now a perch for the hundreds of crows, and the puddle of congealing rot-soup snaking a long slick river across the desert highway. He wasn't hoping for anyone to stop now.

He watched some of the police cars keep going after the Honda, but more than a few were peeling off from the pack to crunch onto the roadside, slowing, the officers inside all drawing guns before stepping out, using their open doors as shields.

Ted raised his hands, let the damp bills get snatched away by the wind, joining to float and flutter with the vultures circling and watching and waiting high overhead.

# CHAPTER TEN

In the church basement filled with the smell of coffee and the sound of the snow melting off everyone's shoes, a woman stood behind the podium in front of the many folding chairs and said, "So, we have a newcomer here with us tonight. Would you like to come up and introduce yourself?"

Amber pressed her cane down and struggled to stand. Some of the others around her tried helping her but she smiled, thanked them, and said she had it. She moved up to the front of the room with one shoe holding a flesh-and-blood foot and the other a foot of titanium and carbon fiber – the stuff inside space ships, the physical therapist had said the day they fitted her with it.

Amber got behind the podium, leaned her cane against the wall, and looked out at the fifteen faces, strangers every one of them. But she could see it in their eyes as they sat and waited for her to begin that they'd been here before, done this same initial introduction, and that made it feel better. She wasn't the first. It was just the first time for her.

"My name is Stella Artois and I'm an alcoholic. Sorry. You guys have probably heard that one before. I just thought because of the whole anonymous part, it might be funny to…ahem, let me try that again. My name is Amber and I'm…."

Her jaw clenched closed on the rest of that declaration. She looked out toward the back of the room where Jolene, with the same titanium carbon fiber leg peeking out at the cuff of her jeans, stood. Her friend smiled, encouragingly, and rolled her hand on her wrist and mouthed, *You got this.*

Amber cleared her throat. "My name is Amber and I'm an alcoholic."

All together: "Welcome, Amber."

"Thanks. So, I guess I'll just jump right in. I brought notes. I'm lucky to be alive today. I don't know how many of you remember last summer. But I was there during what the news ended up calling the Summer of Blood. I wasn't there for the first massacre, but I sure as hell was for the second. For a while I blamed everyone but myself for what happened to me. I didn't think it was my fault. But, as my friend helped me realize, I only had myself to thank for winding up in that situation, one where I ended up paying the price by losing part of myself – literally. And I got there because of many factors. I was greedy. I didn't want to work a regular job. I wanted to cut corners and cheat and steal to get ahead." She stopped reading her index cards. "And when the day was through of lying and cheating and taking advantage of my best friend's patience and loving heart, I drank myself into oblivion to try and numb myself from facing who I was rapidly becoming. It took having a piece of my body cut off to realize I was clearly heading down a bad road. Now, I'm being sued by two different families because the funeral home I used to own – before the bank took it back – the power got turned off and both of their loved ones ended up rotting in my basement and...."

Jolene, in the back, wasn't smiling encouragingly anymore but swiping a flat hand across her throat again and again, eyes wide behind her glasses.

"So much for being anonymous," Amber said, and it got a small chuckle from a few people. Most of them were staring at her, frowning, confused, looking sickened. "Anyway, I'm lucky to be alive. Even if it means having to work off two impending lawsuits and court costs and whatever my lawyer ends up costing me, I'm alive. I have my best friend. I nearly lost her. A bunch of times in the past few years, and again just recently. She's given up so much for me. Countless hours of her life worrying about me, trying to help save me and my business that ended up going under anyway – because of me. So much. So, so much. And more, which I'm sure she probably doesn't want me to discuss."

Jolene in the back was shaking her head.

"Anyway, I just want to say if you have people in your life who have stuck with you as you tried to make yourself better, or helped you see you needed to make that change, you owe them everything. My friend never gave up on me. My sister, I like to call her, because she is my sister." Amber thrust a finger over the podium toward Jolene in the back, who immediately tried to shrink herself, face reddening. "Her name is Jolene – or, you know, Jane Doe since this is AA which I'm not sure extends to friends of drunks – but I love her. I love you, Jo-Jo."

Jolene smiled. "I love you too."

"That's it. I'm done. My name's Amber and I am an alcoholic."

★   ★   ★

Stepping outside, Jolene and Amber donned sunglasses and sparked up cigarettes, passing the pack of smokes and a lighter back and forth until each had what they needed. They moved on down the street, shoes crunching over the thin layer of snow covering the sidewalk.

Inside the prosthetic's soft rubber socket holding her stump, it still ached. Jolene was getting used to the weird pressure she felt when it rained and the imbalance and asymmetry her body would have forever. And worst of all, the sense of loss came at her anew each time her missing leg itched and, forgetting, she reached down to scratch and only brushed her fingernails against cold metal. It was easy to forget it was gone in the morning, when warm in bed in her new apartment. Where she lived alone, and missed sharing a kitchen table with somebody or having someone to talk to first thing about what the day had in store. She wasn't as busy anymore. She didn't wear black to work. She didn't arrange flowers or set up a casket elevator or try talking people up into Egyptian silk linings or platinum handles or cherry over oak because it shined nicer. She didn't spend more time with the dead than the living anymore.

Jolene and Amber came to the bus stop and both stepped inside the fiberglass enclosure. The ad for swimwear next to them had been marked over to put devil horns on the busty model's perfect head.

It wasn't so cold today. In Minnesota you learn, real quick, what's tolerably cold and what kind of cold can kill you. But today it wasn't windy and the snow wasn't falling and the sky, full of dark clouds, was even kind of nice – the occasional sunbeam cut through and found things to spotlight below, briefly. Even in the bus stop where they sat, an occasional drifting ray of warmth on their faces as they both angled their chins up, eyes closed, and savored it. They savored a lot of things now, noticed small stuff more often. Nearly dying can do that. It was coming to them automatically but Jolene, who had to undergo an evaluation following her two months in the hospital, had gotten a few good lessons on appreciating what she had from her new doctor. They didn't see any need to put her on pills and figured being done with her old life would probably help to automatically adjust her attitude. Her doctor recommended not seeing Amber anymore. And Jolene said in reply that she wouldn't be coming in anymore, and left. Only she could say what she needed – and she was ready to speak up and ask for it, no matter the situation. Life was too short. She'd seen a possible end reaching up to grab her, to steal her down into nothingness. It could come any time. And she was surprised she hadn't realized that sooner, given she'd helped bury hundreds of people. But sometimes things can stare you right in the face for years, and never be seen.

"Thanks for coming and being moral support today," Amber said, snapping Jolene back to the present. In the bus stop enclosure, in the not-so-bad cold, right here, right now. "I really appreciate it, Jo-Jo. I would've been pissing my pants up there without you."

"You always did hate public speaking."

"And yet that's all we've been having to do at the trials."

"Yeah, well, that sort of comes with the territory. Are you worried?"

Amber sighed, a little white ghost of her breath. "I was at first but whatever happens happens, I guess. Do they know about it at work, you having to go to the courthouse so often?"

"My boss does but everyone else, I think, is under the assumption I'm going to physical therapy for the leg."

They were quiet awhile. The buses, because of road conditions, had been running late.

"So, what're you up to this afternoon, little lady?" Amber said.

"Well, I've got to go grocery shopping, then after I drop that off at the apartment, I have the closing shift at work." Jolene noticed Amber was using her knee as a desk to fill out an application. "I could put in a good word for you with my boss, if you want."

"Thanks, but I have a good feeling about this one. Kiss it."
Amber held the finished job application out to Jolene.

Jolene kissed it. "Good luck. Did I see that's for a pet store?"

"Yeah. The one downtown."

"I can picture you working there. Might make a good fit."

"Are you liking the bookstore?"

Jolene nodded. "I am. A lot. I wish you'd come in and see me more, though."

"Minute I have something full-time and I know my schedule, consider me there, every lunch break you have."

They were quiet awhile again.

"Still think about the money?" Amber said. It had been the first thing they'd done once the doctors and physical therapists had said they could leave, that their injuries were now healed enough and chance of infection was low. They bit their nails the entire cab ride out to that part of town. It took days of calling junkyards and scrap places to see if a wrecked hearse had come in, passing the hospital room's phone back and forth as the other scoured the White Pages. And when they finally got a hit, they begged and pleaded to the ether hoping the paper bag of money would still be there – a lawyer had come to inform them he was representing not one but two families, the Tamblyns and the Wicks, in a lawsuit against the Hawthorne Funeral Home for criminal negligence. But arriving in the junkyard and walking around the leaning piles of dead, rusty cars all crushed flat, tires level with their roofs, and they finally found the hearse, it took two hours of prying with crowbars to get the back hatch to open far enough for Amber to slide a hand inside. She drew out only scraps of brown paper bag, no money. Not even a single dollar. Neither said a word as they returned to the waiting cab. Now, in the bus stop enclosure, that felt a lot longer than four months ago. And in all the commotion, to add insult to injury, they'd missed Slug's funeral.

"Once in a while," Jolene finally said. "I think it worked out like it was supposed to."

"What about Frank?"

The news of his suicide didn't make national news, but the local papers ran every single detail they could squeeze out of his life, looking to fill the minutes with whatever they could dig up. There wasn't much. He had no online presence. The paragraph in the obituaries summed everything up pretty nicely.

"I thank him every night before I go to sleep," Jolene said.

Amber nodded. "Me too." She ran a gloved hand over her knee, down to where her skin under the jeans ended, and metal began.

For a third time they said nothing. They sat watching the traffic collect at the intersection, then watched it move away when the light changed, and collect again. They heard, with the next approaching mass of vehicles, the grumble of a city bus. They helped one another stand, and waited at the opening of the enclosure, squinting into the cold wind and drifting flakes falling through the leafless trees.

"I think that's yours. Uptown, right?" Amber said.

"Yeah, that's me."

The bus sidled up to the curb and its doors hissed open.

"Guess I'll see you when I see you."

"Call me tonight," Jolene said. "Tell me how it went."

"How dropping off an application went? I don't have an interview yet, Jo."

"I know. But I want to hear about it anyway."

"Okay, weirdo. I'll call you tonight to describe dropping off my application if it's so important to you."

"It is important." Everything, to Jolene Morris, was important now. She didn't want to have a single detail, at all, go unnoticed ever again.

They hugged. The bus driver was patient as Jolene struggled up the bus steps. Amber waved goodbye as they pulled off. Jolene waved too, even for a little while after she couldn't see her friend anymore.

Jolene watched the city move past her. People bundled up walking on the sidewalks. People scraping ice from their windshields. Other drivers in their cars, trying to get somewhere. No one was lying still, no one was on a slab, all of them were still trying to be places, see people, do things, fall in love, work hard enough to go on long trips, have kids, take their dogs for a walk, buy a house, cook dinner for the people they love. Jolene had forgotten about all this life out here, having spent so many hours in a cold, sterile white room putting chemicals into people who'd already lived. She was living about as much as they were, then. But now she was gone from them, the last one put in the ground, burials and solemn words and sobbing and fake flowers and caskets – all of that was over with.

Now it was her turn to live.

# FLAME TREE PRESS
## FICTION WITHOUT FRONTIERS
## Award-Winning Authors & Original Voices

Flame Tree Press is the trade fiction imprint of Flame Tree Publishing, focusing on excellent writing in horror and the supernatural, crime and mystery, science fiction and fantasy. Our aim is to explore beyond the boundaries of the everyday, with tales from both award-winning authors and original voices.

•

**You may also enjoy:**
*Second Lives* by P.D. Cacek
*The Gemini Experiment* by Brian Pinkerton
*The Bad Neighbor* by David Tallerman
*Night Shift* by Robin Triggs

**Other horror titles available include:**
*Thirteen Days by Sunset Beach* by Ramsey Campbell
*Think Yourself Lucky* by Ramsey Campbell
*The Hungry Moon* by Ramsey Campbell
*The Haunting of Henderson Close* by Catherine Cavendish
*The House by the Cemetery* by John Everson
*The Devil's Equinox* by John Everson
*The Toy Thief* by D.W. Gillespie
*Black Wings* by Megan Hart
*Stoker's Wilde* by Steven Hopstaken & Melissa Prusi
*The Playing Card Killer* by Russell James
*The Siren and the Specter* by Jonathan Janz
*Wolf Land* by Jonathan Janz
*The Sorrows* by Jonathan Janz
*Savage Species* by Jonathan Janz
*The Nightmare Girl* by Jonathan Janz
*The Dark Game* by Jonathan Janz
*House of Skin* by Jonathan Janz
*Dust Devils* by Jonathan Janz
*Will Haunt You* by Brian Kirk
*Creature* by Hunter Shea
*The Mouth of the Dark* by Tim Waggoner

•

Join our mailing list for free short stories, new release details, news about our authors and special promotions:

flametreepress.com